Realm of the Vermilion King

The Tick-Tock People

by
Ken Turner

Bloomington, IN Milton Keynes, UK

AuthorHouse™
1663 Liberty Drive, Suite 200
Bloomington, IN 47403
www.authorhouse.com
Phone: 1-800-839-8640

AuthorHouse™ UK Ltd.
500 Avebury Boulevard
Central Milton Keynes, MK9 2BE
www.authorhouse.co.uk
Phone: 08001974150

© 2006 Ken Turner. All rights reserved.

No part of this book may be reproduced, stored in a retrieval system, or transmitted by any means without the written permission of the author.

First published by AuthorHouse 4/11/2006

ISBN: 1-4259-2822-6 (sc)

Printed in the United States of America
Bloomington, Indiana

This book is printed on acid-free paper.

Second Printing

For Stacy and for Christopher

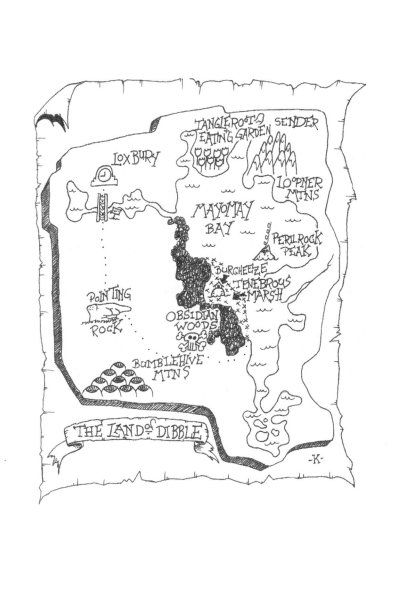

ONE

"Get your shoes on," Mrs. McAllister shouted angrily. "We're leaving." Alistair and Allison were upstairs, in Alistair's room, packing his bag. Allison had already packed hers, but Alistair tended to be a little slower at getting tasks completed on time. He hastily shoved underwear, socks, a semi-clean pair of scruffy blue jeans, a green sweater and a yellow t-shirt (which he quickly sniffed to make sure it was unsoiled enough to bring along) into his back-pack. The weekend was a bleak one for the McAllister children, as they were on their way to see Auntie Bernice, who lived on the other side of their home town of Schmendricktonville, Saskatchewan.

Alistair and Allison were twins. Alistair was a little on the husky side, with a wide bottom, big chubby cheeks, fiery red hair and a splash of freckles speckled his entire face. Allison, on the other hand, was a tiny waif of a thing. She was a little shorter than Alistair and wore thick, round glasses. Her hair, also a shocking red, was pulled into two tidy braids that hung down her back and she wore heavy silver braces on her teeth. Unlike her brother, however, she had only a small smattering of tiny freckles dotting both cheeks. They were nine years old and, as Allison was fond of bragging, exactly three minutes and seventeen seconds apart. "And I'm older," she would always conclude.

Alistair and Allison got along rather well, at least most of the time. But Alistair was a rather rambunctious child and this would often get on his sister's nerves. However, being the older sibling, Allison felt she needed to maintain a certain level of decorum and seldom reacted to her brother's raucous displays. Never to be labelled a tattle-tale, she rarely told on Alistair when he was up to no good. It was her observation that in due time Alistair would tell on himself simply by getting caught. Besides, as a rule, Alistair never really did any thing that was all *that* bad. But every once in a while, he would go too far. And this time, Alistair *had* gone too far.

Far, *far* too far.

It seems that on that particular afternoon, Alistair had decided to go for a ride. Not in the car. Not on the bus. But rather, on the back of their Great Dane, Oscar. Now Oscar was an even tempered sort, who put up with a lot of Alistair's silliness, shenanigans and generally questionable behaviour. Oscar hadn't minded mind the time Alistair had decided to dress him up as a Frankenpooch for Halloween. Nor did he seem to care when Alistair had decided his rusty brown fur would look better with purple and green polka dots, which had been applied freely using paint from his father's garage. And Oscar had not appeared too put out when Alistair tried to hitch the lawnmower to his back in order to get out of his Saturday chores. But on that particular day, Alistair had a wonderfully mischievous idea, much to the dismay of the ill-fated canine.

Careful to not draw attention to himself, he quietly gathered the materials he needed. It was his experience that his mother and father, as well as Allison, tended to frown on his escapades and would undoubtedly try to stop him. By the time he was finished, Alistair was absolutely satisfied that should anything go wrong, neither he nor Oscar would be hurt. First off, he took a large fluffy pillow from his bed and intended to tie it to Oscar's back. However, he couldn't find any string and after giving it a lot of thought, he finally came up with a solution.

Duct tape.

At first, Alistair had planned to wrap Oscar up in plastic wrap so that the tape wouldn't pull out his fur. But after careful experimentation, he found that the plastic wrap just slipped around and around and didn't really stick at all. So he had only one alternative.

"Don't worry, boy," he said to a sceptical Oscar. "It'll grow back."

The decision being made, Alistair had then used his father's clippers to carefully shave Oscar from shoulders to hips, leaving the poor pooch with a brown furry head, a brown furry bottom, long, brown furry legs and a pink, decidedly *unfurry* body. He carefully placed the pillow on Oscar's back, making sure it was positioned just so, then he took the duct tape and wound it around and around and around and around, until he was satisfied that the pillow couldn't possibly fall off. The tape stuck firmly and after making his final adjustments, Alistair carefully positioned Oscar at the end of the long upstairs hallway.

Alistair himself was prepared for any potential mishap as well. He wore a pair of long johns stuffed with toilet tissue, hockey shoulder pads, soccer shin pads, a pair of his Mom's gardening gloves, running shoes and another pillow was taped around his tummy, just in case. A football helmet was strapped securely on his head. He had also, just for good measure, fitted a hockey helmet on Oscar's head. And to ensure he didn't fall off, he carefully wound the tape around both himself and Oscar, until he was satisfied he couldn't accidentally slip free. As wild as the pair looked, it was the two pair of roller-skates that Oscar wore that really made them look absolutely mad. Oscar wobbled nervously on the skates, glancing over his shoulder with doubtful eyes, as if to question his young jockey's plans.

"What are you doing?" asked Allison as she peeked out from behind her bedroom door.

"Nothin'," Alistair said casually. "What are you doin'?"

"Building a model volcano for school," she replied.

"School doesn't start for another month!" he exclaimed.

"Well," she said snidely, "unlike *some* people, I like to be prepared. And I happen to know that we're doing a section on volcanoes this year."

"Yeah," he teased, "I bet it's a perfect specimen. Now if you don't mind, I'm kinda in the middle of somethin'."

"You're going to kill yourself," she said matter-of-factly.

"Just go back to your volcano, nerd-bomber."

Allison simply shook her head and disappeared back into her room. "Boys," she muttered as she closed the door.

"It's OK, fellah," said Alistair with a self-assured grin as he scratched Oscar under the chin, "what's the worst that could happen?" With that, Oscar just sighed and Alistair pulled down a pair of swimming goggles he had resting on the top of his helmet. He grabbed hold of Oscar's neck with one arm and gave him a slap on the bottom with the other. At first all Oscar did was stand there, trying uselessly to take a single roly-poly step. But with an added push from Alistair, they finally started to move, skating smoothly down the hallway. As they went, Oscar let out a deep growlf, which Alistair took for approval.

For the first few seconds, everything seemed about right. But almost immediately, things began to go terribly, terribly wrong. Oscar's legs started to spin wildly, slipping and sliding in every direction. In no time at all, the pooch was not so much rolling as he was simply rocketing down the hall. How Oscar managed to even stay on his feet is anyone's guess, but stay on his feet he did and they were quickly gaining speed. "Oh, NOOOOO!" Alistair yelled as they began to careen out of control. "Stop! STOP!" But it was too late.

The plan had been to ride Oscar to the end of the hallway, turn around and come back and that would be that. However, there was one fatal flaw in Alistair's scheme and only after it was too late did it occur to him.

"I CAN'T STOP!" he shouted.

"What's going on up there?" shouted Mrs. McAllister as she started up the steps. No sooner had she said it than Oscar and Alistair came bounding toward her, a total of two arms, six legs and sixteen roller-skate wheels, all barrelling out of control. Alistair held on tightly, his eyes wide as saucers, as they crashed past, sending Mrs. McAllister toppling to her bottom.

"ALISTAIR!" she bellowed. She couldn't believe her eyes.

They thumpity-thumpty-thumped down the stairs and immediately upon hitting the landing, Oscar took off toward the living room. As a rule, no children were allowed into the living room at the McAllister house, as it was strictly reserved for adults and company. They invaded the small room like savages, crashing into the coffee table with a cacophony of shattering ceramic unicorns, which Mrs. McAllister had been collecting for many, many years. If that wasn't enough, they rebounded off the coffee table and smashed head first into a large vase that held fresh flowers. The vase smashed into a billion pieces, sending petals, flower stems, glass and water in every possible direction. Magazines and a dish full of pistachio nuts flew everywhere. Doilies and lampshades leapt into the air and Mr. McAllister's favourite chair was violently upturned. No harm came to the chair itself, although Mr. McAllister, who happened to occupy the chair at that particular moment, was less than thrilled by the monumental disruption. As a coffee cup went flying in one direction and a newspaper flew in another, Mr. McAllister went tumbling into the air, a hodgepodge of flailing arms and legs. He crashed to the floor with a resounding *thud*, knocking a family portrait from the wall, which then smashed over Mr. McAllister's head.

Now, one would think that the coffee table and vase would be enough to stop them. And if not the coffee table and vase, then surely Mr. McAllister's chair and even Mr. McAllister himself would bring the thunderous chaos to a halt. Well, this was not the case at all. In fact, as it was nearing the supper hour, Oscar had suddenly caught a sniff of dinner. This managed to do nothing less than fuel his charge to inconceivable proportions as he sought the source of the delicious aromas. The boy screamed again for Oscar to stop and Mrs. McAllister was quick to follow the marauding pair as they charged into the dining room. Trying desperately and ultimately unsuccessfully to wriggle free, Alistair had no other choice but to hold on as tight as he could until the ride was over.

In the dining room, they hammered into the china hutch, sending Grandmother McAllister's fine bone china crashing to the floor in a symphony of shattering plates, cups and saucers. Mrs. McAllister shrieked as her mother's heirlooms smashed to the floor and Mr. McAllister bellowed from the living room, "What in Sam Hill is going on here?!"

For reasons that only Oscar could know, he circled the dining room table six or seven times, sending chairs tumbling every which way. More china fell and smashed and more unicorns toppled from a nearby shelf. Oscar then did something that no one thought he would do.

He stopped.

Mrs. McAllister stood transfixed, eyes wide, mouth agape as Oscar stood panting, his long pink tongue lolling out. His tail wagged furiously as Alistair still clung for dear life to the dog's neck. Alistair slowly looked at his mother, his eyes still like saucers, and tried to speak. At that same moment, however, Mr. McAllister came dashing into the dining room. He stood beside his wife, hands on his hips. His hair was tousled and his glasses hung askew on his reddened face. A delicate white doily rested on his shoulder, his shirt was untucked and ruffled and it could be argued that he was the very picture of absolute dishevelment.

"Alistair!" he began to scold, but he got no further than that. At the sound of Mr. McAllister's voice, Oscar leapt back into action. His feet scooted in the same place for a second or two before the roller-skate wheels allowed him to move, but when they did, the two-man demolition team went bounding over an upturned dining room chair and bolted toward the swinging doors that lead to the kitchen. Alistair let out a meek yelp as they went, still firmly attached to Oscar's back. They crashed through the doors, which fluttered back and forth like butterfly wings, as the distinct sounds of glassware, plates, knives, forks, pots and pans came crashing from inside the kitchen. Mrs. McAllister remained statue still, one hand over her mouth, the other resting on her forehead. Mr. McAllister held her close, cringing each time he heard something fall, clatter or smash.

He cringed a lot.

Finally there was nothing but silence. After gathering as much courage as they could muster, Mr. McAllister took his wife by the shoulder and simply said, "Come along, dear. Let's see what *your* son is up to." She went, hand still covering her mouth, the other carefully reaching out to push open the kitchen door.

They peered in together and Mrs. McAllister let out a simple whimper as she took in the scene. Mr. McAllister's jaw dropped as far as it could, maybe even further, as he tried to comprehend what he was seeing.

Everything that had once been placed on the counters and stashed in the cupboards was now all over the floor. Sugar, flour, coffee beans and tea bags, the little bowl of fruit that Mrs. McAllister always kept on the countertop for snacks - all of it was upturned and everywhere. The dinner dishes, which had been stacked on the counter to be set on the dining room table, were scattered all over the place, smashed into hundreds of tiny bits. The coffeemaker, tea pot, kettle, can opener and even the microwave oven were either overturned or laying on the kitchen floor. And dinner was everywhere. Sauce and noodles were splattered all over the walls and even up to the ceiling. Meatballs dotted the floor. A dish of grated cheese had been strewn everywhere around the room and would be found in every corner, nook and cranny for days and days to come.

Alistair sat in the middle of it all, cross-legged on the floor, tatters of duct tape wound around him, goggles askew and his football helmet rested crookedly on his head. On top of his helmet was an upturned saucepan that had once been boiled spinach but was now just an inedible mush of green goo. His entire body was smeared with spaghetti noodles and gobs of rich, red sauce. A strand or two of spaghetti dangled across his freckle-spattered nose and over his shoulder and a meatball was jammed into his left ear. And as for Oscar, well, he stood on the counter, tail wagging like crazy, happily devouring the delicious remnants of their demolished dinner.

Again, Mrs. McAllister simply let out a helpless whimper as she looked around her ravaged kitchen. Alistair's father simply glared at him, his arms folded across his chest. Allison slipped quietly into the kitchen and peered around her mother's back.

"Wow!" was all she said.

"I can explain," said Alistair.

At that moment, Oscar's feet rolled out from under him one final time and he went crashing to the ground, taking the upturned pot of sauce with him. He landed with a wet PLOP! and let out a whimper, then looked at Mr. And Mrs. McAllister with big, sad, brown eyes, as if to say that no matter how bad things looked, it wasn't his fault.

TWO

The McAllister children climbed into the back seat of the family car and buckled in as Mrs. McAllister pulled out of the driveway. Neither Mrs. McAllister nor the twins noticed that Oscar had come bounding around the corner of the house, running after the car, his incredibly long tongue flopping from the corner of his mouth as he galloped along behind them.

The ride to Auntie Bernice's house was a long one. Longer than usual, or so it seemed to Alistair and Allison, though by Alistair's watch, it only took the usual twenty-five minutes. Not a word was exchanged as they rumbled along in the family station wagon towards 634 Bleeker Street.

"I hate going to Auntie Bernice's," Allison grumbled, slouched in the back seat. "It smells bad."

"That's enough," warned Mrs. McAllister, looking at the twins through the rear-view mirror.

"Why am I even being punished?" Allison demanded. "I didn't even do anything."

"You knew what your brother was up to," Mrs. McAllister explained flatly, "and didn't do anything about it. That makes you an accomplice."

"Fine," she snorted. "But I have a book about Canadian Law practices you might be interested in. There's a chapter on how the punishment should fit the crime."

"I think a weekend with Auntie Bernice *is* a punishment that fits the crime," Mrs. McAllister replied, "considering the house is all but uninhabitable thanks to you two. Now I don't want to hear another word about it."

"But Mom, she's *horrible!*" Alistair wailed, his arms flailing theatrically. "You know she is, that's why you're making us go there."

"She means well," said Mrs. McAllister, but even she wondered if that were actually true.

Auntie Bernice was actually Mr. McAllister's aunt. In all the years she had known her, Mrs. McAllister had never known Auntie Bernice to be anything less than eccentric, obnoxious and oftentimes, downright distasteful. Always one with a flair for the dramatic - a trait Alistair inherited from her, no doubt - Bernice was never at a loss for large, wet kisses and rib-shattering bear hugs. She had always been a generous woman, but her tastes were nothing if not unique and her gift-giving skills were somewhat . . . stunted. When Mr. And Mrs. McAllister had been married, for example, Auntie Bernice had arrived dressed in an extremely obnoxious yellow- and green-striped dress with a bow on the rear that served to enhance her already formidable rump. It had large, poofy sleeves which tightly pinched her upper arms, making them resemble two ruptured tubes of pre-made cookie dough. She had also worn a large, floppy green hat that was encrusted with hundreds of little multi-coloured flowers and tiny plastic bees and dragonflies. Her wedding gift had been an equally hideous mantle clock. It was quite large and appeared to be hand carved, however the craftsman's skills left something to be desired. The carved grapes, pears and apples, for example, looked more like basic, almost-round, unidentifiable shapes. From the day it had been received, the clock had never kept proper time and the McAllister children had never known it to ever have been wound. Auntie Bernice, however, would always ask about it whenever she and Mr. or Mrs. McAllister spoke. Not wanting to hurt anyone's feelings, the McAllisters placed the clock on the mantle, tucked behind some family photos and various other nick-knacks, though its enormity made it impossible to conceal entirely.

"And she has all those weird pictures all over the place," continued Allison. "Pictures of her when she was a little kid, when she was a teenager, all with some creepy, weird looking guy beside her. They're everywhere."

"Yeah," Alistair chimed in, "who is that guy, anyway?"

"Just never mind," Mrs. McAllister replied quickly, her voice suddenly taking a sharp edge. "I don't want you kids asking her about it, either. She's very sensitive about it and I don't want to upset her."

"Fine," they said in unison as they slumped deeper into their seats.

The rest of the trip was utterly silent. Finally, with a sense of dread washing over the kids like ocean waves, they pulled into the drive.

The front door swung open and Auntie Bernice came charging out of the house, one mammoth arm waving in the air. To Alistair and Allison, it was sort of like watching a freight train come thundering out of a tunnel, and they were helplessly tied to the rails.

"HELLLOOOOOO, HELLLOOOOOOOOO," she shrieked as she rumbled toward them. She was an extremely large woman, and Alistair guessed she was around eight hundred pounds, but was probably closer to about three hundred and fifty. She had jet black hair that she wore piled high in a beehive, giving her the illusion that she was well over seven feet tall. When she smiled, she revealed a row of impossibly white teeth that seemed just a little too large for her mouth. The hand that wasn't waving feverishly in the air gripped a long wooden cane that bowed significantly under her weight; her short, stubby, sausage-like fingers were wrapped tightly around the carved handle. Auntie Bernice wore a large muumuu that reminded both Alistair and Allison of a circus tent; a garish pattern of red, green, yellow and blue polka dots. As if to maintain some sort of demented colour scheme, she wore bright red lipstick that made her lips look humungous, bright smears of rouge on both cheeks and glittery blue eye shadow that went from her eyelashes right up to her uneven, penciled-in eyebrows. A heavy string of red, golf-ball sized beads hung around her neck and big, yellow and orange bangley bracelets encircled both wrists like manacles.

"I think I can feel the ground shaking," Alistair said half under his breath as his aunt hurtled onward. Allison giggled, quickly slapping both hands over her mouth and darting her eyes toward their mother.

"That's enough," Mrs. McAllister said dryly. "You two be nice to Auntie Bernice. She might be large, but she's also very kind and gentle."

"Yeah, right," muttered Alistair. "So are humpback whales." Allison stifled another giggle, though much less successfully than before.

Ignoring her son's ill attempt at comedy, Mrs. McAllister turned to look at her children. "And when you kiss her hello," she said, "I want you to remember why you're here."

"*Kiss* her?!" Alistair blurted. "No one said anything about kissing her."

"She always smells like pickles," groaned Allison. Mrs. McAllister didn't seem to share their reservations.

"I can't believe Dad approves of this," Alistair moaned mournfully.

"Actually," replied Mrs. McAllister with a mischievous grin, "it was his idea."

"WHAT?" blurted the pair.

"Quiet," said their mother as she opened her door, "here she is." She slipped from behind the wheel and opened her arms very wide. Alistair thought that just for a second, a look of revulsion shivered across his mother's face. "Bernice, how nice to-"

"MY SWEETUMS!!!" bellowed Auntie Bernice as she shambled passed Mrs. McAllister as though she didn't know anyone was even standing there. Allison's fingers were nearly pulled off as the car door was wrenched from her grip. "MY SWEET, SWEET BABIES!!!" Auntie Bernice reached into the back seat and with a deftness that seemed impossible, she single-handedly lifted Allison up and into the folds of her arms as though the girl were made of tissue paper. Auntie Bernice hugged Allison for what seemed an eternity, and the girl got a strong notion that it had been several days since her great aunt had washed under her arms. By the time Auntie Bernice finally set her back onto solid ground, Allison's face was covered in smears of red lipstick.

Auntie Bernice then crammed her massive frame into the backseat to reach for Alistair, the car's shocks working overtime to absorb the weight. Alistair pressed himself as close to his door as he could, reaching blindly for the handle in a frenzied effort to escape her clutches. Unfortunately, he was at an awkward angle and couldn't seem to find the handle. As her ruby coloured fingertips groped for him, Alistair sputtered, "I-I-I have a cold, Auntie Bernice. You better not kiss me."

"*Nonsense,*" she cooed as her powerful fingers dug deep and painfully into Alistair's thigh. Imagine, if you will, old gym socks mixed with boiling cauliflower. Throw in a handful of spoiled eggs, skunk juice, wet dog and a dash of pickled onion for good measure and it would almost describe the hot, putrid air that filled the car as she huffed her way into the back seat. "Come give your auntie a great big smoochy-poo." With that, she dragged him into her clutches and showered him with wet kisses that reminded him of Oscar and his big, slobbery tongue. Soon, he and his sister were wearing identical masks of smeared crimson.

"Now you two do as Auntie Bernice tells you," said Mrs. McAllister. "I don't want to hear about any of your wild shenanigans."

"She means you," said Allison, elbowing her brother in the ribs.

"I mean both of you," came the reply. "I'll be back on Sunday to pick you up. It'll take that long for your father and me to clean up the house."

"Mom, this is why some kids divorce their parents," Alistair whined. She was not amused.

"Toodleoo," said Mrs. McAllister with a wave of her fingers. "Be good. See you Sunday."

Allison, Alistair and Auntie Bernice stood on the sidewalk as Mrs. McAllister drove off, Auntie Bernice once again waving her massive arm and grinning from ear to ear. The twins simply stood silently defeated, wiping lipstick from their cheeks, foreheads, noses and chins as the station wagon disappeared around the corner and out of sight.

Overhead, a cloud drifted in front of the sun, casting a gloomy shadow on the afternoon. A distant rumble of thunder filled the air and both Alistair and Allison felt a deep sense of despair sink into their hearts. It was going to be a looooooong weekend.

Allison and Alistair followed Auntie Bernice into the house, their shoulders drooping and heads hung low.

"I wish Oscar was here," Alistair said forlornly.

As the door closed behind them, the first spatters of rain began to dollop the front stoop.

***

The rain came in torrents, streaming down the window panes and running through the streets like miniature rivers as bits of paper, candy wrappers, pop cans and other bits of litter were carried in its current. Thunder rumbled and lightning flickered somewhere high in the sky. Alistair was worried about Oscar, who hated thunder and lightning. Right now he was sure that his poor little pooch was huddled under his bed, frightened and alone. Little did Alistair realise that Oscar was only a few blocks away, galloping toward Auntie Bernice's house.

The house smelled like moth balls and mildew and the furniture was old, worn and ragged. The window curtains looked like they might have once been white, but now they were a dull yellowish brown. The carpet was old and worn with large, strange blotches that made it difficult to determine its original colour. Wispy cobwebs dangled and clung in every corner and a thin layer of dust seemed to cover every surface. The only thing that they had seen that wasn't dusty was the TV, which sat in the middle of the musty living room. There were no lamps in the gloomy little room and what little light there was came sifting through the glass of one grimy window. The walls were covered with old photographs, most of which were pictures of people the twins had never known. Many of them, however, were of Auntie Bernice and a strange looking boy. There were no baby pictures, but there were photos of Bernice as a very young child, as a teenager and many years in between. The pictures had been taken at birthdays, Christmas, in the woods, one was taken in a boat floating in a lake. In all of these pictures, Bernice was all but glued to the young boy. They looked remarkably similar and Allison and Alistair wondered if he had been her brother. It was obviously a touchy subject, however, and even Alistair knew that to ask would be to push things too far. It was worth noting, though, that this strange, mysterious boy was present in every photo of Auntie Bernice right up until she looked to be in or around her early twenties but then he was suddenly absent. In those latter pictures, Bernice stood alone and the judging by the look on her face, though smiling, her eyes conveyed a sense of deep sadness that wasn't present in the others.

The twins leaned on the windowsill, heads propped up in their hands. Allison simply starred out into the wet afternoon while Alistair absent-mindedly drew little patterns on the dusty ledge with his finger. Auntie Bernice sat in her lounge chair, which seemed to bulge and almost groan under her ample weight, with her feet propped up on a battered old foot stool. In one meaty hand, she held a large jar of baby dill pickles, which she absently munched on as she stared blankly at the television, which was blaring and buzzing, clanging and bleating as game show contestants won cars and boats and trips to the Bahamas. Once in a while, their aunt would blurt out the answer to a quiz show question, but she was always wrong.

"This sucks," groaned Allison.

"I know," replied Alistair. "What do you want to do?"

"I dunno. What do you want to do?"

"I dunno. There's nothing *to* do."

"I know what you can do," croaked Auntie Bernice.

The pair jumped, startled, as she loomed behind them. How she managed to get up from the chair and approach them so quietly is anyone's guess, and before the twins could even ask what she meant, she had grabbed them by the arms and was dragging them toward the kitchen.

"There are mops and buckets in the cellar," she said, pointing a sausagey finger toward an old wooden door. "There are rags under the sink and you can each have a cookie when you're done."

"Well," said Allison, somewhat confused, "what do you want us to clean?"

Auntie Bernice looked at her niece as though she had just asked the silliest question in the world.

"Everything," she finally said. "We have the whole weekend. Now get to work. I'm going to watch my stories."

Alistair and Allison stood silently for a moment as Auntie Bernice waddled back to her chair. The theme music for a soap opera came crashing through the room as she turned up the volume on the TV.

"Is she kidding?" Alistair asked, unable to grasp what had just happened. As he spoke, his voice began to rise in volume, as though competing with the television. "She's kidding, right? Clean the whole house? Has she even *seen* this house? This house hasn't been clean since the Civil War, for cryin' out loud!"

"Quiet," Allison hissed. "She'll hear you."

"So?"

"So, Mom said we had to behave and do whatever Auntie Bernice says."

"Yeah, but she didn't mean *this*. Come *on*, she *couldn't* have meant *this*. I mean, really, I'm serious. Has she even *seen* this house?"

The Tick-Tock People

"Well, I'm going to start cleaning," she said as she approached the cellar door. "If we don't do what she says-" she paused. "If *you* don't do what she says, *we'll* be in even more trouble. And next time it could be even worse."

"Nothing's worse than this."

"Well, do what you want. When Mom comes to get us, I'm not going to have a guilty conscience. And I'm not going to get in trouble again because of you and your stupid nonsense. So you just better do what Auntie Bernice says. It's only for two days. Two . . . long . . . rainy . . . days." She sighed hollowly as she opened the cellar door.

"What?" Alistair asked. Allison was standing in front of the doorway, unblinking, jaw hanging open, as she stared into the darkened void.

"What?" Alistair repeated. He stepped beside his sister and followed her gaze.

By the looks of things, the door hadn't been opened for a long, long time. A labyrinth of thick cobwebs criss-crossed the opening at the top of the stairs, reaching from floor to ceiling. The smell that spilled out was that of old, wet dirt, mould and rotting vegetables and a host of other odours that were sickly and sour and disgustingly indistinguishable. It was pitch black and there was a sharp, scurrying sound as something (or some things) skittered about somewhere down in the dungeon-like depths of the basement.

"Wow!" exclaimed Alistair as his eyes widened and a familiar, mischievous grin crept across his face.

Allison's face remained carved in fright and disbelief. "I am *not* going down there," she finally said.

"Oh, yes you are," said Alistair. "This is going to be so cool."

Allison grabbed her brother by the wrist. "No, we can't. We don't know what's down there. What if we fall and hurt ourselves? What if one of us steps on a rusty nail? We could get tetanus. Who's going to take us to the hospital? No, I think we should go tell Auntie Bernice that it's too dangerous."

"Too dangerous or too scary?" Alistair asked. His sister stood staring at him for a moment before he pulled his arm away from her. "Is little baby Allison a little baby scaredy-cat?" he taunted.

"I'm not scared," she said defiantly. "And I'm not a baby. It's just not a good idea, that's all. Besides, if something happens, we'll never convince Mom it was an accident. She'll probably think we did it on purpose, just to get back at her for sending us here."

Alistair stared at his sister for a second, and then simply said, "Well, I'm going." He carefully reached out and gently pulled away the silky strands of cobwebs. A light switch was just to the left and he gave it a flick. There was a dull buzzing noise as dim, yellow light flickered on in the depths below. It wasn't much, but at least it was light. A thick layer of long undisturbed dust and bits of debris littered the stairs. A small stack of yellowed newspapers sat on the top step. The top paper was dated September 10, 1939, it's bold headline declaring **IT'S WAR!!**.

Alistair looked back at Allison, grinned a grin that never meant anything good, and started down the steps, stirring up the long dormant layers of dust. As he went, his heart thumped heavily in his chest, a combination of nerves and excitement.

"Alistair," Allison said nervously, but he didn't seem to hear her. He slowly crept down into the cellar, careful to manoeuvre around the litter and debris. Finally, he reached the bottom and was almost enveloped by the gloom. Allison could barely see him as he descended the stairs and soon, she couldn't see him at all. "Alistair," she repeated, a little louder. There was no reply.

The TV still blared as Auntie Bernice watched her stories in the other room. For a moment, Allison considered going to her aunt and telling her she was too afraid to go down into the basement, but then she remembered her mother's warning not to upset her. With Allison being a fairly level-headed little girl, she knew when she was beaten. She had no choice. It was either follow Alistair into the cellar or wind up in a worse predicament than they were already in. Although, just as her brother had said, what could *possibly* be worse.

"Come on," Alistair half-shouted from somewhere in the darkened depths below. "You gotta see this. It's awesome."

As Auntie Bernice cackled at something on TV, Allison took a deep breath and readied herself to take her first step into the unknown. "I'll never understand boys," she said, then cautiously slipped down the stairs into the gloomy darkness.

THREE

The foul, wet odour of the basement got more pungent as she descended the stairs. The old wooden steps creaked underfoot and she was positive that one of them would break at any moment, sending her tumbling to the ground and breaking her neck along the way.

At the bottom of the steps, she noticed that the floor was neither cement nor wood, but rather a soft covering of earthy dirt. There was a single light bulb in the middle of the dingy space, giving it an ominous glow. The solitary bulb swung back and forth slowly, moved by a slight breeze that didn't seem to come from anywhere in particular. Shadows crept and leapt like inky ghosts, yet the light never quite reached the deepest corners.

Cobwebs hung and wafted everywhere and it didn't look like anyone had been in the basement for years and years. *And they probably haven't*, thought Allison. *No way could those steps hold Auntie Bernice's weight.* But what struck her as odd was a strange, dull tick-tock noise, like a clock.

But surely there couldn't be a clock running in a basement that hadn't been used in so many years. Could there?

Old boxes and crates were stacked everywhere. A few had fallen over and their contents spilled out; mostly they were old clothes, mouldy and stinking as they rotted on the moist, dirt floor. There was some furniture down there as well; what looked like and old sofa, a chair, some sort of large cabinet as well as a couple of old tables, all of which had been covered in heavy sheets. There was also an old bicycle with no tires, what looked like ancient, rusted tools of some sort, stacks and stacks of old yellowed newspapers that had been bundled up with twine. Like the stack of papers at the top of the stairs, they all had grim headlines; **CANADA RAIDS DIEPPE**; **MORE TROOPS SENT TO EUROPE**; **BRING OUR BOYS HOME**. There were also cartons of old books and magazines, rusty car parts and a few toys that looked like they had been discarded years and years ago.

A shiver went down Allison's spine as she spied an old doll with matted hair, a moth-eaten blue dress and was missing one glassy eye, leaving nothing but a creepy, empty socket. It was lying sideways, on top of a pile of old rags and clothes and a few forgotten toys. Something in its features (perhaps it was just the dreariness of the basement playing tricks on Allison's eyes) made it look old and spooky. Another shiver snaked around Allison's spine as it seemed to stare at her in the dim light, it's single, unblinking eye never leaving her as she made her way through the room.

"Alistair," she whispered, partially to break the spooky silence. There was no answer. "Alistair, where are you?"

She stopped and listened carefully, but she could only hear the muffled sounds of the TV from upstairs, the dull tick-tock clock sound and then the same skittery noises she had heard before.

Definitely mice, she thought. *Disgusting.*

As she crept slowly through the cellar, careful to stay in the dim light, she wondered what vile nastiness lurked in the dark, inky corners. She had no intention of investigating to find out.

The tick-tock sound got louder as she moved deeper into the cellar. Finally, she stopped in front of a tall piece of furniture covered in a musty sheet. It was maybe six feet in height, rather narrow and it was from here that the tick-tock sound came.

She whispered for her brother once more, but still there was no answer. Then, as though she were not even in control of her own hands, she reached out toward the sheet. Her heart pounded as she touched the tarp, finding it rough and heavy and it seemed to feel just a little damp. With trembling hands, she began to lift it. A thin sheath of nervous sweat quickly slicked her brow despite the musty coolness of the cellar, and her nose tickled as she disturbed the long dormant dust particles and peeked beneath it. Her heart leapt into her chest as she locked eyes with the ghoulish image of a person staring back at her from behind the covering. Just as she did so, Alistair jumped up from behind a covered sofa.

"BOOGA BOOGA!!" he bellowed, his face twisted into a freakish grin in the shadowy light. Allison shrieked, dropping the sheet and clapping her hands across her mouth as she leapt straight into the air. Her brother howled with amusement, having successfully frightened his sister.

"You should see your face," he guffawed. "You look like you saw a ghost. Oh, boy, I wish I had a camera."

"That's not funny," she almost screamed. Her heart thundered in her chest as her fear turned to anger. "You scared me half to death."

"Kinda my plan," beamed Alistair as he motioned around the room with his hand. "Isn't this stuff cool?"

"No," she said, remembering the frightening image she saw behind the sheet. It had wide, wild eyes, huge, razor-sharp teeth and its hair seemed to not actually be hair but rather a nest of repulsive serpents, writhing and tangled. "It's scary. I don't want to be down here anymore. Let's just get the mop and bucket and go back upstairs."

"Are you kidding?" Alistair asked incredulously. "This is great. Look at all this stuff. It's like a haunted house or something."

"There are mice down here," she said matter-of-factly. "I heard them."

"I heard them too," he replied. "Mice won't hurt you. Don't be such a baby."

"I'm not a baby," Allison almost whined. "I'm three minutes and seventeen seconds older than you, you know."

"Yeah? Well, you're acting like your three minutes and seventeen *seconds old*, ya big baby." Even in the dim light, he could see her cheeks begin to redden. Sometimes Alistair found it a lot of fun to taunt his sister and this was one of those times. Usually, she would get all worked up, start huffing and puffing and her face would go beet red and then she'd storm off into her room and that would be that. Not once had she reacted any differently. Her anger never got the best of her and she was far too level-headed and even-tempered to simply fly off the handle in a rage. This time, however, there was no room to which she could storm off. But Alistair didn't really think of that.

"Don't call me that!" she growled slowly through gritting teeth. Her face was getting redder and redder by the second. "I want to go upstairs."

"Why, is it almost nap time, baby?" He knew he had struck a nerve and revelled in its effects.

"I want to go upstairs right *now*!" She sounded like she was beginning to cry.

"OK. Fine. We'll go upstairs. It's almost time for Auntie Bernice to change your diaper anyway."

He knew he had pushed too far even as he was saying it, but it was too late. Allison's eyes squinted into narrow slits, spilling fearful tears down her cheeks and her face looked almost purple in the gloomy room. She opened her mouth and out spilled a squeal of rage as she lunged over the sofa and tackled her brother.

They rolled around on the floor, a tangle of flailing arms and legs. Allison wailed in anger and Alistair screamed in fear of his life as they crashed into the covered furniture, boxes and other brick-a-brack. Stacks of cartons toppled over, spilling their contents every which way. They rolled through stinking piles of old clothes, getting some sort of feather scarf entangled between them. Allison grabbed something soft and started beating her brother over the head with it. It was the doll, but its age and decay didn't allow it to stay in one piece. After four or five good, solid whacks, the plastic head went sailing off somewhere and clattered to the floor as stuffing flew about in musty greyish-white tufts. The two were soon covered in filth and smudged with grime as they rolled about, grunting, screaming and pulling at each other's hair. Finally, Alistair broke free and scrambled furiously over the sofa, trying to escape his enraged sister. She climbed after him, grabbing the feather scarf that was still tangled around his foot, and soon they were twisted together again in a knot of fear and anger.

The struggle stirred up dust and dirt and served to only enhance the rancid, mildewy smell as they rolled about on the floor like this for the better part of five minutes, crashing into everything and anything that was in their path. One of the things that were in their path was the sheet-covered clock. They slammed against it with a sharp *thud*, knocking the wind from both of them. The sheet had slid off during their scuffle and now they lay on the ground, staring up at the elaborate time piece. Its hands were set at 3:16 in front of an ornately decorated, yet tarnished gold face. The rich, wooden frame was carved in flowing ivy and what appeared to be strange-looking fruit which crept around the circular face, intertwining among itself and flowing down the body of the clock, creating a base upon which it stood. A brass pendulum swung back and forth rhythmically behind a muddy-looking, dusty glass pane.

Dull glimmers of dust hung in the air and tickled their noses as they looked up at the looming timepiece. A wave of relief and foolishness washed over Allison as she realized that the great ugly creature that she had seen under the sheet was only her own reflection. She was also relieved that she hadn't told Alistair about her vision. She would never live it down:

"You should have seen her," he would undoubtedly chortle at any opportunity. *"Scared out of her wits by her own ugly reflection. I'd be scared too if I looked like her."* The fact that they were actually twins would be irrelevant to him.

The clock itself was now leaning forward, knocked off balance when they had slammed against it. The only thing stopping it from toppling down on top of them was the fact that it was leaning against the arm of the old sofa, which suddenly shifted under its weight and the clock lurched forward, ever so slightly. The feather scarf in which they were still entangled had somehow managed to find its way under the clock and was now stuck. If either of them moved in the wrong direction, it might mean toppling the clock on top of them both.

The twins looked at each other, eyes wide, hair dishevelled, covered in grime as the sofa slowly began to scrape sideways, giving in to the weight of the old clock. In a frantic scramble of hands, the two struggled to detangle themselves before the clock finally gave in to the forces of gravity.

"OK, OK," Alistair finally said. "I have an idea."

Knowing that nothing good ever came from one of Alistair's sentences that began with that phrase, Allison emitted a low moan.

"No," he said, trying to keep an eye on the clock and his sister at the same time. "I saw a magician do this on TV once with a table cloth. He pulled it off the table without spilling all the plates and stuff. I think it'll work. Just trust me."

Before Allison could express just how little she trusted her brother under even the greatest of circumstances, he had grabbed the loose end of the scarf and gave it a sharp yank. Miraculously, the scarf was suddenly free and Allison stared incredulously at her brother.

"It worked," she said with genuine astonishment. "I can't believe it. You actually . . ."

"Uh oh," Alistair muttered. Allison slowly turned her head as the clock wobbled slightly backward, then slightly forward and finally lunged toward them. Its minute hand clicked into the 3:17 position as it fell toward them.

"I'm telling," Allison muttered.

Then there was nothing.

FOUR

Alistair tried to stir, but found his arms and legs tangled in something that didn't seem to want to let go. His head buzzed and thrummed and for a few seconds, he wondered what had happened. Then he remembered the old clock. And his sister. *Allison!*

He tried to open his eyes, but the glaring light made it impossible. It felt like sharp, pointed sticks were being jabbed into his brain.

Wait a second, he thought to himself. *Bright light? But we're in a basement.*

Suddenly he was aware of other things that didn't quite make sense. He could feel a cool breeze caressing his skin and he was absolutely positive he could hear the shrill cry of birds somewhere off in the distance. He breathed deeply and suddenly realised that the musty smell of Auntie Bernice's cellar had disappeared. Instead he could detect fresh, salty air that reminded him of the beach. He tried to move again, but he was still entangled.

The feather scarf, he remembered.

He slowly opened his eyes, bracing against the bright light. Something wasn't right and once his eyes adjusted properly, he knew what that something was. Above them, a brilliant blue sky stretched out as far as he could see. A few round, billowy clouds floated like wispy cotton and birds like he had never seen drifted lazily above him.

They weren't tangled up in the feather scarf after all, he quickly realised. In fact, they were both laying in a tangle of thick, heavy vines which had wound themselves around Alistair's arms, legs and stomach. Dangling from the vines were large, bulbous, orange and yellow orbs. They gleamed in the bright sunlight and a sweet, tangy aroma seemed to almost cling to them. Their slick, shiny skins were glistening with moisture and a fat drip of juice fell from one and splattered Alistair in the face. The juice was sweet and delicious and his stomach immediately began to grumble and his mouth started to water.

"Alistair," croaked his sister, not far away. "Where are we?"

"I don't know," he replied as he easily pulled himself free from the vines. "This is pretty weird."

"Are we . . ." Allison began nervously as she slipped a loosely tangled loop of vine from her wrist, ". . . you know . . . dead?"

"I don't think so," he said, looking at his sister's filthy clothes and face. "I think we'd be all clean if we were dead."

"Then where are we?"

"Not really sure," he said.

"Well," said Allison, "let's get out of this stuff and find out."

Alistair agreed as his stomach made a wicked rolling sound. Remembering the sweet deliciousness of the orange/yellow orb, he plucked one from the stem and bit deep into the sugary flesh of the fruit. Sticky yellow juice oozed out and dribbled down his chin as his mouth practically absorbed the scrumptious nectar.

"You gotta try this," he said through a mouthful of pulp, handing the half-eaten fruit to his sister. She looked at him hesitantly, then took it from him and nibbled cautiously. The moment the delectable flavour touched her tongue, however, her taste for it was insatiable and she devoured the remaining fruit, leaving only a small reddish pit, which she tossed to the ground.

It was as though they hadn't eaten for weeks and the fruit had somehow opened an empty vault which absolutely had to be filled. They picked and devoured the wonderful treats as though it were candy and before long, they had no choice but to lay back down on the ground, holding their stomachs, which were absolutely stuffed.

"Ohhhh," Allison groaned, "I'm so full."

"This is the greatest thing I've ever tasted," moaned Alistair through a heavy yawn, still clutching a half-eaten orb. He longed to finish it but had absolutely no room left in his bulbous belly.

"Are you getting sleepy, Alistair?"

"Yeah, are you?"

"Yeah. Maybe we should just rest a little while before we go anywhere. You know, to gather our strength." She let out a loud yawn and stretched her arms as wide as they would go, her eyelids becoming heavier and heavier by the minute.

"Good thinkin'," he agreed, rolling onto his side and tucking his hands beneath his head. "Just a short nap, then we'll get going."

"Just a short one though," she said dreamily. "Set your watch."

Alistair hadn't heard this last part as he had already drifted into a deep sleep. In less than a minute, Allison was also out cold.

As they slept unsuspectingly, the vines began to rustle about them, gradually reaching for the children. Slowly and silently, they encircled their arms, legs and middles and began to drag them along the dirty ground. A few metres away, the ground began to crack and fissure, suddenly rumbling open like a great mouth. The sound awoke Allison, who didn't understand what was happening at first. She thought she was dreaming for a moment as she was slowly dragged along, but a small stick jabbed her in the left nostril and she suddenly knew she was wide awake.

"Alistair!" she screamed. "Alistair, wake up!"

Alistair muttered something, but didn't wake up at all. She screamed his name again, louder this time, then screamed at the top of her lungs. When her brother finally opened his eyes, they were only a few metres away from the gaping hole in the ground. He watched in terror as the vines and fruit slipped into the large crack, dragging them closer and closer.

"Holy smokes!" he bellowed, struggling against the vines, but the harder they struggled, the tighter the vines seemed to become.

"It won't let go," screamed Allison, as panic clearly enveloped her. She tried to pull her feet from the thick, cable-like grip of the vines, but with each tug, the vines seemed to actually tug back. The thought of being devoured by a tangle of carnivorous ivy terrified Allison and she began to thrash about in a desperate effort to pull free.

"Allison!" screamed her brother as he fought against the pull of the ivy. "Hang on. I'm coming."

It wasn't easy, but he managed to inch his way to his sister, who was now flailing frantically, only a meter from the yawning maw. "Don't struggle, it's pulling you in," Alistair shouted.

"I know it's pulling me in," she screamed. "Pull me out!"

By a stroke of sheer luck, Alistair's left wrist sipped from its restraints and he fumbled with the vines that had hold of his other arm. With great difficulty, he managed to pry himself free. Now able to use both arms, he untwisted the vines from around his middle and bent awkwardly until he could reach those around his feet. These proved to be less willing to relinquish him, so he did the only thing that he could think of; he bit into the vine as hard as his jaws could manage. With a strange squealing sound that seemed to come from within the pit, Alistair's teeth punctured the thick skin as sweet, gooey fluid spurted from the corners of his mouth. Then the vines let go and reeled away, leaving him unfettered. Alistair then leapt through the air toward his sister, landing with a *thud*, grabbed a vine that had wrapped itself around her wrist and gave it a hard tug. It was thick and heavy under his grasp and seemed to be almost warm to the touch. It bulged and rippled and Alistair thought they seemed to be flexing muscles, but of course this was impossible. No matter how hard he tried to pull, however, the ivy was stronger.

"It's not working," Allison cried. "Alistair, it's not working! It's getting tighter!"

"I know it's not working," he screamed back at her. "Shut up and let me think."

Allison squirmed under the weight of the ivy, which was now slowly winding its way around her stomach and up her chest, inching toward her neck. She was finding it difficult to breath as she become more and more constricted and her feet slipped over the edge of the crevice and into the cavity. Tiny white dots seemed to swim before her eyes as the ivy weighed heavy on her chest. She was a goner. *That much*, she thought, *was certain.* Alistair stared at his sister as she was slowly drawn down. She was still struggling and seemed to be disappearing at an alarming rate. He looked at his own feet, and gave a quick kick at a length of vine that was trying to sneak up on him.

"Wait a second," he cried. "Wait a second. Stop pulling."

Allison looked at him. Terror was strewn across her tear-streaked face, which seemed to have taken on a slight pinkish-purple hue. Alistair kneeled above her with yellowish-green fluid still dribbling from his chin. His clothes were filthy and he had a scratch over his left eye. To Allison's terrified eyes, Alistair looked more like some sort of sinister monster than her chubby-faced younger brother.

"It's Finger Torture," Alistair finally said. Her eyes flickered, not understanding what he meant. "The more you struggle, the tighter it gets. I have one at home. Remember? I got you with it at Christmas time."

Allison nodded her head weakly. The previous Christmas, her brother had coaxed her into placing her fingers into a small paper tube. She did so with reservations, knowing it was some sort of trick, and soon discovered his scheme. Her fingers had become trapped in the tube and the harder she tried to pull them free, the tighter the tube became. Only after Alistair had a good, strong belly-laugh did he finally tell her the secret to escape. She had to stop pulling and simply relax. When she did so, the trap simply let go. Just as she had been finger-trapped in the paper tube, she now found herself unable to struggle free of the ivy, which seemed to take its time in its simple victory.

"OK, don't move." This was a silly thing for Alistair to say, since Allison was unable to move a muscle below her chin anyway. "Just relax your whole body. Pretend you're . . . you're . . . just pretend you're not getting eaten by killer fruit."

Being reminded that she was being eaten by killer fruit didn't help the matter, but she tried and it felt as though the vines had loosened their grip ever so slightly.

"I'm going to pull you out," Alistair said calmly. "Now just stay calm and don't try to help. Just let me do it." His sister's eyes looked up at him hopefully. She tried to speak, but the weight on her chest made it almost impossible to draw more than a miniscule breath.

He slowly slid his hands between the heavy tangles of vines and managed to slip his fingers under Allison's arms. "Just remember to relax," he said softly as he carefully pulled up. He was grateful that she was so slight, weighing almost nothing compared to his own ample size. She slipped out of the ivy's grip with relative ease. The moment she was free, they ran as fast as they could in the opposite direction, hurdling tentacle-like vines as they tried to ensnare their ankles. This proved to be difficult as the sleepiness that had gripped them was slowing their reflexes. At one point, a thin vine had wrapped around Alistair's ankle, but he was able to kick it off before it had gotten a firm grip on him.

"It tried to gobble me up," she wheezed when they felt they had finally outrun the vines. Her hands were pressed flat against her chest and the pinkish-purple colour had drained from her face.

Suddenly, panic seemed to wash over her again as she dashed her hands to her face.

"My glasses," she wheezed. "Where are my glasses?" Alistair looked around, but he couldn't see them anywhere. Allison was going to be overwhelmingly useless without them since she needed to them to see pretty much anything that wasn't three inches from her nose. Then he saw a thin plastic arm jutting from a small mound of churned up earth not a few metres away from them. He went over and carefully plucked them from the ground. They were a little bent out of shape, but Alistair twisted them back and handed them to his sister.

"Come on," he said. "We gotta get out of here."

"Where are we, anyway?" she asked slowly.

"I dunno," he replied. "But it sure as heck isn't Auntie Bernice's basement, is it?"

"Alistair, look," Allison gasped, as she slid her glasses on.

"Wow!" they said in unison as they looked amazingly at their surroundings.

They were in some sort of garden, but it was like no garden they had ever seen before. There were flowers that looked sort of like roses, but their petals were each as big as a car. Pansies and tulips were everywhere, but there was something about them that didn't seem right. The pansies were kind of glowing and shimmering and the tulips were sort of opening and closing ever so slowly, almost as though they were breathing.

There were other unrecognizable flowers too. Big, bluish green stems seemed to almost reach the sky, topped with flowing golden petals. Large, thorny bushes poked out of the ground here and there which looked sort of like giant, deformed dandelions with bright yellow spikey-looking things poking out of them. Lush green grass was all around, but the blades were extremely wide with thick, heavy veins. The air around them was sweet-scented, like their mother's back-yard garden smelled in mid-summer, only a hundred times more fragrant.

"What is this place?" asked Alistair. He almost seemed to breathe the words rather than speak them as they stood quietly stunned.

The flowers loomed high above them, swaying gently in the breeze.

"They're so pretty," Allison said aloud as she placed a hand on one of the massive stems. The flowers shifted sharply in their direction as she spoke. Both Allison and Alistair looked at each other, matching puzzlement drifting across their faces.

"Did you see that?" Alistair asked. The flowers shifted again and they appeared to lean closer toward them, ever so slightly.

"I don't think I like this place," Allison shuddered. "I want to go home."

Before they knew what had happened, one of the giant tulips swiftly dove toward them, its large, heavy petals opening like a giant mouth. To their horror, it looked as though there were hundreds of tiny spikes within the petals. The twins leapt out of the way just in time as the tulip struck the ground with a tremendous crash. Dirt and grass showered the pair, who were now huddled on the ground, covering their faces.

"RUN!!" screamed Alistair, grabbing his sister by the arm and pulling her along behind him. His pudgy legs pumped as fast as they could as the tulip made another dive. It crashed only centimetres behind them, sending up another shower of earth and grass and almost knocking them off their feet. They weaved in and out of the giant stems, all of which were now beginning to swish and sway under their own volition. Alistair's husky girth didn't allow him to run very fast and soon it was Allison who was dragging him. They ran for cover, but didn't really know what to do or where to go. Suddenly the ground beneath their feet began to tremble violently as the flowers all seemed to become aware of their presence. Large yellow spikes began to whiz past them and they saw that it was the spikes from the giant dandelions. The green grass immediately wilted and browned around each spike as they pierced the ground and it was clear that they were full of some sort of poison. If one of those spears even nicked their heels, it would surely be the end.

They ran on, not knowing where to turn. It was like trying to find their way through a living, moving maze. Every time they turned left, a giant leaf or petal would block their path. If they turned right, another spear would come hurtling toward them. A long stem studded with dark green, razor sharp thorns swung toward them. Each thorn had an angry-looking red tip and Alistair was fairly sure that they, too, were deadly to the touch. They ducked just in time, one of the thorns just nicking Alistair's shirt collar. All they could do was keep moving, dodging one pouncing flower after another, but they couldn't help but feel as though they were being directed, almost herded by the giant, menacing flowers. Two tiny insects of some sort appeared out of nowhere and began to buzz around their heads. They were brown, about the size of an adult's thumb, with no actual physical features to speak of except for two long wings that were little more than a silvery blur. The insects circled about their heads and zipped around their feet a few times as Alistair and Allison tried to swat them away. Finally, they zoomed away, easily dodging the movements of the attacking flowers. Allison pointed to a slight gap between two stems the size of oak trees. They saw a small clearing just beyond another row of the looming green and blue stems. They bolted toward the gap, leaping through just as a half dozen poison spikes pierced the ground right where they had just been standing.

They were indeed in a clearing, but it was not the relief they had hoped for. Rather than an open field, which would allow them to put ample space between themselves and the killer garden, they stood in the centre of a large empty patch of grass which was surrounded by hundreds and hundreds of the flowers, all of which were swaying back and forth feverishly. It soon became obvious that they had indeed been herded right to this very spot. There was nowhere to run and nowhere to hide. The flowers, a gigantic mass of fragrant and beautiful purple, mauve, pink, yellow, red and blue petals loomed over them maliciously. Their stems were trembling, as were the twins, and the petals twitched with anticipation. As unlikely as it seemed, these flowers almost appeared to be savouring the victory and subsequent feast.

The twins stood huddled together, fully aware that their adventure was about to meet a horrible and undoubtedly painful end. Tears streamed down their ruddy, speckled cheeks as they trembled in each other's arms.

"Allison, I'm sorry for all the rotten things I did to you. I'm sorry for the time I glued your diary shut. I'm sorry I told everyone at school you pee the bed. I'm sorry I put a booger in your baloney sandwich. I'm so, so sorry for all the times I made you smell my fingers."

'And I'm sorry I told on you the time you tried to . . . wait . . . When did you put boogers in my baloney sandwich?"

Before Alistair could answer her, a low, droning noise filled the air, seeming to approach them from every direction. Alistair was about to ask what it was when they saw for themselves.

A swarm of flying insects was streaming towards them. At first they didn't look like anything but a large mass of dark specks against the crisp blue sky, but soon they could see that they were actually bees. But the bees were like nothing they had ever seen before. For one thing, they were humungous. They had large black and red striped abdomens, thick, shiny black bodies and long, thin legs with pincers at the end. Their wings looked massive, but it was hard to tell because they were beating so fast they weren't much more than a fuzzy blur. The strangest of all (as if they weren't strange enough) was that they each seemed to have four remarkably large and glossy green eyes.

The sound was getting louder and louder as the bees came nearer. The ground below them began to tremble and the twins didn't dare move. All around them, the strange flowers began to stir violently, jerking toward the sky. The bees were almost upon them and the twins were absolutely terrified. They closed their eyes as tight as they could and held onto each other, waiting to either be torn apart by giant bees or gobbled whole by killer flowers.

Suddenly the earth beneath their feet trembled violently, sending them tumbling. Somehow, they managed to hold onto each other and they could feel a strong wind begin to whirl around them as the flowers thrashed about in a frenzy. The deafening drone of the bees was all around them and although neither could hear the other, they were both screaming as loud as possible into each other's ears. They huddled together for a long time, surrounded by the thunderous beating of giant insect wings, wet, tearing sounds and the occasional splatter of unidentifiable liquids. Then, it was suddenly quiet. The wind stopped and the buzzing drones were abruptly silenced, replaced by a low, creaking noise that sounded like tree branches swaying in a strong wind. Alistair slowly peered out from a half-squinted eye, not knowing what to expect. Somehow, they were still alive. Once again, he was amazed by what he saw.

"Allison, look." She shuddered, terrified to open her eyes. "It's ok. It's safe. Look."

She cautiously lifted her head from the crook of her arms, pushed her glasses up on her nose and peeked out. Then her eyes bolted open in absolute astonishment.

The flowers that were within striking distance had been completely demolished. Their petals were tattered and shredded; some were nothing more than headless, wilting stems, and their colourful, if heavily damaged, remains littered the ground. The twins watched in awe as the stems seemed to shrink before their very eyes until they returned to their original height. Bits of what looked like legs and antennae also littered the ground, some of which were slightly twitching and one large, translucent wing the size of a palm frond gently fluttered down directly in front of them. Everything, including them, was covered in some strange, sticky fluid and Allison informed her brother that it was probably sap from the flowers. Whatever it was, it proved difficult to get off and Alistair would complain that his hands were sticky for days to come.

"I think they . . ." Alistair began as he tried slowly approached one of the fallen insects. As he cautiously reached out to touch its furry abdomen, one of its legs twitched and Alistair quickly jumped backwards with a sharp yelp of surprise.

"Ate them," his sister concluded. "The flowers and bees . . . they ate each other." As soon as she spoke, one of the tattered tulip-like flowers started to creak, slowly bending in their direction. The twins stood perfectly still, terrified to move, as the ragged flower slowly inched closer and closer. Its petals bulged and relaxed slowly as it approached but rather than eating them, it let out what sounded like a burp and another piece of bee leg spat out. The tulip then thudded to the ground and lay unmoving.

"OK, let's go," Alistair said, not taking his eyes from the flower.

Behind them, flying high above the garden, came yet another large, single insect, though this time it wasn't a giant bee. It looked a lot like a dragonfly, with a long, thin body, four large, buzzing wings and six long, thin, dangling legs. It was flying right toward them at a tremendous speed and the pair quickly began to run once again, but they were no match for the speeding dragonfly, which was quickly gaining on them. The undamaged flowers lurched and lunged upwards at the insect, but it managed to avoid their attack, expertly manoeuvring between their strikes.

The twins could soon hear the buzzing of the giant bug's wings and it wasn't long before it was right behind them, though still high in the air. Then, all of a sudden, it swooped downwards. The flowers darted at it, but it managed to swoop around them with little difficulty, swooshing through the stems and petals like an acrobatic stunt-plane. One of the flowers managed to nip one of its legs, but it expertly jerked away, unharmed. The children ran as fast as they could, but the humungous insect was bearing down on them quickly.

"It's coming! It's COMING!!!!!" screamed Allison. Then the dragonfly swooped down and grabbed them with the sharp claws on two of its legs.

They went soaring up and up, dashing and darting between flower attacks. Both Allison and Alistair kept their eyes clenched tight for the entire flight, terrified of what they might see. Were they being taken to some sort of web, where they would hang helplessly until it's time for dinner? To a nest, where they would be fed to weird little baby dragonflies? Or would it be something even more horrible, more unimaginable, than either of them could possibly conjure up in their frantic minds?

Before too long, they could feel that they were slowing down and then gently came to rest on solid ground once again. They were placed on what felt like soft grass, then the pincers (which had not actually pinched them but rather their shirt collars) let go.

They both opened their eyes in time to see the giant dragonfly soaring off in the distance. It did a strange little loop-the-loop twice, flicked its bulbous tail and then was gone from sight.

The twins clung to each other, still trembling. They were on a grassy ledge that seemed to jut out of the side of a large mountain. It was lush and beautiful. Far below they could see nothing but luxurious, green pastures and the sandy shores of a large body of water that stretched to the horizon, in the middle of which they could see a large island. Far below them they could see the people-eating ivy, which seemed to stretch out for hundreds of miles. Had they been anywhere else amidst the tangles of vines, they never would have gotten free. They could also see the large flower bed, which looked beautiful and harmless from such a distance. The patch of flowers that had been demolished was clearly visible and it seemed difficult to believe that they had been right in the centre of it only a few moments ago.

"What just happened?" Allison asked. Alistair just looked at her, unable to speak, and shrugged his shoulders.

"You were almost lunch," said a little voice which came from behind them. They both jumped, startled by the unexpected voice. They spun around and before them stood a little man wearing funny red pants, a brown shirt and a furry yellow vest. He wore shiny brown boots that laced up the front and leaned on a long, wooden staff. He had long silver hair and a long silver beard. His bulbous nose was a perch for tiny, wire-rimmed glasses and behind them were the kindest eyes either of them had ever seen. He smiled kindly at them, holding out one wrinkled, knob-knuckled hand. "Welcome," he said.

The twins stared, terrified, yet somehow a feeling of safety and comfort quickly set in.

"H-h-hi," said Allison. Alistair offered a slight wave of his hand. "How's it goin'?"

FIVE

Allison and Alistair sat silently, eyes wide and mouths agape, staring at the strange little man. His smile was all but toothless, just one yellowed and crooked tooth jutted from his pink gums, right in the front.

"Come, come," the strange little man said in a slow, slurred voice. "You must be hungry. You've had quite an adventure." With that, he turned and started up the hill with careful and deliberate steps. With nowhere else to go, they followed him, though somewhat reluctantly.

He led them to a little wooden cottage not far up the hill. It was obviously very old and had it appeared as though it had been repaired so often that very little of the original shack even remained. The roof was awkwardly shingled in several layers of wood and a crooked, stubby stone chimney poked up awkwardly. Gentle tendrils of smoke drifted from the chimney, however, which made the odd little cabin seem warm and inviting. Inside, he offered them a seat at a little hand-crafted table and chairs and then handed them each a cloth. It was soaked in a pungent liquid that smelled remarkably like Alistair's gym shoes.

"It will get the sap off," Sender said kindly, taking the cloth from Alistair and rubbing the boy's cheek with it. The sticky sap wiped away as thought it were water. "See?"

Something that smelled delicious simmered in a pot on a little stove and after they had managed to wipe themselves down adequately, the little fellow served them both without asking if they even wanted any.

Both Allison and Alistair were surprised at how hungry they suddenly were and devoured the delicious concoction of broth and unidentifiable vegetables.

"My name is Sender," the little man said as they devoured the soup. "You had us worried there for a while. It's a good thing the flowers were moving so slowly or you would have been killed."

Alistair choked on a spoonful of broth. "Slowly?!" he chortled. "Are you kidding me? Those things were like lightning. I thought we were dead."

"Believe me," said Sender, "under other circumstances, you would have been. The Eating Garden is not usually a playground for children. Or anyone else for that matter."

The Eating Garden, thought Allison. *That makes sense.* She didn't think she had to ask any further questions regarding the garden. Its actions and name spoke for themselves. The sooner they forgot about it, the better. Alistair didn't share his sister's desire to forget recent events, however.

"What's an Eating Garden?" Alistair asked.

"The Eating Garden is extremely dangerous," Sender explained. "I don't remember the last time anyone, or anything, has entered and lived to speak about it. Which reminds me . . ." Sender plucked a tiny wooden box with several small holes drilled into the sides from a nearby shelf. He opened it carefully and a small brown ball rolled into the palm of his hand. He then stroked it gently with one long, gnarled finger and the ball slowly unrolled until it revealed itself to be one of the strange insects that had been buzzing around their heads while they were fleeing the Eating Garden. Sender carefully brought the little insect to his lips and whispered something softly to it. Its wings immediately began to whirr and the low hum quickly became a steady buzzing sound, the same one it had made when they had first encountered it. Opening a shuttered window, Sender sent the insect flying off into the rain, then gently closed the shutter and returned his attention to the twins.

"So, how come we're so lucky?" Alistair asked.

"Everything in due time," said Sender. "Now eat up. You'll need your energy."

"Well, all I know," Alistair continued, "is that if it wasn't for those bees, we probably would have been killed."

"Ah, yes," Sender said sadly, lowering his eyes. "The Bumbles. They were very brave."

"You mean-" Allison began, her soup momentarily forgotten. She stared at the little man, absent-mindedly pushing her glasses up the bridge of her nose. "They died to help us?"

"Indeed they did, young lady," Sender said softly. "The Bumbles live in the Bumblehive Mountains, not too far from here. They're not terribly social creatures but they are brave and come when they are needed. They sacrificed themselves to save you. Of course, that's what they do, but it always saddens me when I see it happen. Yes, they were very brave indeed."

Allison no longer felt like eating. The news that the Bumbles had died to save them twisted in her stomach. She lowered her spoon slowly and slid down in her chair as the little man approached her.

"They'll be missed," he said, kindly patting the girl on the shoulder. "But they will be remembered for their bravery." He stood for a moment, his eyes focused on nothing in particular, as though dreamily off in his own little world. Suddenly he seemed to snap back to consciousness. "Now then," he said as he sat down on a rather uncomfortable looking sofa made of bark and carefully woven twigs, "do you have names or shall I simply call you Boy and Girl?"

A broad grin flashed across Alistair's freckled, chubby face as he smiled at the sarcasm. "I'm

The Tick-Tock People 59

Alistair," he said. "And this is my sister, Allison."

"Hi."

"Twins, I dare guess, eh?" Sender said, his eyes a-twinkle. "And you," he said to Allison, "are about three minutes and seventeen seconds older, correct?"

"I am," Allison said, obviously bewildered. "But how did you—"

"Well," he interrupted, his eyes slowly drifting from one child to the other, "here in Dibble we have a way of recognizing the preciseness of time. I see age has little to do with appetite, eh?"

Alistair flushed at this, but Allison grinned. It wasn't very often anyone commented on her brother's size right to his face. Usually it was Alistair making the colourful remarks. She delighted in the brief moment as she watched her brother squirm with embarrassment.

"Did you say Dibble?" asked Alistair, trying to shift the subject.

"Yes. You are in the Land of Dibble," said Sender. "On the outskirts of Mayomay Bay. Although technically you're in the Loopner Mountains, where I live."

"How did we get here?" asked Alistair.

"Well, you came through a gate, of course," Sender replied, as though it was the most obvious question he had ever answered.

"A gate?"

"Yes," he said. "There are several gates all over Dibble. They link our world and yours, among others. There used to be hundreds of them, but over time, they have slowly been destroyed or simply worn out. Only a few remain now. You fell through one of them."

"You mean the old clock?" Alistair asked as realization washed over him.

"Yes," Sender replied. "I thought that particular gate had been lost. It hasn't been used for many, many years. Good thing too, because it opens right in the middle of a patch of Tangleroot, as you well know."

Sender explained that Tangleroot is a subterranean plant species that feeds on other living organisms. It sprouts vines that yield large berries with a sweet nectar that acts as a sleeping agent, rendering the unsuspecting victim unconscious. The vine then ensnares the sleeping victim and drags them underground, where the Tangleroot absorbs the body's moisture, leaving only the drained carcass to biodegrade, enriching the soil and ensuring a fertile feeding ground.

As they spoke, Alison carefully gazed around the tiny cottage. There was a small bed in the corner with a three drawer chest pushed against the wall beside it. A tall - for Sender - coat rack stood beside the door, on which hung a woollen overcoat and long cap that looked to be woven of some heavy and unusual cord-like yarn. A small cupboard stood against the opposite wall and on it sat a few earthen dishes, carved wooden cups and a stack of old and cracked porcelain plates. There was a small wood-burning stove on top of which sat a kettle and the pot which contained the stew they were eating; the entire little room smelled of its delicious aroma. Outside, a distant and familiar rumble rippled toward them and at once, they knew it was thunder. The wind began to pick up slightly and Sender edged over to a tiny window, securing a small shutter against the wind.

"Are you some sort of hermit?" Allison asked. Sender smiled his single-toothed smile.

"Of course," he grinned. "I'm a Sender."

"I thought your *name* was Sender," Alistair said.

"Oh, no," he chuckled. "That's just what everyone calls me. I had another name once, but I've just been a Sender for so long, I can't really remember what it is."

"Just how old are you, anyway?" Alistair marvelled.

"Don't be rude," his sister scolded, slapping him on the arm. Sender began to chuckle softly.

"Oh, that's quite alright," he said pleasantly. "To be honest, I don't really know. Quite old, I suppose. Older than most of the people in Dibble, to be sure. But then, you have to be old - and may I be so humble as to say wise - to be a Sender."

"Well," Allison asked, "what does a Sender do?"

The little fellow looked at her as though she had asked another very silly question. "Why," he finally replied, "I send things. My job is to stand watch over Dibble and make sure everything is safe and secure. And if someone needs help, I know about it immediately and I *send* help. For example, when you needed help escaping the Eating Garden, I sent Thurgood."

"Thurgood?" Alistair questioned.

"Yes, Thurgood. He carried you here."

"Oh, you mean the dragonfly."

"Yes. Dragonfly," Sender said, a hint of agitation in his voice. "That's a common human misconception. It seems that a human who had visited Dibble during one of our Loxday celebrations a few hundred years ago saw one of our dragons dressed up in a silly costume. Next thing you know, every human in your world thinks a dragon has leathery skin, bat wings and breathes fire. They're actually quite fuzzy and very gentle. We keep them as household pets. They're very good with children. Dragonfly. Indeed."

The twins both exchanged curious glances.

"No," Sender continued, "Thurgood's a Whipperlooper. There is only about a hundred of his kind in Dibble and he is a very good friend of mine. Very helpful. The rest of our people live in Loxbury, a town not too far from here, just on the other side of this mountain."

After Alistair devoured three bowls of the broth and Allison skimmed her way through half of one bowl, excusing herself by saying she was full, Sender got up and began to clear away the dishes. "Now that your stomachs are appropriately filled," he said kindly, offering a leery glance toward Allison, "I suggest you get some sleep. Tomorrow is a big day. You will need your rest and I have to keep watch. I've been away from my post for too long as it is. In the morning we'll have some breakfast, and then we'll go into Loxbury to see the Mayor. Perhaps he'll be able to figure out a way to get you kids home."

Sender proceeded to place the dishes in a small basin filled with water, then pulled a few thin blankets from the tiny bureau and laid them out on the little bed. He placed two small, itchy-looking pillows on top of the blankets and stood back, admiring his own work. The twins thought the blankets, which appeared to be woven from the same rough twine as Sender's jacket, looked equally itchy and not very comfortable at all. Again, the two exchanged curious glances as Sender beamed at his impromptu sleeping arrangements.

"There we are," he said, waving a little gnarled hand at the bedding, as though unveiling a masterpiece, "I'm sure you will find this quite comfortable. It's not ideal, but it will get us through the night anyway. Rest up now, rest up.

Busy day tomorrow."

The thunder had become more frequent and beyond the shuttered windows, the darkening sky flickered with electricity. Before long, the distinct sound of fat raindrops could be heard pelting the shingled rooftop and it was several minutes before anyone realized that there was something tapping on one of the windows. Sender opened the shutter and the strange little insect whizzed around his head, buzzing excitedly.

"Excellent," said Sender. "Well done." The little insect set down in his palm and curled up into a little ball once again.

"Get some sleep," he said to the twins as he placed the little brown ball into its box and returned it to the shelf. "I'll be back as soon as I can."

Without another word, Sender spun around on his heels, his jacket billowing out slightly, and marched out the door, grabbing the hat from the coat-hook as he went. His footsteps were quickly swallowed by the sound of pouring rain. The quiet crackle of the smouldering fire was drowned out by the thunderous pounding of rain and the wind outside buffeted the little building relentlessly, making Alistair wonder if the shack was even going to weather the storm. Allison and her brother stood for a moment, staring at the scratchy looking bed.

"If you think I'm getting in that thing with you, you're crazy," Allison finally said.

"Oh come on," grinned Alistair as he plopped onto the bed. He rolled himself up in the blanket like a cocoon with only his chubby, ruddy, mop-topped head poking out. "It's not that bad." His sister looked at him with great reluctance for a few more seconds before she slowly and warily sat down beside him and wrapped herself in her own blanket.

"If I hear one noise come out of you that doesn't involve speaking, you're sleeping on the floor."

"Scouts honour," he grinned, his eyes twinkling in the quickly dimming room. "You won't hear so much as a peep."

Alistair rolled onto his side, his back to his sister. She rolled in the opposite direction, facing the little door and shuttered window. It was almost completely dark outside and the full force of the storm began to rattle the tiny shack. The blankets were every bit as itchy and uncomfortable as they looked and smelled oddly of a cross between hay, old books and something that resembled (but wasn't quite) mothballs.

"Alistair," Allison said, her voice sounding as though she were already half asleep.

"Yeah?"

"Do you think we're gonna get home?"

"Yeah," he replied, but he knew the uncertainty in his voice gave away his own doubtfulness. "Sender seems nice. I think he's going to help us as much as he can."

"Yeah," Allison agreed. "He'll help us."

A few moments later, Alistair began to giggle.

"What's so funny?" Allison asked, but no sooner did she get the words out when she knew why he was giggling. It was as though a green, sulphur haze had filled the room, zooming directly toward her nose and attacking her senses. "Alistair! Get off the bed! I told you . . ."

"Nuh-uh," he defended himself. "You said if you *heard* anything I had to sleep on the floor. You didn't hear a thing, did you?"

She decided it wasn't worth arguing about. In a few minutes the rank odour would pass and she wouldn't have to worry about her flatulent brother until morning. As she drifted off, the wind and rain howled and hammered outside as the shack shimmied and shook all about them. Somewhere in her dreamy subconscious, she thought she heard Alistair giggle again but if he had blasted her a second time, she was asleep before she ever knew it.

SIX

A thunderous crash pulled Alistair out of a dream. He had been running through the Eating Garden with Allison and Oscar. The flowers were bombarding them from every direction, lightning fast, narrowly missing them with each violent attack. The flowers were different than those which they had experienced already, which had been frightening enough. The flowers in his dream had rows and rows of razor-sharp teeth, dark crimson tongues lolled about within the savage petals and a foul odour spilled out every time one of them came near. Bumbles swarmed above them and for a moment Alistair thought they were there to save them. Instead, they dove at them like fighter jets, their long, pointed stingers dripping with a greenish fluid that he instinctively knew would be fatal if it even touched their skin, let alone penetrate into their bloodstream. Oscar bounded about the garden like a circus performer, but Allison wasn't so lucky. She stumbled and tripped over every root, stick and rock and it was a miracle that she hadn't been devoured. He could hear the drone of the Bumbles get louder and, looking up, realized that Thurgood - a thousand Thurgoods - had joined them. They swooped and looped like acrobats, high above them, but the flowers paid them no mind. As one of the Whipperloopers swooped down for a closer look, Alistair noticed that its head had been replaced by Auntie Bernice's head. She was laughing hysterically, her eyes evil slits of humourless mirth as she cackled like a wicked old witch.

"The mop and bucket are in the cellar," she cackled. "Don't be afraid. Just go to the cellar." She cackled again, a high-pitched squeal that threatened to pierce his eardrums and then she swooped away from him and rejoined the rest of the flying insects, all of which were cackling in unison.

He could see the clearing before him and ran for it, but his legs were heavy and difficult to move. As though running in slow motion, he finally pushed through the opening and then everything changed, as often happens in dreams. He suddenly found himself hurtling through empty space. Looking back over his shoulder, he saw that he had run right over a jutting cliff. Above him, savage man-eating flowers writhed and lashed at empty air. Looking down, he saw that he was plummeting toward a large patch of Tangleroot. Allison and Oscar were nowhere to be seen and a second or two later, he landed with a heavy crunch, immediately entwined in the ivy.

He tried to scream for help, but a thick, pulsing vine wrapped around his upper torso and his head, gagging his mouth. His chest was restricted and all that came out was a creaking whimper as his life was slowly being compressed out of him. Somewhere, Allison was calling his name.

"Alistair. Alistair! ALISTAIR!!!"

Alistair gasped for air as his chest was suddenly released from its crushing pressure. His eyes opened (he hadn't even realised they were shut) and his sister was looking him straight in the eyes, her hand covering his mouth. He tried to move his arms, but found he was still wound in a tight embrace, but after a moment, he realised he was tangled in the old blanket. Finally he stopped struggling and tried to catch his breath. Once his faculties were about him again, Alistair realised that he wasn't in an ivy patch after all. Instead, he found himself lying on the cottage floor with Allison kneeling beside him. The storm still raged on outside and the timbers shivered with every rocking thunderclap.

"What happened?" he croaked.

"You were having a dream," she said. "A bad one. You scared me half to death."

"Auntie Bernice," he muttered.

"What? What about her?"

"I-I don't know," he said, detangling himself from the blanket. He was sheathed in sweat and his heart was racing a mile a minute. "But she was there. Laughing at us. And Oscar was there too. I think he got eaten by the ivy. And you . . . You

. . ." Tears were beginning to well up in his eyes and despite his every effort to hold them back, they began to spill down his flushed and freckled cheeks.

"It was just a dream," she said, patting him on the shoulder. "Oscar's OK. And so am I."

At that moment the door burst open and rain began to flood into the shack. Just as Allison got up to shut the door, Sender entered and closed the door behind him. The little fellow was drenched to the skin. He shook his tiny frame, sending droplets of water in every direction, and then wiped his hand across his soaked and grinning face.

"A little moist today," he said pleasantly. "Not the best travelling weather, eh? Oh well. Hungry?"

He shrugged out of his waterlogged coat and then went about the kitchen, peeling and chopping little roots and strange vegetables into a pot. He placed a log in the fire and in a few minutes the shack, which had become cold and damp over night, was warm and comfy. It wasn't long before the pot was simmering and a scrumptious aroma filled the room. Alistair's stomach rumbled at the delicious redolence and his sister's stomach gurgled audibly. She flushed a little as her brother and Sender both looked at her, grinning.

"Pardon me," she almost whispered, pushing her glasses further up the bridge of her nose. Her reluctance to eat was forgotten and she devoured three bowls of the wonderful concoction. Alistair, usually able to out-eat his sister by leaps and bounds, only managed two, his stomach still somewhat uneasy from his traumatic nightmare.

After they had finished eating, Sender handed each of them a heavy overcoat. Allison's fit almost perfectly, though a little short in the arms, while Alistair's was terribly tight across the shoulders and the buttons at the front were under tremendous stress as he tried to fasten it across his ample belly.

"So," Allison said reluctantly as she slipped into her jacket, "we're going out in that?" She pointed toward the window, indicating the storm raging outside.

"Yes," Sender grinned. "Why not?"

"We'll get soaked. Can't we wait until it stops?"

"Stops?" he asked, a queer look crossing his ruddy face, quickly replaced by a strange look of revelation, as though he had just remembered something of great importance. "Oh, no," he said quickly, "Hurry along, now. We haven't time. We have to get you to the Mayor. Why, if you two were still here when it stops, well, it would be catastrophic."

"Wait," said Alistair, "what do you mean? First you say it's lucky the flowers are moving so slowly or they would have killed us and now you say it'll be a catastrophe if the storm *stops*? That doesn't make any sense."

"Oh dear," Sender said, his voice trembling ever so slightly. "I don't want to worry you. We'll get you home before anything terrible happens.

But we *must* go now. The Mayor will know what to do. He's very wise. He's also the town barber, you know."

"Well, I'm not going anywhere," Alistair said. He stamped each foot once on the ground, as though anchoring himself.

"There isn't time, boy," Sender almost wailed. His wild eyes seemed to be bulging almost right out of their sockets and his already frizzled hair seemed to be even more untamed. He fidgeted for a few moments, shuffling back and forth on his feet, until finally, in one swift move, he scooped the hefty boy into his tiny arms.

Alistair couldn't believe that the tiny little man was now carrying him across the floor as though he were a sack of potatoes. Sender huffed and puffed as he shuffled toward the door, asking Allison to open it for him. He lugged the boy outside, where they were immediately soaked by the cold, sharp rain. Thunder rolled and lighting flickered in the sky. Thurgood was waiting patiently not far from the cottage. He wore a sturdy looking harness on his back which resembled a horse saddle and his wings fluttered almost lazily as they were buffeted by the wind.

Sender heaved Alistair onto Thurgood's back, and then cupped his hands so Allison could use them as a stoop. She quickly alley-ooped up and sat in front of her brother, who was still speechless. Fearing she may lose them in the strong winds, Allison quickly slipped her glasses from her freckled face and tucked them into her pocket.

"You'll be going to Loxbury to see the Mayor," Sender shouted above the wind and rain, though his voice was almost lost. "He'll help you. Don't worry. You're in good hands. Well, wings, as it were. Just hold on tight." With that, he patted Thurgood on his head and gave him a gentle slap on the tail. Thurgood's wings began to hum as they beat faster and faster and in a few seconds, they were slowly rising from the wet and muddy ground, climbing higher and higher into the sky. Allison clutched the saddle horn tightly as Alistair slipped his hands around her waist. Both squealed in fear, clenching their eyes as tightly as they could as they lifted off. After a few minutes, Alistair's fear gave way to curiosity and he opened his eyes and looked down. They had risen to what seemed to be a few hundred metres and Sender was little more than a tiny brownish-black speck beside his little cabin. He was waving in the air, one little arm arcing wildly back and forth. Alistair cautioned a wave back, a little nervous to let go of his sister. Then, in a sudden burst of speed, they were off and for a second or two, he thought he might topple end over end, right off the back of the Whipperlooper.

They flew over the Eating Garden, which seemed to go on forever and ever, and then crossed the waters of Mayomay Bay. It was difficult for Alistair to see much due to the rain that pummelled them relentlessly and the hazy, silvery fog which seemed to hang lifelessly in the air.

It seemed as though they were right in the middle of a war zone with booming explosions detonating to their left and right. Every clap of thunder and lightning seemed to envelope them, almost shattering their ear drums (or so it seemed). At one point, a bolt of lightning zipped toward them and Thurgood swooped out of its path with only centimetres to spare. Even in the frigid rain, they could feel the heat emanating from the bolt and although he wouldn't notice until much later, the little hairs on the back of Alistair's neck were singed. All three of them bounced around on the turbulent air and the twins were both pretty sure they were going be killed before they set foot on solid ground ever again.

They had been swooping and swirling, riding the violent air currents, when Thurgood lurched suddenly to the left. It felt as though they had been hit by a freight train and Alistair let out a loud yelp of shock and fear.

"Are you OK?" Allison bellowed, barely able to hear her own voice, let alone her brother's. She had clenched her eyes so tight in fear that she was absolutely terrified to open them. He didn't answer. "Alistair? Are you OK?" He still didn't answer. Her heart leapt to her throat as she opened her eyes and looked behind her. She was alone on Thurgood's back.

"ALISTAIR!"

Her fear was suddenly gone. Looking over Thurgood's back, she could see her brother tumbling freely through the non-colour grey sky and then disappear into the thick, angry clouds below.

"Thurgood, wait!" she bellowed, slapping the Whipperlooper on the back. "Alistair fell off. He's gone. Stop. STOP!!"

Thurgood sharply banked right and Allison almost fell off as well. They dove straight down like a torpedo, thunder and lightning blasting around them like artillery fire. She could hear a strange wailing noise and at first she thought it was the wind, or perhaps Thurgood, then she realised that it was her own voice as she was screaming out of fear, not only for her life, but also her brother's.

It was difficult to see through the heavy rain and grey, foggy sky, but something dark and rather large seemed to be climbing toward them. At first it was little more than a murky grey smudge, but it quickly grew larger and darker. Soon it was a dark grey smudge, and then black, then she saw what looked like another Whipperlooper. As it approached at great speed, she could see that something was on its back.

"What the-" she began, then she could see her brother's big head grinning from ear to ear as he sat astride the Whipperlooper as if he was riding a bronco. He was holding onto his own saddle horn with one hand and waving the other wildly in the air. "Yaaa-hooooooo!!!!!!!" he bellowed, barely audible over the wind and storm. His red hair was plastered to his head and face; his cheeks were the colour of ripened apples and from what Allison could see, he was having the time of his life. Her panic quickly turned to annoyance. Alistair obviously didn't appreciate the gravity of the situation. Deep inside, however, she was relieved. As scared as she was in this strange land, she was glad she had Alistair with her. He may be big, dumb and ugly, but he was her brother and she was pretty sure he wouldn't let anything *really* bad happen to her.

They climbed higher and higher, each astride their own Whipperlooper, zigging and zagging through the raging sky. The surrounding noise was deafening and the pressure on their inner ears was tremendous. Neither thought they could take much more of the onslaught of sound and the fear of being zapped by a stray lightning bolt when all of a sudden they burst through the heavy cloud cover and into the calm, morning sky.

Below them, they could see nothing but swirling thick clouds rippling with electricity and muffled thunderclaps. Above them, the sun shone brightly and the sky was a shade of blue the likes of which neither had seen before. The air was warm and it wasn't long before both were completely dry. The sight was magnificent and the twins looked about in utter astonishment as they sailed effortlessly across a denim sea of sky. They grinned and laughed as they glided along on calm air currents, their hair blowing off of their freckled faces. Allison's braids fluttered behind her head as they soared, their overcoats billowing like capes. Alistair let out another "Yaaaaaa-hooooooo!!!" as his Whipperlooper dropped and arched, flipped and loop-the-looped, as though it were a ride at a carnival. Thurgood was a little less flamboyant, only swaying lazily from left to right, as though he understood that Allison wasn't the a thrill-seeker that her brother was.

Before long, the sky below them became less of a dark and angry grey, giving way to light grey, then white and billowy clouds. The lightning became less and less frequent until it had disappeared altogether and the thunder had ceased completely. Soon, the clouds began to break up and lush green grass could be seen through the fluffy gaps. In no time, the cloud cover disappeared completely and they saw that they were soaring over beautiful meadows dotted with little houses. They could see a few rivers and ponds, what looked to be fences along a number of winding roadways, and here and there were a few thickets of rich, green forests. The Whipperloopers began their descent, giving the twins identical Tummy Tippers - that strangely fun feeling one gets in their stomach when they drive up and down a small hill very quickly.

They skimmed along the surface of the meadows, only a metre or so from the ground, and the sweet aroma of fresh grass tickled their nostrils and warm air caressed their skin. They continued on this way, barely touching the ground, for what seemed to be several kilometres. When they came to a small pond, Thurgood just skimmed the surface, his dangling legs leaving identical trails of water in their wake. Alistair grinned at his sister as he leaned over as far as he could and let his fingertips drag along the water's surface.

"You're going to fall off again," she shouted. Alistair just rolled his eyes at her and leaned further as he laughed with genuine, heartfelt delight.

They approached a series of small hills and crested each of them with only a few metres between themselves and the ground, which again caused a series of Tummy Tippers in each of their stomachs. As they slipped over the final hill, an entire village came into view. This, the twins surmised, was Loxbury.

SEVEN

The tiny hamlet was bustling with dozens upon dozens of little people, all of whom looked a lot like Sender. They were crowding the town square, each one garbed in brightly coloured clothes that seemed to have been woven from the same itchy-looking fabric. The little men all had facial hair of varying lengths and colours, from the younger looking fellows who had only little bits of fuzz on their chins to the elderly looking ones, who all had long and flowing, if somewhat unkempt, beards. The women were wearing long dresses made of a more delicate looking material and most wore little hats or bonnets. The children all wore simple shorts and shirts.

The streets were lined with buildings, though unlike Sender's shack, these were larger and finely crafted from stone blocks, wood and sturdy-looking straw. Some had hand-painted signs out front that read 'Barber', 'Bakery', 'Blacksmith', 'School' and so on while another had a large sign which read 'Doc Foober', accompanied by a crudely drawn and undoubtedly inaccurate picture of a little bald-headed man with a long beard and frizzy hair that jutted out wildly from his impossibly large ears. All eyes were skyward as the twins rapidly approached on the Whipperloopers.

What struck the twins most strangely, however, was the fact that there were an extremely large number of clocks all over the town. From their altitude, they could see that there were clocks on the front of every building. There were pictures of clocks on large signs, gardens had been cultivated to resemble clock faces, even the clouds which drifted lazily across the clear blue sky seemed to vaguely resemble clock faces. The townspeople also wore small clocks or watches on leather straps, which hung around each of their necks and many of them wore several wristwatches on their arms.

The town was literally bedecked with large clocks, small clocks, pictures of clocks, even the town square was designed to look like a clock and wasn't really a square at all. In the centre of the town square stood a large bronze pillar which was easily two stories tall, festooned with clock faces of all different shapes and sizes, not to mention several hourglasses and sundials. Dozens of tiny posts jutted out in every direction, each affixed to one of the clocks. It looked as though there had once been something attached to the topmost peak of the tall spire, perhaps another clock-face, but had apparently been removed rather forcefully, judging by the bent and mangled empty bracket.

Wooden carts pulled by tiny brown and white horses were lined up along the earthen streets. *But they're not quite horses*, thought Allison. They had the broad and powerful body of a horse and the long faces, but their legs were very short and almost stumpy, and rather than hooves they had little feet with three webbed toes. Instead of long flowing tails, they had what looked quite similar to large, flat beaver tails.

Beside one little boy sat a dragon; a small furry dog-like creature with a long snout from which protruded four long, thick whiskers which appeared to be quivering in anticipation as it shifted excitedly from paw to paw. It had a long furry tail, which wagged gleefully back and forth and a long black tongue which lolled out of its open mouth, dripping gobs of saliva onto the earthy ground. Alistair wasn't sure, but the little creature seemed to almost be smiling; there was a twinkle in its eye that made the odd little fellow appear harmless and kind. When it let out a few barks, it sounded more like a frog with a bad cold than it did a dog.

Most of the buildings had trickles of smoke rising lazily from their chimneys and the square was engulfed in a medley of delicious aromas that drifted up to them. Fresh bread, ginger, straw and mint were a few that the twins could recognize, but there were others, equally redolent, which were entirely unfamiliar. A few of the little people were dressed in light brown uniforms, police of some sort, and they were carefully keeping people off the street and on the wooden sidewalks as they tried to get a good look at the strangers who had just flown into town.

Across the street from the growing, curious crowd stood a much larger building with big wooden pillars, a large pair of wooden doors and a sign which read 'Town Hall'. Oddly enough, beside the sign hung a red and white barber's pole.

There was also a small group of people wearing matching bright green uniforms consisting of long jackets, shorts and tall furry hats with straps that attached just below their noses. Beautiful brass clocks hung from a gold chain around each of their necks, their shiny faces glimmering in the bright sunlight. They were all holding strange looking musical instruments, some of which were *almost* recognizable. One fellow was holding what looked to be a large trombone, but it had three bell sections and two slides rather than the usual one of each. Another fellow, heavy-set with large rosy cheeks and a white beard that came to two separate points, carried a tuba, but the tuba was larger than he, with coils and coils of brass tubing that went every which way, fully encircling his ample body, and there looked to be about a hundred valves. It looked more like a giant brass pretzel that had gone terribly wrong than a musical instrument. There were other instruments as well that seemed particularly odd, but most of them didn't actually look like anything either of the twins had seen before. There was something that resembled a large bass drum but it had a series of strings stretched across the skin and from the centre jutted a long brass pole with a pair of cymbals on the very top. There was also a flute with bright red, blue and green feathers poking out of it at very odd angles; a lady stood teetering awkwardly as she held what looked like a large double bass (twice as large as she) as though it were a violin. A lonely looking little old fellow with long, gangly arms, a bent and stooped back and tremendous puffs of silvery hair poking out of his ears held up a circular brass ring with one trembling hand, his other clutching a tiny brass rod, ready for his cue. As the twins approached, this little fellow smiled and revealed a gummy, toothless grin amidst a white frizzled mass of wiry whiskers. After a moment, Allison recognised the little man as Doc Foober, whose crude drawing on the sign wasn't entirely inaccurate after all. The Whipperloopers came to rest in front of the Town Hall doors as the band struck up a tune which was decidedly tuneless, but very, very lively. The large tuba player blew into his instrument with great gusts of breath, his already chubby cheeks stretching to almost impossibly large proportions as his stubby fingers manipulated the keys. His eyes were squinted so tight they almost seemed to disappear. Doc Foober stood almost statue-still in concentration, hand poised, ready to strike his instrument at just the precise moment. The other musicians played with equal enthusiasm and although they were not what one might call *good*, they certainly seemed to put a great deal of enthusiasm in their efforts.

As the band played on, the large wooden doors of the Town Hall opened and a long red carpet rolled toward the twins, unfurling as it approached and ended in a tiny *flop* at their feet. The first to come out of the building was a tall, lanky man with a long, sour-looking face, wearing a dark blue suit. He wore tiny glasses that pinched the very tip of his long, beak-like nose and he walked in long, broad strides, reaching the twins in only a few extended steps. Attached to his lapel was a shiny silver badge which read "Welcoming Committee". He carried a rolled up sheet of paper tucked under his arm. As he stepped up to the Whipperloopers and without looking at either Alistair or Allison, he unrolled the paper and held it out at arms length.

The lanky man squinted his little black eyes to read the paper as he cleared his throat. The band awkwardly stopped playing as the lanky man held up a long-fingered hand.

"Esteeeeeeeeeemed guests of Dibble," he said in a nasally tone, his Adam's apple bobbing up and down as he spoke. The band surged and the lanky man shot them a sharp look. Immediately, the band music trailed off awkwardly, the musicians looking somewhat embarrassed. The lanky man returned to the paper.

"Esteeeeeeeeeemed guests of Dibble," he repeated. At that moment, Doc Foober *'tinged'* his brass ring, eliciting another sharp glance from the lanky man.

"Sorry," Doc Foober croaked, a weak smile trickling across his wrinkled face.

The lanky man rolled his eyes as he returned to the paper again. He cleared his throat, and then glanced cautiously at the musicians. The chubby tuba player giggled nervously and grinned, waving at them with a wiggle of his sausagey fingers.

"Esteeeeeeeemed guests of Dibble," he said for the third time, much louder than he had before. He paused for a moment as Alistair and Allison sat atop their Whipperloopers, not sure what to say or do at this point. "Welcome."

The band struck up again, even louder and more enthusiastically than they had before, and the lanky man rolled up the paper, turned on his heels and returned to the building, his nose held high in the air.

The twins looked at each other curiously as another person, a woman this time, emerged from the building. She stood perhaps two metres tall and about four metres around and wore a shiny green and yellow striped dress that would look right at home in Auntie Bernice's closet. The dress skimmed the ground as she walked, concealing her feet and giving her the illusion that she was rolling rather than walking. Her smile was very wide and cheerful and her glistening green eyes conveyed a kindness that seemed to radiate around her entire being. She had bright bluish hair, which was piled high atop her round head in grand, swooping curls, giving her the illusion that she was actually taller than her true height, and adorning her tresses were beautiful white, yellow and blue flowers. The band trailed off once again as she approached and she too, pulled a roll of paper from beneath her arm. She unrolled it and began to read.

"Ladies and gentlemen," she began. Her voice was very squeaky, almost like a cartoon mouse. This amused Alistair, who let out an audible giggle. His sister jabbed him sharply in the ribs with her elbow and he slapped a hand over his mouth to try to stifle his chuckles. "May I present to you, his honour and esteemed leader, our most valued citizen, cherished by all, despised by none and is offering a two for one special if you book your haircut before next Loxday..." She turned to the open doors and her grin widened even further, "Our Mayor!!!"

The crowd, which had grown to what looked like the entire town, erupted in applause. The band struck up yet again and this time, their playing actually hurt the twins' ears, it was so loud and terrible.

A stubby little man emerged from the Town Hall. He wore a long and shimmering robe that glistened like spun gold. Under the robe he wore a light green tunic and dark green trousers held up by rainbow-coloured suspenders. Atop his head sat a tall top hat, the same dark green as his trousers, adorned with a beautiful clock which was set into the pipe of the hat. Across his ample torso was slung a large white sash which read 'Mayor Maynott' in large blue script. He had a kind, cherubic face with large chubby cheeks, twinkling and crinkled blue eyes and half-glasses that sat high atop his tiny little button nose. He was beardless but wore a long white moustache that grew down to his knees, the tips coming to little screwy curls. He beamed with delight, waving enthusiastically at his fellow citizens as he passed. It took the Mayor almost ten minutes to walk the thirty or so metres between the doors and the Whipperloopers as he stopped repeatedly to shake hands, kiss babies and pat little children on the head. At one point, a little man with a funny brown hat quickly set up what appeared to be a sort of camera on a creaky-looking tripod and snapped a photo, the large flashbulb giving off a blast of light so sharp and brilliant that for the next half hour, Allison and Alistair could see little blue smudges everywhere they looked.

The Mayor finally reached Thurgood, who stood closer than Alistair's Whipperlooper, and extended a soft, pudgy hand. He continued to grin with delight as Allison reluctantly took his hand and allowed him to help her to the ground. Alistair slipped from the back of his Whipperlooper and stepped alongside his sister. The band again came to another awkward and somewhat uneven stop as the Mayor turned to them and raised both hands. He turned back to the twins and bowed graciously.

"Welcome to Loxbury," he said cheerfully. His voice was surprisingly deep.

"Thanks," said Alistair as he sheepishly jammed his hands into his jeans pockets.

"Yes," said Allison awkwardly, still somewhat apprehensive of the entire situation. "Thank you."

The look of kindness on the Mayor's face quickly turned to worry as he spoke. "I trust you had a satisfactory flight? Did you? Oh, I certainly hope you did. Maybe you didn't. If not, I'm terribly sorry. Oh my, oh my, I knew the flight would be terrible. Here you are, guests in our little town and already you've been made to feel uncomfortable. Oh dear, oh dear, I am so sorry, I do apologise. Or *did* you have a nice flight? Perhaps you did. Oh, I don't know. Did you? I'm always so worried about these things. My, my, my, I do certainly hope you had a nice flight and nothing terrible happened. So, you did have a nice flight, then, or didn't you? Yes? No? Yes? Oh dear."

By the time the Mayor was finished speaking, neither Allison nor Alistair even knew if he had asked a question. He hadn't even paused to take a breath before he finished so everything he had just said sounded like one extremely long word. The twins looked at the surrounding crowd, who looked on anxiously, awaiting their response.

"Um," Allison said slowly. "Y-yes?"

The crowd erupted in grand applause and the Mayor clapped his hands together like a delighted child as another broad and beaming grin washed across his relieved face.

"Magnificent!" he boomed. The crowd was suddenly upon them, cheering and laughing, as though she had just presented them with the most wonderful news they had ever heard, patting them on the back and hugging them tightly. The band struck up another tune and before they knew what had even happened, Alistair and Allison had been hoisted up onto people's shoulders and were being paraded through the town square.

As they marched around the square, the twins noticed a few very peculiar things (as though things weren't peculiar enough). First of all, all the street names were all somehow clock related. They saw Watch Road, Pendulum Boulevard, Spring Avenue, and the Town Hall sat at the corner of Tick and Tock Streets.

"Alistair, look," Alison gasped as they passed a statue of a little fellow who looked just like Sender. On the brass plaque was inscribed:

'Horatio Q. Loxbury - Our Founder'.

As they passed through the throngs of people they were forced to stop over and over again, shaking hands and accepting hugs, head rubs and the occasional good-natured noogie. Alistair revelled in the attention, a cheesy, self-satisfying grin spilling across his freckled face, as he gladly shook hands and waved his arms in the air. Allison, on the other hand, was beginning to feel somewhat nervous over all the attention. She was relieved when Mayor Maynott leaned toward them and shouted "Come, come, let's get indoors, where we can talk with fewer distractions." The band played on, their warbling tunes combining awkwardly with the shrill din of the excited crowd.

EIGHT

The large doors swung closed behind them, muffling the whoops, shouts and applause from outside. The interior of the Town Hall was simple but quite nice. The floor was covered in rich, red carpeting, which appeared to be hand-woven, in the centre of which was an intricately embroidered clock face. There were a few furnishings here and there such as chairs and tables but all in all, it was a rather humble little building that was awash with natural light spilling through two large windows. Candle holders hung on the walls, their wax drippings reaching almost all the way to the floor like stalactites. As they approached a small door, it was opened from within by the same little circus tent lady who had introduced the Mayor. They stepped into a small office which had been crafted in dark wood and more red carpeting. A large desk sat in the centre, behind which stood an entire wall of shelves packed with hundreds of books and reams upon reams of paper as well as candle holders similar to those which adorned the outer foyer. In front of the desk were three emerald green barber's chairs. A portrait of Horatio Q. Loxbury along side a portrait of the Mayor. A large mirror hung on the other, in front of which stood a shelf table with an assortment of combs, brushes, what looked like a straight razor and a large glass jar containing a strange blue liquid.

"Thank you, Verona," the Mayor said with a slow nod of the head and it occurred to both Allison and her brother that the Mayor's voice was slow and slurred, much like Sender's had been. Verona offered a slight curtsey and motioned for Allison and her brother to have a seat in the very comfortable looking chairs. The Mayor sat in down behind his desk as the twins settled in their soft seats. Verona quietly left the room, shutting the door softly behind her.

The Mayor crossed his arms over his ample belly and laced his fingers together, smiling broadly at the twins for several moments. His twinkling eyes darted back and forth as Allison sat motionless, bolt upright, her hands nervously kneading the padded arms of her chair. The sudden silence made her uncomfortable, as she was not used to being the centre of attention *and* at a loss for words. Alistair, on the other hand, appeared right at home as he almost lounged in his chair, sitting cross-legged, one arm dangling over the armrest, and the other absently picking at a little stone which was lodged in the tread of his shoe. A moment later, Verona returned, carrying a tray with a tea pot and three little cups along with a dish holding several delicious-looking sweet-cakes. She poured the tea, which smelled tantalising, and handed a cup to Allison.

"Thank you," she said softly, taking the cup.

Verona handed another to Alistair, who took it absently. "Thanks," he said, eyeballing the sweet-cakes.

"Please," said the Mayor, as though he knew exactly what Alistair was thinking, "help yourself."

"Can I have two?" he asked.

"Alistair!" his sister hissed. "Don't be rude."

"Well, I'm hungry!"

"Not at all," the Mayor chuckled. "The boy has an appetite, that much is obvious. Of course you may have two."

Alistair quickly snatched two cakes from the plate, dropping one in his lap as he stuffed the other in his mouth, sending sticky, red jelly dribbling down his chin.

"Ugh!" Allison grunted. "You're such a slob."

Alistair mumbled something indistinguishable through a mouth full of sweet-cake as he wiped his chin with his sleeve.

"I presume Sender explained how you came to find yourselves in the Land of Dibble?" the Mayor asked as he stood up from his chair. The twins watched as he absently moved the papers and documents around on his cluttered desktop.

"Sort of," Alistair replied. "He said we came through a gate, whatever that is."

"Ah, yes, a gate," said the Mayor. "Yes, well, there are many gates which act as passageways between our world and many others." He had begun to sit down again, but appeared to be dissatisfied in the way he had arranged his desk. He continued to shuffle the contents of his desktop as he spoke, never seeming satisfied with the results. "At one time it was not uncommon for a human to visit the Land of Dibble and sometimes a Boffle would venture into the human world, though it was usually far too frightening and dangerous to stay for any extended amount of time."

"A Boffle?" Allison asked.

"Yes," he explained, "Our people are called Boffles, though humans often referred to us as Tick-Tock People. You see, we enter your world through your clocks. Well, not *all* of your clocks, just certain ones. There used to be hundreds of gates in your world, as I believe Sender told you, but over time, they would simply wear down or became damaged or destroyed."

Mayor Maynott stepped back from his desk to consider his current arrangement for a moment, and then began to shuffle them together once again.

"Are all the clocks here gates to other worlds?" Alistair asked.

"Oh, yes," said the Mayor. "Well, most of them, anyway, but we don't really use them anymore, as I said. It's been a long time since a Boffle dared enter the human world."

He had fanned the papers out so the entire desktop was covered, then paused for a moment, scratching his chin as he contemplated what to do with the clutter. Finally, he opened a drawer and simply scooped the papers inside, quickly closing the drawer with a dull thud.

"So Auntie Bernice's clock was a gate?" Allison marvelled.

"Precisely," the Mayor said, "but as Sender told you, that gate hadn't been used in a number of years. To be quite honest, I find it remarkable that you even came through at all."

"Well, it shouldn't be too hard to get home then, should it?" asked Allison. "I mean, if there's a bunch of gates still around, can't we just use one to get back?"

"Well, I'm afraid it's not quite that simple," the Mayor said as he began removing the sheets from the desk and placing them squarely on the desktop, careful to uncrease the ones which had been crumpled when he shoved them into the drawer. "You see, you can't simply go through just any gate. You must go through the very one from which you came, since each gate on this side has a counterpart on your side, what we call a counter clock. If you were to try to get through a gate whose counter clock was, oh, I don't know, sunk on a ship, for example, you might very well come out on the ocean floor. Why, you may find yourself half way around the world, or in a different world altogether, with no way to get home. Or the human gate may no longer exist at all and you could be trapped between-time."

"Between time?" Allison queried.

"Yes,"explained Mayor Maynott. "That's when you slip through a gate and there is no exit. You simply drift between-time, lost between both worlds for all eternity."

"That's gotta suck," Alistair mumbled.

"Yes. It's always best to use the gate from which you came, that way you know where you're going on the other side."

"OK," said Alistair, licking the final remnants of his second sweet-cake from his fingers, "so we use the gate we came from. We know it exists, right? Can't we just go through that one?"

A look of concern washed over the Mayor's face. "That's not going to be quite so simple," he said regretfully.

"Why not?"

"Well," he continued, "we've had a bit of bad luck, I'm afraid." He began to pace back and forth in front of the twins, his papers forgotten, as he worriedly rubbed his hands together. "Oh, I had hoped we might have avoided this. I really do dislike bearing bad news."

"What is it?" Alison asked, getting up from her chair. The Mayor stopped pacing and looked first at her, then at Alistair.

"I-I-I'm afraid there's been an . . . incident," he said, "involving your gate."

"Well, what kind of incident?"

"Ohhh," he fretted, "I do so hate to have to tell you this, but I suppose I must."

"Would you just tell us?" Alistair demanded, a hint of nervousness in his voice.

"I don't know how to say this," said the Mayor, "but your gate is . . . well . . . missing."

"Missing?!"

"Not missing, exactly," he said. "We know where it is. At least, we do now. Perhaps I had better explain from the beginning."

Mayor Maynott called for Verona to bring more tea, and then began to explain why he was in such a panicked state.

"On the other side of Mayomay Bay," he began, "there is a terrible place called Tenebrous Marsh. There lives a man named Burcheeze. Now, as you may have gathered, we Boffles like to celebrate when there is reason to and, to be honest, we're a very cheerful community and we celebrate quite often."

"I hadn't noticed, actually," said Alistair, making no effort to disguise his sarcasm. Allison rolled her eyes at her brother's bluntness.

"Yes, well, Burcheeze noticed and it wasn't long before he began to get annoyed by our constant revelling. There were several occasions when he would storm into town and ravage everything in sight. We've rebuilt our Bakery three times and the school house is brand new, we've only just finished it last week. And, I'm saddened to say, we have lost a few of our own citizens during his frenzied tirades. Very good Boffles, each one of them, and very dearly missed. He's a terrible, terrible man."

"And this guy took your clock?" Alistair asked.

"Yes," the Mayor replied. "Two days ago, he came charging into Loxbury like a rampaging monster. We were in the middle of our annual Loxweek celebration."

"Loxweek?"

"Yes, Loxweek marks the first of seven days before Loxday. It's a week long celebration that leads to the Turning of the Key."

"Wait," said Allison, "I'm confused. What key?"

"Every year, on Loxday, we turn the Great Key one full revolution. It keeps the Grandfather Clock running for another year. Except this year, the key is missing."

"Missing?" asked Alistair.

"Yes. You see, we have a wonderful parade to commemorate the Turning of the Key. It begins in our town square and travels throughout Loxbury. Everyone comes out for the parade. Oh, it's wonderful. There are brightly coloured streamers and confetti, balloons, acrobats and clowns as well as a multitude of delicious cakes and sweets. The marching band plays on for hours and everything is always *so* lovely." His voice, which had escalated in genuine pride and desire as he spoke, now dropped to a very serious tone. "Except this year. As we began our parade, Burcheeze charged into our town in a thunderous rage, demanding that we cease immediately. Infernal racket, he called it. Of course, we couldn't. This was our tradition, we've been doing it for hundreds of years, and we couldn't simply stop. It was out of the question, as we tried to explain to him. But he would have no part of it. He was so angry; he was beyond reason. When we refused, we all thought he was going to go mad and start stomping our little town to bits. I almost wish he had. At least then we know we could have a chance to recover."

"Why?" Alison asked. She was trembling as she absently pushed her glasses up the bridge of her nose.

"He took the key."

"What a jerk!" Alistair bellowed, thumping a pudgy fist into the soft armrest, sending little plumes of dust into the air. "So you couldn't even have your parade?"

"I'm afraid it's much worse than that," the Mayor continued. "Without that key, we wouldn't be able wind the clock on Loxday, and we simply must, must, *must* wind that clock, or else . . ." he trailed off, his voice trembling. Genuine fear had gripped him as he leaned against his desk, nervously fiddling with the ends of his moustache.

"Or else what?" asked Allison. The Mayor looked deep into her eyes, then at Alistair's.

"Or else we simply . . . stop."

The room was silent for several seconds; the only sound was the slow, monotonous ticking from the clock which adorned the Mayor's hat.

"W-what do you mean, stop?" Allison finally asked. At some point, Alistair had slipped from his chair and was resting on the arm of his sister's.

"The key which was stolen by Burcheeze must wind the clock once per year. If not, the clock will wind down and eventually stop. When that happens, well, so does the Land of Dibble."

"So that's what Sender was talking about," Alistair almost shouted, snapping his fingers in the air as he spun to look at his sister. "Remember, Allison? He said something about us escaping the Eating Garden because it was moving so slowly. That's because time is slowing down." He turned back toward the Mayor. "Right?"

"That's correct," said Mayor Maynott. "Time *is* slowing down. If we don't get the key back by Loxday, it will cease entirely and I'm afraid we'll never get you home."

"Well, that's no problem," Alistair said. There was something in his voice that made his sister nervous and she recognised it right away. It was the same tone that always precluded one of his more sinister plans. They were seldom successful, of course, but that seldom, if ever, stopped him. Unfortunately, experience was no teacher as far as Alistair was concerned. "We'll just go and get your key, bring it back, wind that sucker up and we'll zip back to Auntie Bernice's basement. Simple, right?" Mayor Maynott didn't respond. "Right?" The edge had already begun to dwindle from Alistair's voice. "What?"

"There's more," said the Mayor. "The reason we were so surprised that you appeared in the Land of Dibble is not simply because you fell through a gate. It was actually the gate itself which surprised us. The spire you saw in the Town Square - the one with the multitudes of clocks, hourglasses and sundials - is the main gate to every world to which we are connected. Until a few days ago, there had been another clock affixed to its peak. The Grandfather Clock."

"What's a Grandfather Clock?" Alistair asked.

Mayor Maynott continued to explain that the Grandfather Clock was the oldest clock in Dibble. Its history is timeless and it is widely believed to have been the first clock to bridge the between-time gap of two worlds; The Land of Dibble and Earth.

"This is the clock which you came through," he further explained. "Until yesterday, that clock had remained unused for a very long time. We had assumed that its counter clock had been destroyed or hidden, but apparently this isn't the case at all."

There was a gentle knock on the door and Sender entered, smiling pleasantly as he settled into the third barber chair.

"I'm sorry to interrupt," Sender said. The Mayor waved his hand as though it was of little consequence.

"I was just explaining to them the history and significance of the Grandfather Clock."

"I see," said Sender. "Then you understand why it was so surprising to have found that you two had come through."

"I don't understand anything," Alistair whined. "What happened to the clock?"

"Burcheeze," Allison said with great assurance. The Mayor and Sender both nodded their heads.

"Yes," said Sender. "He must have come back and stolen the clock through the night. Apparently he threw it into the Tangleroot, thinking that even if we discovered its whereabouts, we would never go looking to retrieve it."

"And he was right," said the Mayor as he swooned dramatically. "As long as the clock is in the Tangleroot and winding down, we Boffles are doomed." He slumped deep into his chair, appearing as though he were a man in the deepest depths of despair.

"*And* without the clock," said Sender quietly, "you are trapped here. Perhaps forever."

"Oh dear," moaned the Mayor. "Oh dear, oh dear, oh dear."

The room suddenly seemed extremely gloomy despite the bright light that spilled through the windows. The Mayor and Sender were all but lost in despair as Allison and Alistair sat in silence, not sure what to say or do. A look of confusion crossed Alistair's face as he looked about the room. Allison could see that his mind was spinning, the wheels turning as he processed the information Sender and the Mayor had just presented to them. She had seen that look many times before; it was another tell-tale sign that her brother was only moments away from an idea that would undoubtedly result in trouble, chaos or worse.

"But that's not true," Alistair finally said. Mayor Maynott and Sender both looked at him, puzzled.

"What do you mean, Alistair?" The apprehension was evident in Allison's voice, fearful that she knew where this dialogue was leading.

"I mean, *we* were able to escape the Tangleroot. If we did it once, we can do it again. All we have to do is go and get the clock and bring it back here."

"Oh, no," said Mayor Maynott. "No, no, no, no, no. It's far too dangerous. Besides, even if you did manage to get the clock from the Ivy, we still don't have the key."

"So, we go get that, too. All we have to do is sneak over to this Bluecheese guy's house and snitch the key. I can do that in my sleep."

"Burcheeze," said Sender, "and I'm afraid it's not that simple. He is a terribly dangerous man, capable of killing without hesitation. If you were to be caught -" He shuddered, unable to say any more.

"He's right," Allison said nervously. "We were lucky to escape anything the first time. We might not be that lucky again. And if Burcheeze is anything like they say," she motioned to Sender and the Mayor, "then he'd squash us like bugs before we got fifty metres from his front door."

"No way," Alistair said. "It's a cinch. Remember last summer when all those police cars got covered in smiley face stickers? From inside a locked and guarded parking lot?"

"So, it *was* you!" she shouted, pointing a finger at his nose. "I *knew* it! I told Mom and Dad it was you, but they said it was impossible. I am *so* telling on you when we get home."

"Whatever," he said, rolling his eyes. "I bet I could get in and out of that place and get your key back and he wouldn't even know we were there."

"We?!" Allison said incredulously. "Wait a minute. I'm not going into some giant's house and stealing anything, never mind going back through the Eating Garden and purposely jumping into that patch of killer ivy! No way. There must be something else we can do."

Everyone looked at her for several moments as she searched their faces, hoping someone would offer an alternate solution. None came.

"I'm afraid," said Sender, "there is nothing else we can do. If we don't have the clock *and* key, we're doomed." Mayor Maynott pulled up the sleeve of his robe, revealing several wrist watches. The second hands, which should have all been turning smoothly about the watch face, moved in tiny, hitched increments every few seconds. "If we don't get the clock wound in three days," he said slowly, "we're finished. Alistair. Allison. We need your help."

NINE

"This is absolutely crazy," Allison said. They had asked the Mayor and Sender to leave them alone for a few minutes to discuss their decision.

"No, it's not," said Alistair, bubbling over with excitement. "It's awesome! When will we ever have a chance to have another adventure like this? It makes rolling Oscar down the stairs look like a Sunday picnic."

"You're crazy, you know that? We could die, Alistair. We could go out there, find Burcheeze and he could kill us. Or we could stumble into another Eating Garden. Or fall off a cliff. Or get bitten by a poisonous . . . who-knows-what. You may be used to just jumping around and not caring what happens, but I'm not."

"You know what?" he sighed. "You're right. This *is* nuts. What were we thinking? I mean, it's not like these are our friends. We don't even know these guys, right? So what if they all die because we could have helped them and didn't. Who cares? It's not like any of them will know what happened, right? Yeah, we should just sit in these comfy chairs and wait for time to stop. That's a nice safe way to handle this. Oh, by the way, I hope you like Dibble tea, because that's all we'll have to drink for the rest of our lives, since WE CAN'T GET HOME!!!"

She stood silently for a moment, head hung low, as her brother spoke.

Finally, she turned to face him and said, "Well, you don't have to be a jerk about it."

"Look," he said quietly. "I know this is crazy. Believe me, I've done some pretty stupid stuff, dangerous stuff, I *know* crazy. But this is different. We gotta help these guys. They need us. And if we want to go home, we have to do it anyway, or else we're stuck here. Forever. Come on, Allison. We don't have a choice."

"Fine," she finally said. "But if we live and somehow figure out a way to get back home, I'm telling Mom everything. Even about the police cars. *And* the time you put boogers in my sandwich."

"*Splendid*!" roared Mayor Maynott as the door suddenly burst open and he and Sender tumbled in. "Delightful. Wonnnnnderful!!!" He hugged the twins tightly, squeezing the air from their lungs as their faces turned a deep scarlet. Allison's glasses flew from her face and clattered to the floor.

***

The next few hours were spent working on a map which would get them to Burcheeze's shack.

Allison stuffed a few itchy garments and a few other essentials into a satchel which had been provided by Mayor Maynott. Alistair said nothing, handing her a few items to put in the bag: an old compass, a canteen full of water and a small packet of dried berries, fruit slices and nuts. "We're going to get killed," Allison huffed as she crammed a small blanket into the bag. "Actually, *I'll* probably get killed. You'll be fine, as usual. Why do bad things always happen to me and never you?"

"In case you haven't noticed," Alistair said, "I got sucked through the clock too. I think that counts as a bad thing happening to me, don't you?" Allison said nothing as she buttoned the bag closed.

"I have nothing but faith in the both of you," said Sender. He had been standing quietly in the corner, watching the twins pack for their journey. "The map shows you exactly where to find Burcheeze. It won't be easy, but if you stay the course, you should be fine."

"Why can't we just take Thurgood?" Alistair asked. "Wouldn't that make the trip a lot easier?"

"Not at all," said Sender. "As you may have noticed, our movements and even our speech are gradually slowing down. I'm afraid Thurgood or any of the other Whipperloopers would not be dextrous enough to effectively manoeuvre through any threats or obstacles. Burcheeze would spot you almost immediately. No, this is the only way we can be sure there is any chance for you to approach unnoticed. Now, on to the map."

The map itself, which had been crudely drawn up on an old and yellowed piece of parchment, showed the safest way to get to the shack. A sketch of a small clock marked Loxbury, their starting point, and a dotted line marked their path. "You will leave Loxbury and proceed due south," Sender said as they studied the map, "crossing the bridge at the Shallows of Mayomay River. You will then continue until you come to Pointing Rock." He placed his finger on a small picture of a rock, indicating their first landmark. "From Pointing Rock," he continued, "you are to travel south east until you come to a large patch of wooded forest." Again, he pointed to a crude drawing of trees that seemed to stretch on for what looked to be miles and miles. "On the other side is Tenebrous Marsh, and thus, Burcheeze. His is the only structure in the Marsh but it is well hidden. To find it, simply follow the odour. Now listen to me carefully." His voice turned icy cold. "Under no circumstances are you to go through that forest. You *must* go around. Do you understand?"

"Why not?" asked Alistair, that familiar gleam sparking in his eyes. "There's a clearing right there and Burntcheese's house is just on the other side. It'll take all day to go around."

"Oh, no, no, no, it's very dangerous," said Mayor Maynott in a nervous, shaky tone. "Very dangerous indeed. Oh, maybe this is not such a good idea. Maybe there's another way to solve this.

Oh my, oh my, what are we to do? There *must* be another way, but there isn't, is there? What *shall* we do? *Will* you go in the forest? You won't, will you? Will you? Oh, please say you won't. Please!"

"Why not?" demanded Alistair, "*What's* in the forest?"

"Ohhhhhhh," wailed the Mayor. He swooned, grabbing his head in his hands. "They're going to go in the forest. Please, *please* don't go in the forest. I beg you. You will, won't you? I know you will. But don't. Oh, pleeeeeeeease, don't go into . . ."

"I promise," Allison interrupted, her hand held in the air, "we will *not* go into that forest."

"Oh, thank goodness," the Mayor sighed, all but spent after his little outbreak. He dropped his head to the table and for a moment, it appeared as though he had actually fainted. Alistair began to giggle at the Mayor's antics, but Sender's voice stopped any humour he may have made of the situation.

"The Obsidian Woods are very, very dangerous, Alistair," he said. His voice was deep and serious and the look in his eye sent a bit of a chill down Alistair's spine. The room darkened a little as the sun was obscured by a heavy cloud. "There are things in those woods that will make your blood run cold; deadly plants which make the Eating Garden seem tame by comparison; creatures that will not think twice about killing you if you should happen to set foot where you don't belong, which is essentially the entire forest. No, you must not enter that forest under any circumstances. You must swear to me that you will keep your word." He stared directly at Alistair as he said this, as though he knew how easily the boy's longing for adventure can overcome his good sense.

Alistair had fallen silent, that mischievous glimmer suddenly absent from his eye and it looked to Allison as though he may just be trembling ever so slightly.

"I swear," he whispered.

"I swear," said Allison, again holding her hand in the air, the other across her heart.

"Good," said Sender, his demeanour suddenly less sombre. "Now then, I must apologize but as much as we would love to provide you with a grand send-off, we cannot risk it. If we upset Burcheeze and he comes here on a rampage, all could be lost. We must act with stealth. However, if you . . ." he paused for a moment, ". . . *when* you return, we will have a grand celebration the likes of which Dibble has never seen."

"Sounds great," said Alistair with a weak grin. "Can hardly wait." He was thinking of the marching band and their desperate attempts to make music. The assault on their hearing would no doubt border on being violent despite their good intentions.

"I have one question," said Allison. "Why does Burcheeze want time to stop? Won't he be stuck too?"

"Oh, no," groaned Mayor Maynott. "If only that were true."

Sender explained. "Time doesn't affect humans the same way it affects Boffles, otherwise, what you say makes sense." He pointed to Alistair's wrist. "Only those of us who are native to Dibble will be affected."

Alistair looked at his watch. It ticked away the seconds as it always had, yet Sender's watches were all ticking much more slowly.

"Weird," Alistair muttered.

"With our time stopped and Burcheeze's time running along as per usual," Sender continued, "he is in a position to do to us whatever he wants at his leisure. He is not a nice man and he loathes Boffles a great deal. We fear he will find many imaginative ways to destroy us. And it will be torture. When time finally does stop, we will all be stuck, captured in a moment, but I assure you, we will have all our faculties about us."

"And whatever torture Burcheeze has in store for us," the Mayor moaned, "it will not be painless." He swooned again, wailing even louder this time, and then dropped his head to the desk top once again with a hearty thud.

***

Alistair and Allison stood in front of the Town Hall, shaking hands with Sender and Mayor Maynott. The rest of the town had gathered as well, just as they had when the twins arrived. This time, however, they were all but silent, the only words muttered in hushed voices. Alistair held the map firmly in his pudgy hand and Allison had the small pack slung over her shoulder.

"Guard that map," Sender said as he patted Alistair on the shoulder. "You'll need it to get back as well."

"I will," said Alistair.

"You will also need this," Sender said as he handed Alistair a gold pocket watch attached to a long gold chain.

"That's OK," said Alistair. "I already have a watch."

"You have a human watch," Sender said. "This is a Dibble watch." Alistair stared at him blankly.

"It's so we can see how slow time is going," said Allison as she rolled her eyes at her brother's incomprehensiveness. To Sender she said, "Do you have a vaccine against stupidity he could have?"

"She is correct," Sender smiled, choosing to ignore Allison's jab at her brother. "Keep a close eye on it. It will tell you how much time is left. Quite literally."

"OK, I will," said Alistair as he compared it to his own watch. His read 11:29 while the Dibble watch told him it was 11:07 - almost twenty minutes behind.

"And you won't go into the Obsidian Woods?" asked the Mayor. Just the mention of the forest elicited a hushed gasp from the gathered crowd.

"No, we promise," Allison replied. Alistair could see that she was nervous as she stood there absently fiddling with her braids.

"Mind your compass, then," Sender said, "and try to get back as quickly as possible. We have about four days before we'll all be stuck."

"We'll be back in time," Alistair promised. "Don't worry."

"Good luck," Sender said as he embraced the twins once again. "Have a safe journey."

"We will," Allison said. Her voice trembled. The townspeople had gathered all around them as they spoke to the Mayor and Sender, but they now stepped away, creating a passage through the crowd. As Allison and Alistair slowly made their way out of Loxbury, they were wished good luck, patted on the backs and shoulders and Verona, the woman who had greeted them in front of the Town Hall and again in Mayor Maynott's office, gave each of them a tight hug and a slobbery kiss on each cheek. It was a full minute before she let them go.

Geeze, Alistair thought, *it's not like she'll never see us again.* An icy snake entangled his spine at the thought. Perhaps she wouldn't.

TEN

The trip was uneventful as they headed for the bridge that crossed the Shallows of the Mayomay River. They had been walking for several hours, having stopped briefly to rest and munch on a few nuts and berries and have a sip of water from their canteen, and still there was no sign of the bridge. While the countryside wasn't what one might call barren - they walked briskly through knee-high grass most of the way - there were few trees and thus little protection from the hot afternoon sun. Alistair periodically checked the compass to make sure they were heading in the proper direction and assuming it was correctly calibrated, they were still headed due south. The sun beat down on them, but there was a soft breeze which abated the heat, although both Allison and Alistair wished they had brought hats to keep the sun off their heads. Both were sheathed in sweat and their clothes clung to them, as though they had just climbed out of a swimming pool. It wasn't long before they had turned a deepened red hue, their skin very delicate and easily. Allison's glasses had also developed an annoying habit of repeatedly slipping down her nose and she absently pushed them back up, over and over, not realising she was even doing so.

"It sure doesn't look this far on the map," Alistair said as he wiped his arm across his sweaty brow. Due to the heat (coupled with the fact that they had walked further in the past four hours than he had in the past six months), the boy was breathing laboriously, lagging behind his sister, who had to stop several times in order for him to catch up.

"Well, we must be almost there," she said as she pushed her glasses up again. As she said this, something glimmered in the distance, having caught and reflected the blazing sun. "Wait!" she shouted. "What's that?"

They pushed on, following a glimmer which occasionally flashed in the distance. As they approached, they realised it was a signpost, at the bottom of which lay a few old, discarded bottles, a weather beaten pack and a pair of odd little shoes, set neatly on the bank of the river. It looked as though the owner of the items had rested at the river, taken a moment to cool down in the water before continuing their journey, and never came back for their belongings.

"What do you think happened to him?" Allison asked, looking worried at the sight of the forgotten items. Alistair, too, felt a pang of doubtfulness as he gazed upon the strange little pile.

"I dunno," he said. "Maybe he got into a boat or something and paddled away. Or maybe he -" He was going to say 'drowned', but he didn't think Allison would have appreciated the morbid - but probable - idea.

"Yeah," she nodded, not daring to consider otherwise. "He probably got into a boat."

"Well, there's no boat here for us," said Alistair. "Looks like we keep walking."

They considered the bridge for some time. It seemed to be ancient and rickety, little more than a series of old, sun-bleached planks held together by dry and brittle looking rope. Beside the bridge lay a wooden sign, face down, which must have once been affixed to the post. Alistair picked it up to read it but the sun and outdoor elements had long ago faded any writing that might have once been upon it.

"I bet it said 'Use at your own risk,'" said Allison, eyeing the bridge suspiciously. "I don't think that thing will hold us."

"You mean you don't think it'll hold *me*," Alistair said accusingly. "Because I'm too fat. Right?"

"I didn't say that," she replied, though that was, in fact, what she had been thinking. "It just looks old and dangerous, that's all. I don't know. It's not that far across. Plus, it's better than being baked alive in the sun."

"There's only one problem," said Alistair. "I can't swim."

Allison considered the bridge, then the water, thinking carefully. "Yeah, that could be a problem," she finally said. "But then again, if that bridge breaks, we'll be swimming anyway. Besides, it doesn't look that deep."

"OK," said Alistair as rolled up the bottom of his pant legs and took a deep breath. "Last one in is a rotten Whipperlooper."

Allison was about to ask why he rolled his pants up but left his shoes on, but decided it didn't matter. If he wanted to squelch around in soggy shoes for the rest of the trip, it was his problem. He waded into the water, somewhat apprehensively, though he was also looking forward to the reprieve from the heat and sweat.

"It's warm," he called back to his sister. She stood far back on the bank, warily watching as Alistair tested the water. "Come on, we don't got all day, ya know."

He waded further into the water, swishing his arms about as it rose to his midsection, then his chest. Allison followed behind, holding their pack over her head to keep it dry.

"This feels great," she shouted, since her brother was several metres ahead of her, almost to the other bank.

"I know," he shouted back. "And it's not very deep." With that, he dunked under the water completely.

Allison watched the spot where he went under for a few seconds, waiting for him to emerge. When he didn't come up, she immediately began to fear the worst.

"Alistair?" she called nervously. "Alistair, stop it, you're not funny." She looked around the surface of the water, searching for any sign of him.

As a glint of worry began to creep into her stomach, Alistair burst up in front of her, waving his arms wildly about.

"Boogidy boogidy boo!!!" He screamed. Allison yelped as he splashed her with the water.

"Alistair, you stupid jerk!" she snorted. "Look at what you did. You soaked the pack. Now our things are going to be all wet."

Alistair just looked at his sister, wailing with laughter as he playfully continued to splash her. She tried to ward off the attacks, but it didn't seem to work. Her only retaliation was to strike back, so she began splashing as well. Her annoyance with her brother quickly dissipated and they played in the water for several minutes, splashing and dunking each other.

"OK, that's enough," Allison finally wheezed, winded by the impromptu water fight. "Come on, we don't have time to waste."

"OK, OK," said Alistair, looking at his waterproof Timex watch. They had been on their journey for a little over four hours. "Boy," you sure looked scared. Ha ha, that was better than in Auntie Bernice's basem -"

Alistair suddenly dropped below the surface again, much to the great annoyance of his sister.

"Alistair, it's not funny any more," she called. "Come on, we have to go. We don't have time for your stupid games."

She waited a few seconds for him to emerge, prepared to tear into him with a violent volley of verbal abuse at his tired tomfoolery. But he didn't come up.

"Alistair?" she shouted again, that creeping feeling of worry slipping over her once again. "Alistair, this isn't funny." She looked around for a sign indicating where he might be, but saw nothing. Then, looking behind her, she saw a few bubbles gurgle to the surface. She let out a deep sigh of relief, which quickly slipped into anger once again.

"Alistair, stop it, you big stupid jerk!" she shouted. "Come up here right now, before I -"

With a violent splash of water, Alistair burst to the surface. He gasped for breath, eyes bulging, arms whirling. At first, Allison thought he was playing another one of his crude pranks, but then she noticed that he was clutching at something wrapped around his neck. Something big. Something green. Something *bad*.

"Allison," he glubbed through a mouthful of water, but was then yanked back below the surface. The water churned violently where he had just appeared and a couple of times she saw his hand or foot briefly slip above the water and back again. The water quickly became still and there was no sign of her brother. Not knowing what to do, all too aware that whatever had grabbed him may not be finished torturing young kids, she scrambled out of the water on the opposite bank.

She scanned the river carefully, though the sun was directly overhead and glimmered blindingly off the surface. A few more bubbles gurgled to the surface and something began to rise slowly and deliberately from the water. Allison stood in awe, unable to believe what she was seeing. Two large, bulbous green eyes emerged from the water very slowly, each glistening orb attached to a long green stem of scaly skin. They stared at her for several seconds, blinking lazily. Allison was paralysed with fear, knowing that this creature may well have just killed her brother and she would undoubtedly be next. It rose upwards and the eyeball stems turned out to be attached to a large, misshapen head that resembled some sort of snake, except that it had a long snout and large jagged teeth which jutted out in all directions. It was a mottled brownish green, its scaly skin dripping with foul smelling mossy tendrils. There were three rows of brown stony ridges running from the tip of its snout, over its head and down its back. She could see a small sliver of blue denim hanging from one of the teeth and her heart skipped several beats as she recognized it as a shred of Alistair's blue jeans. Then, to her bewildered amazement, it lifted two long tentacles from the water and Alistair was entangled in one of them. He hung lifelessly, jeans torn, a smear of blood dribbling from behind his left ear and down his cheek. His arms and legs dangled freely, his eyes closed and his mouth open. The other tentacle began to slowly reach toward her and she saw that there were hundreds of tiny pulsating suction cups on its underside.

For a brief moment, as she looked back at the creature, she almost thought it was smiling as it reached for her. The creature gave a sudden quick flick of its scaly appendage and connected squarely with the side of Allison's head. She went tumbling, her glasses flying from her face and the contents of the pack were sent scattering across the bank. She slowly picked herself up, looking almost blindly for her glasses. Another flick, lighter this time, sent her feet scooting out from beneath her, landing smartly on her rump. It then flicked her again, much harder this time, sending her rolling across the dirt. She could feel her face begin to pulse and she was sure that there was going to be a large bruise on her cheek and forehead, assuming the thing didn't kill her, of course. The tentacle slipped tightly around her ankle and she let out a frightened yelp as it jerked her slightly forward. It was obviously enjoying the hunt, playing with its prey like a cat plays with a mouse. As she slid across the ground, she managed to snatch her glasses, which were lying in the loose dirt. It flung her backwards, somersaulting her away from the waters edge. The creature still had a firm grip on Alistair, but she could now see that he was moving, trying to weakly struggle from the monster's firm grip, but to no avail. The monster began to lower its head toward Allison and she could smell its rancid breath - a combination of sewage, garbage and rotting fish. It slowly slid a long, blue forked tongue toward her, which flickered wickedly before her face, the very tips of the tongue just touching her cheek as she turned away in revulsion. On the ground, within an arm's length, was the pack. The contents had been scattered among the rocks and stones, but most were not too far out of reach. Reaching for the first thing she could, she grabbed the compass and threw it as hard as she could. It connected with the creature's gelatinous left eye with a sickening squelch and it let out a hideous sound unlike anything Allison had ever heard or imagined. She then grabbed the canteen by its leather strap and flung it like a slingshot. It arched high over the creature's head and splashed down uselessly far behind it.

At some point the creature must have let go of Alistair, because he was now splashing his way toward her. The creature's attention was squarely on Allison and didn't pay any attention to the boy as he clamoured onto the shore, gasping for breath. She grabbed blindly for anything she could throw. She pitched rocks, stones, bits of driftwood - anything she could pick up and hurl at the beast's ugly head. Most managed to connect but a few sailed far too high, left or right. Finally, the only other thing that was within reach was the pack itself. She flailed wildly with her arms, finally snatching it as the creature lunged toward her, apparently having had enough of their little game. As the beast bore down on her, mouth agape revealing more of the razor-sharp teeth, she wadded the thick, waterlogged pack into a ball and threw it as hard as she could. It flew from her hand and lodged perfectly into the back of the creature's throat, choking it. The creature let out a very loud, very strange gagging sound as it reeled back, viciously splashing water everywhere. The tentacles thrashed and she had to duck as one of them sailed just a few centimetres above her head. Its eyes bulged grotesquely, the compass still wedged in one of its ugly green ocular membranes and with a heavy splash the creature toppled back into the water and disappeared.

Alistair was lying on his back, taking in large, heavy gasps of breath and Allison stood wheezing and trembling on the bank. She gazed at her brother, who looked terrible. He was soaked to the bones and a smear of deep red was washed across most of the left side of his face. His jeans were torn, one leg still rolled up, the other missing just below the knee and one sleeve of his t-shirt was ripped halfway from its seam. He slowly propped himself on one arm as he looked at his sister.

"What . . ." she gasped, swallowing hard to catch her breath, "the heck . . . was that?"

"A Serpensilicus," he replied through his own heaving breaths.

A perplexing look crossed her face. "A what?"

Alistair pointed toward the bridge. There was another signpost on this side, the large faded lettering still somewhat legible. It read:

'BEWARE OF SERPENSILICUS. ABSOLUTELY NO SWIMMING!!!'

Allison read the sign three times, then looked across the narrow waterway at the post on the opposite side, its faded sign laying uselessly on the ground, then back at the sign before her.

"On the way back," Allison finally said, flopping to the ground beside her brother, "we're taking the bridge."

Alistair nodded in agreement, and then plopped flat on the ground once again. "Yeah," he panted. "That's a really great bridge."

ELEVEN

They rested for almost an hour, well aware that time was of the essence, but to try to continue would have been pointless, they were so exhausted. Even after an hour, it was all they could do to pick themselves up and continue on.

The pack was gone, as was the compass, their ration of nuts and berries (which had scattered everywhere) and the canteen. All that remained were the two blankets Sender had given them, the Dibble watch and (thankfully) the map, both of which miraculously remained tucked into Alistair's pocket. The watch crystal was somewhat cloudy but it otherwise appeared to be in working order, though it was difficult to tell as the second hand was ticking so slowly - one tick for about every five of Alistair's own watch - and it read 2:04. Alistair's watch read 3:37, meaning that Dibble time had slowed down by more than an hour since they left Loxbury.

They found a long, sturdy stick and managed to fashion a crude bindle pack; one blanket was tied to the stick and in it were tucked the other blanket and the few bits of food they managed to salvage from the shore. It wasn't ideal and they had to stop to retie the pack a few times, but it was the best they could manage under the circumstances.

"So tell me" said Alistair snidely as he lifted the bindle onto his shoulder. "Why would you throw away a perfectly good compass?"

"You're welcome," his sister retorted with a leering glare.

"I'm just sayin'," he continued, "now we have to figure out which way is south and hope we keep going in the right direction."

"Well," she said, "the sun moves east to west, right?"

Alistair shrugged his shoulders, looking at her blankly.

"Well, it does," she said. "Now it's three o'clock in the afternoon and the sun is right there." She pointed upward and to the left. "So that's west. Now, we came from that way (she pointed behind them) so it's obviously north. So, as long as we can see the position of the sun, we can tell which way is south."

Alistair looked at her for several seconds. "Is that what you do in your bedroom alone all day?" he finally asked. "Read about astrology?"

"Astronomy."

"What?"

"Astrology," she began, her voice suddenly assuming the authoritative tone that always assured she was about to relay some piece of wisdom that she considered to be particularly intelligent, "is the study of stars and planets for the purposes of divination and fortune telling. *Astronomy* is the observation and explanation of events occurring outside Earth and its atmosphere in order to determine -"

"Forget I asked," he said with a wave of his hand. "Boy, you'd probably flip out if I told you what I do alone in my bedroom."

"Ewwww," she groaned. "I don't even want to know."

"You probably don't," he replied. "Come on, let's go."

They headed in the direction that Allison had indicated, which was actually south west and consequently, they were veering slightly off course.

The land had been somewhat lush and rich with vegetation before the bridge but within about three kilometres on this side, it had become parched and dry. Soon there was nothing to see but ridges and plateaus of caked and cracked earth that obviously hadn't seen rain in quite some time.

By six o'clock, their stomachs began to grumble again and they opened the pack to nibble on a few bits of the remaining morsels.

"OH NO!" Allison wailed as she reached into the pack. They had failed to notice a small tear and the bits of remaining nuts and fruit had fallen out without their realizing it. They were out of food.

By seven their stomachs were almost roaring with hunger and as the brightness of the day began to dissolve toward dark, they began to worry that before they even got to Burcheeze's house they might just keel over from lack of food and water. Alistair noted how funny it was that just a few hours ago they had seen more water than either of them had ever wanted to and now they may well completely dehydrate before morning. He mentioned this to his sister, who didn't find the humour in it at all.

"It's called irony, jerk-wad," she had said, "and it's not funny." He told her to lighten up and that was all that was said between them for another hour.

"I think we should rest at Pointing Rock," Allison eventually said, "and keep going in the morning."

"Good idea," he said. "Except, we don't know where the heck it is. Shouldn't we see it by now?"

"Are you sure we're going in the right direction?" she asked.

"You're the astrologer," he snapped. "I was following your directions."

"Astronomer," Allison corrected.

"Who cares?"

"Well," she said weakly, "I *think* we're going in the right direction."

"You think? I thought you knew what you were talking about."

"Well, I'm not an expert," she said. Tears began to shimmer in her eyes and her bottom lip began to tremble ever so slightly.

"Ah, forget it," he said. "Don't get all cry-baby about it. Geeze! It can't be far. Come on, we gotta find it before it gets dark."

They walked on for another half hour and the sun was well into its slow descent toward the horizon. The azure sky had become a deep orange and before too long it was a striking palette of reds, oranges and yellows as the sun dipped out of sight. Neither Alistair nor Allison had seen anything like it and they stood for a moment, trancelike, staring at the breathtaking colours.

"Wow," Alistair whispered as he drank in the magnificent sunset.

"It's beautiful," said Allison in a hushed tone. Then something on the horizon caught her eye.

"What's that?" She pointed almost directly eastward. In the distance they could see something that looked distinctly large. In fact, it looked a lot like a rock.

"I dunno," said Alistair, "but I bet it's something we want. Come on. We can probably get there before it gets completely dark."

They kept a sharp eye on the object and as they got closer they saw that it was, indeed, a large rock. It stood perhaps twenty metres tall and was simply majestic against the blazing sunset. It cast a massive, elongated shadow in the fading light and the moment they were in its shade, the heat of the day seemed to dissipate almost immediately.

They walked around the rock and saw that it was as long as it was tall and remarkably, it was shaped very much like a hand, one long finger outstretched, as though pointing. The shapes in the rock even resembled individual fingers, three folded into the palm and a large bulge formed a crude thumb. There was no mistaking it. This was Pointing Rock.

The cup of the 'palm' and the ridge of the 'thumb' had created a natural shallow cave and it was here that Allison and Alistair nestled in for the night. They were glad to still have their blankets, which had quickly dried in the blazing sun, as the absence of sunlight left them far colder than they thought possible. They weren't enough to keep them toasty warm, but it staved of the chill, and that would have to do.

Both were exhausted and Allison had developed a headache after being thumped by the Serpensilicus. She hadn't bruised as badly as she had thought, but it still hurt, thrumming sharply with each pulsing heartbeat. Alistair's head hurt as well, the gash behind his ear stinging smartly and he pretty much ached all over from both the thrashing he had recently taken as well as the extensive walking he had just done. Their stomachs took turns growling angrily, sounding like some sort of rumbling symphony, but there was nothing to eat. All they could hope for was to find something that might resemble food in the morning.

Once the sun went completely down they were blanketed in absolute darkness. It was a moonless night but the stars shone brilliantly in the sky like billions of radiant gemstones. The constellations were none that Allison had seen before and it occurred to her that perhaps the sun didn't orbit this world as it did Earth, explaining why they had veered off course. She decided not to bother mentioning this little detail to her brother who, she was pretty sure, secretly admired her for her superior intellect and she didn't want to spoil his opinion. After all, being three minutes and seventeen seconds older than he, Allison felt obligated to maintain her authoritative position of leadership by constantly setting a good example. It only seemed logical that sooner or later, her younger brother would begin to understand her way of thinking. Her heart, then, sunk with an almost audible *thunk* when Alistair said to her in the darkness, "I guess you didn't figure that maybe we're not exactly on Earth anymore, eh?" She didn't answer. Instead, she wrapped herself tightly in her blanket and rolled over, almost immediately slipping off to sleep.

***

"What was that?" Allison whispered. She had been awakened by a soft rustling sound in the blind darkness.

"Shhhh," whispered Alistair, who had also heard it.

They waited in silence but heard nothing for several minutes. Then they heard it again. Someone - or something - was creeping around the rock. They could hear footsteps and a deep snarfling sound that resembled the noise Oscar made when he had discovered something particularly delicious in the trash can. The thing sneezed, causing both Alistair and Allison to jump. They quickly huddled together, embracing tightly, and trembling.

They could hear it slowly coming closer. Its claws (they were both sure it had razor sharp claws, whatever it was) were clicking softly on the hard, dry ground. Alistair was imagining a large hairy beast with gauzy yellow eyes, long, pointy teeth and a putrid pink tongue dripping with saliva as it licked its chops, ready to pounce on them at any second. Allison's imagination had conjured up something equally horrific and they both began to whimper helplessly as the thing drew closer. They could hear it breathing now, sniffling and snuffling as it followed their scent.

"Allison," Alistair whimpered, "I'm sorry I scared you back at the river. I didn't mean to. And I'm so sorry I got mad when you lost the compass. I know you were trying to save me."

"It's ok," she said. "And I promise I won't tell on you about the police cars and stuff when we get home."

The thing was now only a few feet away and coming closer. And closer. And closer. They could clearly hear its heavy, panting breath.

"*If* we get home," Alistair sobbed. They embraced even tighter as a puff of hot breath washed over their faces. They could only just make out the vague form of the creature in the encompassing darkness. It was massive and doglike, with large pointed ears, quite like Oscar's. Its breath was steaming hot, now only centimetres from their faces, which were pressed together cheek to cheek.

Alistair slowly raised his trembling hands to just below his chin and pressed the illumination button on his watch. A tiny green glow appeared, revealing the beast before them - a savage creature with a long snout, narrow black eyes and teeth like darning needles. Alistair and Allison shrieked in unison, clenching their eyes shut, as a hot tongue washed across their faces several times, then abruptly stopped, followed by a familiar chuffing sound. Slowly, Alistair opened one eye, his thumb again pressing the watch button.

"What the -" he said slowly.

"Wh-wh-what is it?" Allison shuddered as she buried her face in her brother's shoulder. "Is it horrible?"

"No," said Alistair. "It's not horrible."

He blinked his eyes a few times to make sure he wasn't simply imagining things.

"It's Oscar."

"What?" she blurted, her eyes darting open. Before them stood Oscar, his big wet tongue lolling out of his mouth. They couldn't see it due to the absolute darkness, but his tail was wagging excitedly, swoosh, swoosh, swooshing through the dry, cold air. He chuffed again and licked both of them across their faces in one long swipe of the tongue. The twins then realised they were still embraced and quickly pulled themselves apart. Allison even went so far as to brush herself off, as though her brother had left something distasteful on her clothes.

"How is that possible?" Allison asked as Oscar nuzzled in between them, his wagging tail thumping heavily on the ground. He rolled onto his back, inviting any willing participant to rub his belly. "He wasn't even at Auntie Bernice's house. How could he have come through?"

"Who knows?" said Alistair. "Who cares? He's here, that's all."

"But it's impossible, isn't it?"

"I dunno," Alistair replied, rubbing his pooch on the head vigorously. "How is any of this possible?"

Allison tried to consider any way Oscar may have managed to find his way to Dibble, but was absolutely dumbfounded. It simply wasn't possible, yet there he was.

"Well, we better get some sleep," she finally said. "We have a long day tomorrow."

"You mean today," Alistair said. He pointed to the horizon, which was just hinting at a sliver of light. "We should go as soon as it's bright enough."

They nuzzled down, Oscar wedged tightly between them, and drifted off into a deep sleep.

When Allison opened her eyes again, the sun was high above them, blazing down. They were no longer draped in the shadow of the rock and she had already begun to sweat. Oscar lay beside her, snoring deeply, his shaven midsection turning slightly pink from the sun. Alistair was on the other side of him, one arm draped across Oscar's head, a dribble of drool trickling from the corner of his slackened jaw. She could see his watch, which read 9:42.

"Alistair, get up!" she shouted, jumping to her feet. Oscar opened one eye and looked at her sleepily, but her brother didn't move a muscle. She grabbed the bindle stick and jabbed him sharply in the ribs.

"OW!" he groaned, rolling onto his back. Every muscle in his body was now in tightened knots and it hurt even to roll over. "Cut it out!"

"It's almost ten o'clock," she said. "We have to go."

Alistair slowly raised his arm, groaning as he did so, and checked his watch. "Argggg!" he groaned.

They slowly and painfully bundled their blankets then checked the map trying to determine how far they had to go before they reached Obsidian Woods. Navigation was now no problem, they need only follow the extended finger of Pointing Rock.

Alistair checked the Dibble watch, which read 6:14 - it was over three hours slow, each second ticked off for every eleven on his Timex.

By ten o'clock they were again on their way, Oscar bounding well ahead of them, his tongue flapping and his tail wagging. He seemed to be having the time of his life. Though neither of them would have admitted it to the other, both Allison and Alistair felt a great sense of relief and security now that Oscar had somehow come to join them.

Their stomachs roared in contempt as they trundled along and both were well aware that they must eat something soon or else they would be too weak to continue their journey.

Around eleven thirty they began climbing a series of dry, cracked dunes and their trusted pooch darted over its crest, disappearing from sight. Fearful that something may happen to him, Alistair called out feebly but didn't have the energy to chase after the dog. It was almost a miracle when Oscar came bounding back toward them with a branch in his mouth. At first they had thought he had managed to find an old piece of deadwood, but as he drew closer, they saw that something was dangling from the small branch. Oscar growlfed through the branch as he approached, dropping the limb at Alistair's feet. He sat down, tail wagging wildly, pleased that he could help his master.

The dangling branch was tipped by what looked to be a small bunch of tiny grapes, but they were a deep scarlet colour. Immediately, Alistair grabbed the branch and plucked a few of the berries from their stem, poised to pop them into his watering mouth. Before he could do so, Allison grabbed him by the wrist.

"Wait!" she said quickly. "What if it's poison?"

Oscar chuffed softly as Alistair offered his sister a sidelong glance.

"What if it's not?" he asked.

"Well, we don't know if it is or isn't. It could be some sort of horribly toxic plant that melts your stomach or something. I think it's best to side with caution," she said smugly.

Alistair considered this for several moments, and then lowered the fruit.

"Yeah," he agreed. "Maybe you're right. We better not risk it."

"That's the first smart thing you've done on this trip," she said with a relieved smile, letting go of his wrist. "I mean, who knows what that stuff -"

Alistair quickly popped the berries into his mouth, squelching them loudly between his teeth as Allison let out a sharp gasp.

The berries were delicious, not unlike a grape but far sweeter. His dry mouth seemed to explode with passion for its rich flavour and sweet juices began to dribble down the corners of his mouth. He closed his eyes and leaned his head back in complete ecstasy. He grabbed another handful and shoved them into his mouth as his stomach roared for more.

"These are great," he beamed though a muffled mouthful of berries. His already chubby cheeks were even puffier, stuffed with the tiny fruit. To

Allison, he looked like some sort of grotesque chipmunk. "You gotta try these. I haven't had anything like -"

His voice cut off sharply and his eyes bulged wide, a look of shock and horror washing over him. Allison watched in terror as he began to gag, madly clawing at his throat, scarlet juice and chunks of pulpy fruit spilling down his chin. Oscar let out a worried snarf as Alistair dropped to his knees, still pawing at his neck as more juice and fruit chunks gurgled from his gaping mouth. Allison gaped, then gasped, working her way toward a torrent of wails and fear and horror when a broad, crimson-smeared smile crossed her brother's ruddy pink face.

"Stop doing that, you big fat jerk!" she shouted, slapping him across the head. She wiped tears away before they could spill down her cheeks.

"You fall for that every time," he roared as he wiped the mess from his chin with the back of his arm. "You're so gullible." Allison turned on her heels and stormed off, away from her brother and Oscar and over the dune. "I hate you," she whimpered as she went.

"Oh come on," he shouted after her, still kneeling on the ground. "I was just foolin'. Don't be such a cry-baby." If she heard him, she gave no indication. He turned toward Oscar, who sat a few feet away, staring at him. "You thought it was funny, right boy?" Oscar chuffed again and trotted off after Allison.

A few minutes later, Alistair crested the dune. Below him, Allison and Oscar sat on the bank of a small pond which was surrounded by lush vegetation. Green grass and pretty yellow and orange flowers were everywhere as well as several tiny bushes, all bearing bunches and bunches of berries. Beyond that grew a majestic row of beautiful green trees. They had come to the edge of the Obsidian Woods.

Allison was sitting on a rock, slowly munching on some fruit as Oscar lay by her feet. She didn't look at Alistair as he approached, dragging the bindle behind him.

"I was only goofin' with ya," he said reproachfully, but she didn't answer. For the first time, he noticed how tired his sister looked. Her previously tight braids had become frizzled and little bits of dirt and debris clung to her red hair. She looked bedraggled, filthy from head to toe and a slight bruise covered the majority of the left half of her face. Her glasses were resting on the tip of her nose, both lenses badly scratched and two dark patches hung below her eyes. She sat silently crying, tears rolling down her face and forging tiny rivers through the grime on her cheeks. She wiped her nose on her arm as she slowly continued to munch on the berries. Oscar looked up at Alistair with sad eyes, and for a moment, Alistair thought he saw a look of disappointment in them.

"Hey," he continued, tapping her foot with his toe, "come on, Allison, I was just jokin' around. Lighten up."

She looked up at him, her red and puffy eyes drooped with sorrow. "I'm not talking to you," she whispered.

"Well fine," he huffed as he dropped to the ground beside her. "See if I care. My ears can use the rest anyway." Nothing else was said between them for a long time as they sat together, slowly eating the berries. Oscar let out a deep and sorrowful sigh and nuzzled closer to Allison.

TWELVE

"We should get going," said Alistair, looking at his watch. It was half past twelve and the day was sure to be long. The Dibble watch was now just over four hours slow. They were not even half way through their task and assuming time was relatively even between this world and their own, that meant it was Sunday noon and they were to return home within a few hours.

Allison stood up and brushed herself off without a word in response. Oscar stood between them, casually looking back and forth between the pair as Alistair considered the map once again.

"It looks like we're right about here," he said, pointing to a narrow patch of forest on the map. "It'll take hours to go around. This doesn't look too deep here; we could probably make it through in a couple of hours."

"I'm not going in there," she said matter-of-factly.

"Look," he said, "we're running out of time. We can save, like, three hours or so if we just cut through. See? Burcheeze's place is just on the other side of these trees. It'll take an hour, tops. Besides, we have Oscar here to protect us. You won't let anything bad happen, will ya boy?" He scratched Oscar behind the ears. In his usual fashion, Oscar simply chuffed in a disheartened manner, resigned to engage in whatever adventure Alistair had in mind for him.

"I'm not going in there, and that's that," she said coldly, crossing her arms across her chest. "Remember what Sender told us?"

"Oh, come on. How bad can it really be?"

"Did you have an extra large bowl of Stupid Flakes for breakfast? Were you even *at* the river yesterday, Alistair? Or the Eating Garden?"

The words had come out as though a dam had burst, flooding from her mouth and assaulting her brother like a tidal wave. Tears streamed down her face and she began to tremble from head to toe, her hands clenched so tightly they had turned a pale shade of pasty white. What had started out as a soft muttering now escalated to a loud and near-hysterical tirade.

"I'm not going in there and that's final. If you want to get yourself killed, then fine. Go ahead. But I'm not following you on any of your stupid adventures anymore. You tease me and scare me and make me worried and make me mad and I hate it when you do those things. It's not funny. It's mean. Mean and stupid and I hate you so much I want to puke, you big stupid booger. I'm your sister and you're supposed to be nice to me especially because I'm three minutes and seventeen seconds older than you are. I hope you go into those woods and I hope some poisonous snake or something bites you right on the nose and you die a horrible death, because you'd deserve it and I wouldn't even care! So go through the woods and just see if I follow you."

By the end, she was all but hyperventilating, taking deep, choppy breaths, her chest heaving heavily. For a moment Alistair thought she might have a mental breakdown right then and there. He was so dumbfounded at the outburst that before he even had a chance to say anything, she turned and bolted right where she had told Alistair she had no intention of going. She charged headlong through the brush and was immediately swallowed by the thick copse of the Obsidian Woods. Oscar barked loudly and dashed after her, also disappearing immediately in the dark forest and for the first time, Alistair was left standing all alone.

"Allison, wait!" he shouted, suddenly not so sure that cutting through the forest was such a great idea. Sender *had* said that there were things in there that he would never hope to see and it was these types of warnings that he so often overlooked before charging forward with one of his signature schemes. Now, however, he had little choice. Allison was in no state to make any rational decisions and there was no way she could handle this sort of thing under the best of conditions. Heck, she couldn't handle a harmless little snail that had once "accidentally" found its way into her lunch bag one day at school, let alone being lost in an evil forest. He looked around, considering a potential alternate plan, but there was nothing to see but dry dunes behind him and thick forest in front of him. There was little else he could do. His heart thundering in his chest like a jackhammer, he took a few apprehensive steps toward the thickly wooded forest. Then he heard a sharp scream.

"Allison!" he bellowed, charging forward as fast as his legs would carry him. Only a few feet into the woods, he was already engulfed in a shroud of unfathomable darkness. The trees smelled rich and naturally pleasant, but he was pretty sure it wasn't an indication of great things to come.

"A-Allison?" he called in a hushed voice. "Oscar?" There was no response.

Ahead of him he could see a rugged trail where the branches and twigs had been carelessly driven through. It zigged and zagged, going in no particular direction, obviously the path of a hysterical girl and a stupid old dog. There were eerie sounds in the woods too - something that sounded like wind seemed to wail through the trees, though he was met with only a slight breeze. The trees themselves loomed high above him, their thick branches reaching in every direction, intertwining with each other, creating a heavy canopy that obliterated the early afternoon sky. Looking up, all he could see was gloomy darkness and the occasional glimmers of what he was sure were dozens of tiny watchful eyes.

All around him he could hear branches creaking and rubbing against one another, twigs snapping and the shrill sound of strange insects seemed to come from every direction. Something that resembled a big black rat but with a fat, furry tail and large pointed ears scurried in front of him, crossing his path. It stopped and stared at him for several seconds before raising up on its hind haunches and hissing, thus revealing extremely sharp and yellow teeth. He was pretty sure those teeth could shred the meat from his bones in a matter of minutes. It considered him for a few seconds, its long pink nose twitching madly as it sniffed the boy's scent, then disappeared into the brush. Overhead, he heard a heavy flap of wings and something swooped above him, its shape lost among the murky shadows. A moment later, he heard a squeal from the direction the rat-thing had run, fallen prey to an unseen predator. Whatever the predator was, it let out a terrifying, victorious shriek that sent chills down Alistair's spine and he thrust the bindle out in front of him like a sword as he slowly plodded along, following the rugged path.

"Allison," he whispered loudly, trying not to draw attention to himself. "Oscar. Where are you guys?"

Despite his own best judgement, he continued deeper into the forest, following Allison's path. That is, until the path abruptly ended.

It was terribly dark and the sounds that surrounded him seemed to become louder and shriller as he approached the end of the broken trail until they suddenly stopped altogether, leaving him in an eerie silence. In front of him, the trail just stopped and the trailblazers apparently just disappeared, turning neither left nor right, which made absolutely no sense. Alistair looked up but could see nothing but bleak and foreboding darkness. He realised he was trembling terribly and made an effort to steady himself, ignoring the intense urge to hastily turn back the way he had come. It was his fault Allison had dashed off into these woods and therefore it was his responsibility to find her. But what had happened to them? Surely they didn't just vanish. Was he standing on a trap door or something? Had they fallen through a hole? *That doesn't make sense*, he thought. *There wouldn't be all these twigs and stuff on top of a trap door.* No sooner had the thought crossed his mind when something wrapped tightly around his waist and yanked him sharply up into the trees with an audible *gurk*, hitting his head sharply on more than a couple of branches on the way up, leaving a few nasty scrapes and gashes in his scalp as well as his arms and legs. As consciousness threatened to abandon him, he saw something dark and hideous loom in front of him. In the semi-conscious haze, Alistair could only get a vague impression of what it might be. It had eight milky white eyes, which appeared to glow in the murky darkness, a crooked nose that pointed toward its jutting, scruffy chin and gaunt, sunken cheekbones. What sent a jolt of terror though the boy, however, was the fact that it appeared to be laughing softly, revealing a crooked row of sharp teeth.

"Welcome to my web, my succulent little fly," it hissed, exhaling a wave of rancid steaming breath. "You're just in time for lunch."

I'm going to die, Alistair thought as his vision first doubled, then tripled. A second later, his world faded to black.

THIRTEEN

Almost as soon as Allison had sped into the Obsidian Woods, she realised what she had done. Oscar approached her from behind as she stood frozen in fear, staring into the darkened void of the ominous forest. The Great Dane gave her a nervous nudge and chuffed softly, snapping her out of an almost trancelike state of fear.

"Yeah," she said slowly, looking down at Oscar, "this is a bad idea. Maybe we had better go back."

As she turned, she noticed that there was a rugged path cut into the dense foliage where someone (or something) had passed through not too long ago. This gave Allison a decidedly wicked idea, something that was very uncharacteristic of her. It filled her heart with joy at the absolute deviousness of it. She intended to give her nasty little brother a taste of his own medicine.

To the left of the trail lay a large uprooted tree, its exposed roots just large enough to conceal both she and the dog. A mischievous gleam twinkled in her eye as she devised the details of her scheme.

Once she felt she was appropriately hidden, she simply sat and waited, keeping a firm grip on Oscar's collar so he didn't give away their hiding spot. She giggled softly to herself as she waited for her brother to come looking for her. "This will teach him a lesson," she whispered softly in Oscar's ear. "See how he likes it, eh?"

Something rustled in the dry leaves and needles behind her, skittering across her foot. She let out a sharp, quick scream, slapping her hand over her mouth immediately, as a strange rat-like creature scuttled past them and over the rugged path. Her heart raced as she crouched deeper behind the root, peeking around, as Alistair finally stepped into view.

She and Oscar watched in secrecy as her brother looked around. He called out their names, but of course, she didn't answer and since she now had a hand clamped tightly around Oscar's snout, neither did he. It was all she could do to stifle her maniacle giggles as she watched her brother wallow in absolute fear.

Another of the rat-things skittered across the path in front of Alistair, pausing to hiss defensively before scuttling away. A second later she heard what sounded like a large bird take flight with the flap of heavy wings. This was followed by a shrill cry as the rat-thing undoubtedly fell prey to whatever it was that had just taken flight. A second later, there was another high pitched shriek that sent shivers down her spine and Oscar hunched lower to the ground, gently placing his front paws over his nose. Allison almost burst out laughing as the shriek startled her brother and he swung the bundle in front of him as though he were some sort of swordsman.

As scared as she was, she refused to give up her hiding place, determined to let Alistair see what it felt like to be frightened for someone else's safety. He stood frozen with fear as she peeked at him from behind the root and she wore a victorious grin that made her feel very warm inside. Any moment now he would begin to cry, realising what she was doing, and beg for her to reveal herself, sorry for having scared her so often. If he didn't, well, she would simply jump up from behind the root and scare the bejeepers out of him. If she was really lucky, maybe she could even make him pee his pants. *Now that would be awesome*, she thought. But then Alistair did something she hadn't counted on. Rather than stand there and cry (as she would have done), he started further down the path. This was not part of the plan. She didn't want him to go deeper into the forest. She wanted him to stand there and be terrified. Now what?

Now you jump out and scare him, dummy, she thought to herself, *before he goes too far into the woods*. She told herself she didn't want him to go further into the woods so that he didn't get into any trouble, but really it was because she didn't want to be left alone. He had just slowly crept past the root, bindle thrust forward, when she decided it was time to finish the game. *He's scared enough*, she thought.

Allison hadn't realised that the sounds of the forest were so loud and constant until they suddenly stopped. The busy sounds of woodland creatures had ceased and she stood in absolute silence. She once read in Canadian Geographic magazine that animals will cease making a sound if there is a predator nearby. This thought made her knees weak, her hands began to tremble and she decided that it was, in fact, time to call back Alistair and get out of the woods. She stepped onto the path and could just make out her brother, who stood about ten metres ahead of her, almost lost in the shadows. As she opened her mouth to call his name, he suddenly disappeared, yanked upward so quickly that it took her a few seconds to realise what had happened.

Something had taken Alistair.

***

Alistair's eyes fluttered open a short time later. He appeared to be lying in a sort of cocoon that completely enwrapped his entire body from his shoulders to his ankles. He couldn't move his arms or legs and he was finding it very difficult to breathe. Looking around in the gloomy darkness, he could make out very little, just odd shapes here and there, bulging greenish sacks like the one in which he seemed to be trapped, jagged branches with long, fine needles and the bulky, almost shapeless form of his captor, which stood with his back to the boy. He could hear a strange sucking sound, not unlike a drinking straw when it gets to the bottom of a pop can, and a sickly, salty aroma lingered amidst the smell of sap and tree bark. A pair of tiny feet was poking out from the end of the sack, wiggling madly for a few brief moments and then slowly becoming still. Alistair suddenly realised what was happening.

"Allison!" he shouted. His captor jerked sharply at the sudden sound, then craned his head slowly to face him, turning his head completely backward without moving the rest of his body. He - "*No, not he*" thought Alistair, "*It*", made a slick licking sound, and although Alistair couldn't make out what it was doing, he was positive it was licking its lips. It started to chuckle its spine-tingling laugh once more and slowly brought the rest of its body toward him, then creeped forward. As it approached, engulfed in near darkness, Alistair could see that its body was very oddly shaped. It appeared to have the grotesque head of a man, though somewhat misshapen, but its body was almost cylindrical, covered in course hair with eight impossibly long, multi-jointed arms and legs which moved swiftly, carefully holding onto branches as it approached almost soundlessly, reminding Alistair of some sort of nightmarish spider. It lowered its putrid head level with Alistair's and the fetid stench almost made him throw up.

"Tut, tut," it croaked as Alistair gagged. "I expect better manners from my guests." With that, the thing began to make a sickly retching noise, its head jerking forward a few times, and then a thick wad of greenish bile spilled from its mouth, splattering down on Alistair's face. It began to harden almost immediately, obviously the same substance in which he was encased, and his mouth was now bound in a thick layer of rubber-like mucous, leaving only his nose through which to breathe. "You'll taste better fresh." It slowly returned to its previous meal, continuing to slurp disgustingly.

It was all Alistair could do not to panic. When the spider creature had approached him, he saw that the feet jutting from the pod were long with three webbed toes - obviously not Allison's and certainly not Oscar's. That meant they were probably somewhere nearby, wound tightly in their own little green pods. All he had to do was figure out a way to escape his pod, defeat the spider creature and find them. He began to cry.

FOURTEEN

The spider creature turned once again to face the boy who now lay helplessly trapped, encased in his cocoon and positive that he was going to die. Thoughts of what may have happened to Allison and Oscar charged through his mind, but he didn't have a clue as to their actual fate. For all he knew, they could already be dead, having fallen victim to this hideous creature. Or maybe they were still alive, waiting to have their guts sucked out. It was even possible that they had not been captured at all and were safely on the forest floor, looking for him, but that, he thought, was entirely unlikely.

"Ohhhhhhhh," cooed the creature as it slowly loomed over Alistair. It canted its head to the side, its face twisting into a demented caricature of sadness. "Poor, poor boy. Are you scared?" The tip of one long, spidery arm gently brushed the tears from Alistair's cheek, tickling him with tiny hairs. Then its face turned ghastly sinister as its soft voice took a decidedly more ominous tone. It leaned closer, another wave of nauseating breath washing across the boy's face. "Well, you should be," it continued. "This is going to be very, very nasty."

Alistair watched in horror as a long thin tube that resembled a drinking straw emerged from its mouth. It slid forward with a sickening wet sound, dripping with saliva and no doubt a few other juices, pulsing so slightly it was difficult to see at all in the grim light. Alistair struggled in vain as the tube came slowly closer, his muffled screams for help stifled by the wad of thick rubbery bile. As the tube slowly penetrated the outer layer of the pod with an audible snap, something struck the creature on the head, distracting it.

It jerked away quickly, the probe disappearing back into its mouth in a flash, as it looked around with eight squinting eyes. After a moment of careful observation, it decided there was no immediate danger and returned its attention to the boy.

The tube had slowly protruded once again when another object hit the thing on the side of its head. It looked like it might have been a small rock. Suddenly a volley of rocks and stones came sailing through the air, some striking the spider creature about the head and torso, while others sailed too high or too low. The creature's arms began to pinwheel wildly as it tried to cover its head and at the same time bat away the incoming debris. It retreated a few steps, the proboscis having disappeared once again, and it let out an angry bellow of rage.

Most of this was difficult to see once the action was no longer directly over top of him, as Alistair was lying almost flat upon a branch, facing upward, and the denseness of the forest offered little light by which to clearly see. Suddenly, he felt hands all over him, tugging him back and forth and all he could do was close his eyes as tightly as possible. If he was going to be ripped apart by some sort of band of roving scavengers, he didn't want to see it coming.

Though still tightly wrapped in the gummy pod, he could feel himself being torn free from the branch to which he had been fastened. Elsewhere, he could hear sounds of fighting, hissing, growling, a few yelps of pain and a constant low-pitched gibberish. Something warm and sticky splashed across his face and Alistair was sure it was his own blood although in truth it was only tree sap. Bits of tree bark, leaves and needles fell all about him, littering his face and sticking in his hair and suddenly he could feel himself falling though the air, plummeting straight down. He thumped heavily into a number of branches but due to the thick outer layers of the pod he landed unharmed with a heavy thud on the soft forest floor. Above him he could still hear the sounds of the spider creature fighting with whatever little demons had stolen him. There was more thumping all about him as other pods dropped to the forest floor.

Something heavy landed right on top of him and rolled to the side and the boy was sure it was another pod, perhaps the one which encased

Allison or even Oscar. He was now laying on his stomach on the forest floor with his face mashed into the moist ground as another pod landed right beside him, sending a shower of dirt and debris over him. A wad of earth somehow managed to clog his nostrils and suddenly he couldn't breathe at all as the gooey substance was still firmly stuck over his mouth. As his lungs, which were already compressed due to the tightness of the pod, screamed for reprieve, something rolled him onto his back and a warm liquid was poured over his face. It stung his skin a little bit but immediately he could feel the wad of goo loosen and then slip down his chin like a moist slug, plopping wetly to the ground. He gasped for air, which came in short, painful breaths. Opening his eyes, he could see dozens of brawny little people working diligently, pouring soft skins full of liquid over the faces of the pod victims. Looking around, Alistair was amazed at how many pods lay scattered on the forest floor. A few more dropped down, landing heavily and immediately a couple of the little people tended to it, pouring liquid over the victim's faces.

The people themselves were very strange and Alistair wasn't even sure if they were really people at all. They were about three feet tall and very stocky, with stubby little legs and stubby little arms but these arms and legs bulged with powerful musculature. They had broad shoulders and were barrel-chested and their heads looked almost square, propped low on their torso since they appeared to have little in the way of a neck. Their faces were ruddy and scruffy, though none had beards like the Boffles and their eyes were set deep into their skulls with a heavy ridged brow, wide, flat noses and deeply carved slits for mouths. They wore what appeared to be animal skins of varying colours, draped over their shoulders like a toga, bound at the waist by heavy ropes. A few wore leather wrist bands and all were barefoot. Small leather pouches were slung over their shoulders and a few of them held what appeared to be some sort of weapon, not unlike a slingshot. Others had their slingshots tucked into the rope about their waists as they administered the releasing agents to those still bound in their cocoons.

Their powerful hands ripped the pods open like some sort of large paper sack, the greenish substance tearing with a sickly wet sound. It seemed to be made of millions of tiny fibres that were somehow woven tightly together. When they were pulled apart, hundreds of tiny little tendrils hung in the air while still more clung to their victims' bodies.

Alistair simply couldn't figure out what was going on. These people appeared so savage looking he was positive he had simply been snagged from one horrific death only to be thrust into another one. Incredibly, they seemed to be freeing the captives. He watched in bewildered confusion as creatures of all description slowly began to pull themselves from the remains of their cocoons and dash off into the woods.

A heavy pair of hands suddenly grabbed hold of Alistair's pod, eliciting a sharp yelp of fear and surprise from the boy. One of the squat little men stood beside him, ripping apart the thick membrane. The sound was strange - a soggy tearing noise that reminded him of yanking dandelion weeds from his mother's garden - but immediately he could take in a deep breath of fresh air as the pressure was suddenly lifted from his chest. He looked at the little man who stood beside him and saw a kindness in his expression that told him he was safe. Without a word, the little man turned to another pod and ripped it open.

Slowly Alistair pulled himself from the cocoon. Tiny fibres clung to him like hundreds of sticky threads but he easily brushed them away. The air was thick with lingering tendrils and Alistair looked around slowly as he dug the dirt and debris from his nostrils, searching for any sign of his sister or Oscar.

A small row of lifeless bodies, mostly creatures which Alistair couldn't recognise, lay on the forest floor - the unfortunate few who didn't survive. Neither Allison nor Oscar was among them and a wave of relief engulfed the boy. The pods had stopped coming and there was a sound of fury from high above followed by a savage shaking of leaves and branches. One of the little men came crashing down to the ground with a heavy *thunk* but he immediately stood up, brushed himself off and with a stern look of anger and determination, clamoured back up a tree and disappeared into the shadows. A few moments later, there was silence from above. Over a dozen men then carefully inched down the trees, their stubby but powerful arms and legs expertly manoeuvring down the heavy trunks. They were bloodied and bruised, breathing heavily and one of them held a hand over a gaping wound as blood oozed between his fingers and down his arm. Immediately another little man rushed to him and poured more of the liquid over the wound. The blood was immediately washed away and the wound began to heal almost immediately.

One of the little men slowly approached Alistair from behind, placing a dirty, scarred hand on his shoulder. He spun around, startled, and the little man took an apprehensive step back then smiled as he held out Alistair's bindle.

"Th-thanks," Alistair stammered as he took the stick.

"You're welcome," the little man replied pleasantly. Alistair's jaw dropped and his eyes almost popped out of his head as he looked past the little man. Behind him, perhaps twenty metres away, stood Allison and Oscar. They were like statues, Allison's jaw almost touching the forest floor, amazed at what she had just seen.

The little man looked behind him and saw the girl, then looked back at Alistair. "Your sister?" he asked. Alistair nodded wordlessly as his mind reeled in a desperate attempt to figure out what had just happened.

"Come," said the little man, "let's get you cleaned up." He motioned for Alistair to follow as he trudged deeper into the woods but Alistair didn't move. "Come on," he said as a kind smile crossed his face. "It's alright." To Allison he said, "You too. Come." The twins exchanged glances, and then slowly followed the little fellow deeper into the woods. Oscar offered another one of his apprehensive growlfs, and then trotted along behind them.

The remaining little men gathered around the fallen victims and continued to pry them from their cocoons. Then they began to pour a strange liquid into their mouths and within seconds, the once subdued prisoners began to stir and dash off into the forest. A few of the little men expertly shimmied up the tree trunks and disappeared into the dense foliage, obviously hoping to administer more of the elixir to anyone still entrapped among the boughs.

***

They had walked for almost an hour, finally coming to a stop in what appeared to be the thickest part of the Obsidian Woods. The shrill sounds of the forest had continued again and that seemed a good sign to Allison. Neither had spoken on the trek through the woods as the pair stubbornly clung to their vow never to speak to each other ever again.

"My name is Halford Littlejohn," said the little man amicably as they trudged through the thick branches and brush.

"Allison."

"Alistair. And this is Oscar"

Oscar let out a disheartened snarf as they plodded along.

"I'm happy to meet you," said Halford. "I must say, we were surprised to see humans in the woods."

"It was an accident," Alistair said snidely.

"Yes, well, it would have to be," said Halford. "I don't know of very many people who would purposely walk right into Ryvek's lair."

"Who's Ryvek?" Allison asked.

"I bet I know," said her brother.

Halford paused to pull away a thick bramble of tangled branches. It proved to be a hidden passageway that opened into a small clearing.

"Ryvek," said Halford, "is an Arachnoid. Half man, half spider. There are a few of them around, though their numbers are dwindling. We've done our best to rid the woods of their kind, but a few have proven far more difficult to handle. Ryvek is the worst of them all. You're lucky to be alive. If we hadn't attacked when we did, your internal organs would have been liquefied and then devoured. Not one of the better ways to die, I'm sure."

The thought of how close he had come to becoming a protein shake sent shivers down Alistair's spine and Allison let out a pitiful groan at Halford's explanation.

"So, you can speak English?" asked Alistair.

"We speak Giantese," he said. "But we learned your English many years ago from a human who used to visit quite often."

"Giantese?"

"Oh yes," said the little three foot man. "We're Giants. Here we are."

They stood in front of a large row of tall, bristly bushes and shrubs. Halford reached out and shook them violently. He turned to offer a kind smile at the twins. "Just be another minute," he said. The other little men had joined them, carrying the remains of Ryvek's less fortunate victims. The bushes shook again, though this time it was from something on the opposite side. Then Halford barked something in what was apparently Giantese but it sounded more like a walrus with strep throat.

"Gurn tagok. Baktu Kak!"

The bushes then swung inward as though on some sort of hinge and Halford led the group inside. Behind them, the bushes rustled back into place as a little man (with muscles that would rival any of the TV wrestlers Alistair was so fond of) stood guard. He held a long spear that looked dangerously sharp.

In front of them was a small village of crude construction. There were huts and little barns, small patches of garden where vegetables seemed to grow by the bushel. There were little people pushing carts laden with what appeared to be straw or hay down the dirt packed roads. Alistair noticed another one of those dog-looking creatures which they had seen in Loxbury chase a little boy down the road, the boy cackling with glee as the dog-thing clipped his heels. There was a small wood mill where lumber was being cut, a blacksmith's hammer sang its shrill song somewhere in the distance and the pleasant murmur of people buzzed in the small market where people were trading gourds and fruit the likes of which neither Allison nor Alistair had ever seen.

The women were dressed in much the same fashion as the men - little more than animal skins worn like dresses, cinched at the waist by rope. The one thing that Allison found truly intriguing was that every woman wore their hair in long, beautiful braids just like hers. She looked at her own, which weren't even really braids at this point, but simply twisted clumps of red hair tied awkwardly at the ends with little rubber bands. She exhaled a deep, mournful sigh.

"Come along then," said Halford, as he led them toward a small cottage similar to Sender's. As they went, they passed a little woman who was squeezing a yellowish liquid from a strange looking tapered yellow tube. Both Allison and Alistair recognised it as one of the dandelion spikes that had attacked them in the Eating Garden.

"Ah," said Halford, noticing the twins cautiously eyeing the ominous looking spike, "that's Deadlylion. Its nectar is quite lethal on its own but when combined with Tangleroot it has remarkable healing powers."

Inside the shack, they were greeted by a lovely looking woman who stood about two feet tall wearing a soft looking dress that appeared to be suede. Like the others, her hair was pulled back in a tidy braid and adorned with beautiful, multi-coloured feathers. Her features were soft and delicate and she embraced Halford, obviously delighted to see him.

She said something in Giantese, which pretty much sounded exactly like what Halford had said at the bushes.

"Please, Nessa," said Halford. "We have guests."

"I'm sorry," she said with a pleasant smile. She bowed gracefully at the twins, eyeing Oscar with some suspicion. "He's not dangerous, is he?" Her eyes darted toward the furthermost corner where a bassinet stood. The sounds of a cooing baby drifted toward them.

"Nah," said Alistair, rubbing the dog on the head. "He's a good guy. He just looks weird cuz I shaved him. It's a long story."

"Well then, please," she said, gesturing toward two high-backed wooden chairs, "make yourselves comfortable."

The twins sat down as Mrs. Littlejohn placed a plate of biscuits on the table, and then poured them each a cup of steaming liquid that smelled deliciously of cinnamon. "It's Dibble tea," said Mrs. Littlejohn. Famished and thirsty, the twins eyed the cookies and tea longingly, neither wanting to be rude.

"Help yourselves," Halford said with a grin. At that, they devoured the cookies, which were more delicious than anything they had ever eaten before and washed them down with Dibble tea that was ten times better than what they had had in Loxbury.

"So tell me," said Halford, after they had eaten two more plates of cookies and drank three cups of tea apiece. Their stomachs were full and Alistair wanted nothing more than to take a long nap. "How did you come to end up in the middle of the Obsidian Woods?"

They told their tale of adventure in great detail, from Alistair riding Oscar down the stairs in Schmendricktonville to the moment that Allison ran into the woods. Halford and Nessa listened intently, gasping at the story of the Eating Garden, Mrs. Littlejohn saying "Oh, my!" when they told of the Serpensilicus attack and laughing when they recounted their imagined marauder at Pointing Rock that turned out to be Oscar. But when they mentioned Burcheeze's name, Mrs. Littlejohn gasped again, grabbing Halford by the arm.

"Yeah," said Alistair, "the Boffles think he's a big jerk too."

"Well, they have reason to," said Halford. "He's a terrible, terrible man."

"Why does he hate the Boffles so much?" asked Allison.

Mrs. Littlejohn looked worriedly at her husband, who began to explain all about Burcheeze.

"It's not just Boffles that fear Burcheeze," he began. "He is even more dangerous than Ryvek, the Serpensilicus and the Eating Garden combined."

"How can that be?" asked Allison, unable to think that anything could be worse than that which they have already been through.

"Well," said Halford, "in those cases, we always know where the threat lies. It doesn't take long for one to learn where to tread and where to not. Their actions themselves may not always be predictable, but their borders are always precise and limited. Ryvek lives in the Obsidian Woods. Nowhere else. The Serpensilicus lives in the shallows of Mayomay Bay. We know this and thus limit our intrusions to such places. In the case of Burcheeze, he is able to strike wherever and whenever he pleases."

"So who is this guy anyway?" asked Alistair. He leaned across the small wooden table with great interest as Halford explained further.

"Hundreds of generations ago, there lived a great King named Barchod. He wore rich and flowing red robes, sported long, brilliant red locks and everyone referred to him as the Vermilion King. He was a good and kind King until one day, a group of his servants turned against him. Overnight they became marauders, invading his tiny kingdom from within its own ranks. They ravaged the land, burned the villages and stole the Vermilion King's only daughter, threatening to kill her if he didn't step down. You see, the King was a man of his word and the marauders knew that if he agreed, the land would be theirs to plunder forever. Of course, King Barchod agreed and the land of Dibble was reduced to a vast wasteland.

"Now the marauders were a vile group of men and women whose word was as useless as a blind bat's eyes. The King's daughter was never seen again and Barchod wandered the land, mourning the loss of his only precious child.

"One day he found himself wandering in Tenebrous Marsh, weeping and sobbing, when a voice called out to him. It was the Marsh Hag, a powerful sorceress who hated people and lived alone. She offered to grant the King one wish, but only if she asked a favour of him, knowing that the King was a man of honour and would do his best to fulfill her wish. The King agreed and made his wish."

"He wished that Dibble would be peaceful again," Allison said in astonished wonderment.

"Yes. And his wish was granted. The marauders were vanquished and sent into exile and the Land of Dibble once again belonged to the Boffles. There was a grand celebration, a tradition that continues to this day, and all was well. Of course, there was a condition. There always is with the Marsh Hag, and this one was two-fold. The Boffles were to construct a great clock and set it in the middle of the King's courtyard. Every year they would have to wind the key to keep time moving forward. If the clock was allowed to completely wind down, even once, it could never be wound again and time would simply cease for the Boffles. It seemed a small price to pay and in fact it has become a glorious tradition. For generations since, the Boffles would live in peace and harmony, thanks to the selfless sacrifice of the Vermilion King."

"What happened to him?" Alistair asked.

"Well," Halford said, "the Marsh Hag only wanted one thing from the King. She wanted him to stay with her in Tenebrous Marsh forever. And she got her wish."

"Tenebrous Marsh is a vile place," Mrs. Littlejohn continued. "It does things to a person's mind if they spend too much time there. Marsh Fever they call it. No one knows exactly what happened after that, but it is believed that Barchod went mad and killed the Marsh Hag, but not before siring an heir.

"You mean Burcheeze," Allison said slowly.

"Yes."

"But if Burcheeze is the son of King Barchod," said Alistair, "how can he still be alive? I thought this was hundreds of years ago."

"That's the sorcery of the Marsh," said Halford. "Barchod was forced to live there for all eternity, as is his heir. The sins of the father fall to the son."

"So then what happened to Barchod?" asked Allison.

"No one knows," Mrs. Littlejohn replied. "Dead, probably. Perhaps killed by Burcheeze. It's difficult to say. No one has seen King Barchod since he first left for Tenebrous Marsh all those years ago."

"And Burcheeze stays there," Halford concluded, "every day a little madder, loathing the fact that the

Boffles were freed from their enslavement while he was forced to live in wretched, poisoned squalor for something he hadn't even done."

"It didn't take long for Dibble to rise to its former glory and the story goes that not long after the Grandfather Clock was completed, the first visitors began to come through. When word spread of how wonderful Dibble was, several others came, from many, many different worlds."

"In the end I suppose it doesn't matter where he came from," said Halford. "He's here and that's all we need concern ourselves with. If we had known, I doubt the Giants would have ever come here."

"You're not *from* Dibble?" Allison asked.

"So *that's* why you're not slowing down like the Boffles," Alistair said. He had wondered why the Giants had not shown signs of losing time and now he had his answer.

"Yes," said Mrs. Littlejohn. "Our people came here a long time ago, much like the humans. Ours is a proud race and there were some who didn't like us simply because we were different than they. You see, by Giant standards, we are somewhat . . . small."

"Oh really?" Alistair said awkwardly. "I . . . uh . . . it's . . . er . . . you can hardly tell."

"We were hunted," Halford said in a deep, saddened voice. "Destroyed. Simply because we were different. Once we realised there was an escape, we took advantage of it. What few of us that were left immediately escaped to Dibble, where we could live in peace and harmony. We can never go home."

The room was very quiet for a very long time as Halford paused to pour more tea before continuing.

"But that's not the issue at hand. For generations Burcheeze has been terrorizing the Boffles. There are stories where he has burned Loxbury to the ground, cast spells to make the Boffle men turn into Stinkrats and the story of the time Burcheeze stole all the Boffle children is a common one when the wee tykes are too restless to go to sleep at night." Halford chuckled softly. "Of course, some of these stories have been exaggerated, but the horrible truth is that Burcheeze is a mad, angry man who will stop at nothing in his efforts to destroy the Boffles once and for all."

Looking at his watches, Alistair was startled to see that several hours had gone by. It was now almost six o'clock by his watch and the Dibble watch's second hand was barely ticking at all.

"Well, we're almost out of time," Alistair finally said. "We still have to get that key from him. Are we very far?"

"You're still going after hearing that story?" asked Mrs. Littlejohn, obviously startled by Alistair's determination to press onward.

"Of course," he said. "This guy is worse than we thought and you guys might be next. Who cares if he's a wacko prince or just some nut that belongs in a loony bin? He's gotta be stopped.

How do you know he won't start to kill all the Boffles' friends?"

"Y-Yeah," Allison added nervously. "We have to stop him . . . somehow."

"Then we'll help you," said Halford.

"Oh, Halford, no," gasped Mrs. Littlejohn.

"We have to, Nessa," he said soothingly, placing a hand on hers. He looked deep into her eyes and the love they shared was more than obvious. "The boy is right. It's only a matter of time before Burcheeze finds us and he'll think of a way to destroy us as well. We have a chance to stop him *and* save the Boffles. We have to, Nessa. The Boffles would gladly do it for us. You know they would."

"Yes," she said, averting her eyes from her husband's. "Yes, they would.

You're right. We have to help them."

"It's settled then." To Alistair and Allison he said, "We have tunnels. We'll take you to Burcheeze."

FIFTEEN

Halford led them through the village, across a small courtyard, past the blacksmith's shop and into a small bakery. Inside, the redolent aroma of freshly baked pastries and bread lingered and Alistair's mouth began to water. Allison was still somewhat full from the cookies and tea but even she longed to savour the delicious warm baked goods that lined a small wooden shelf. A kindly looking little Giant who was covered in a fine dusting of flour smiled at them as he removed a loaf of bread from a stone oven.

"Boy, those look great," cooed Alistair as he licked his lips and rubbed his hands together. "Don't they Allison?"

Allison didn't respond.

"Oh come on," he said, "are you still not talking to me? This is stupid."

Just then a small group of Giants joined them inside the bakery, each armed with a slingshot and a bulging pouch of ammunition.

"This is Feldon," said Halford, motioning to a blond-haired Giant who stood just a little taller than the rest of them. His face was deeply scarred, as were his hands and arms. This was obviously a Giant to beware of. "He'll be guiding us." Feldon nodded slightly as he adjusted his grip on his slingshot.

Alistair looked at their crude weapons. "You guys don't have any guns or anything?" He had visions of charging into Burcheeze's house like a wild west desperado, shooting first and asking questions later.

"You are *not* going to give him a gun," Allison blurted loudly before Halford could answer.

"Oh, *now* you're talking?" Alistair scolded.

"I was talking to Halford," she said flatly. "I'm not talking to you until you say you're sorry."

"Sorry? Sure, I'll say I'm sorry. I'm sorry I ran into the woods to save your scrawny neck. I'm sorry I almost got eaten by a mutant spider. I'm sorry I fell from the top of a giant tree all because I was worried about *you*." He paused for a moment, considering what he just said. "Actually," he continued, "I didn't even do it for you. I was worried about Oscar."

Oscar let out a gruff that seemed to say 'Leave me out of this'.

"He'd probably end up shooting himself in the foot," said Allison in an icy tone.

"I'd probably shoot you in your big stupid butt," retorted her brother.

"You wouldn't dare!" she almost screamed. Their voices had gradually grown to a near shouting match and Halford had to step in between them, fearing they might actually start to physically assault one another.

"Enough of this bickering," he shouted. "We have a task to accomplish and you must remain focused. You can argue all you like once we have retrieved the key from Burcheeze."

He nodded to the baker, who removed a small section of brick from the oven, uncovering a sunken handle. With great effort he pulled on the handle and the entire oven began to shift, scraping heavily across the floor to reveal a dark cavern. Feldon took a small torch and used the oven's fire to set it ablaze.

"Follow me," Feldon said in a deep, serious tone.

The tunnel was almost as black as pitch, the only light coming from the torch. Orange light and dark, inky shadows danced across the earthen walls and the smell was very similar to Auntie Bernice's basement. Every so often they passed what appeared to be doorways which had been blocked off either with loose dirt, heavy brambles of thick branches and twigs or sometimes completely bricked over.

"Some of these tunnels are no longer accessible," explained Halford. "Some have caved in or become overgrown. Some are simply too dangerous to use all together."

As they continued along the tunnel, its ceiling gradually became lower and lower and the twins had to stoop slightly. The walls now seemed to glisten and shimmer and a quick touch told them that they were cold and damp. Soon, the hard packed dirt beneath their feet had given way to a soft, mushy texture and every step was accompanied by a sickly wet squishing noise.

"We're under Tenebrous Marsh now," Feldon finally said in a hushed voice. "It's only a little further."

A moment later they stopped at a small opening that was covered by dripping tendrils of seaweed and moss, though the tunnel itself went further along. The stench was almost unbearable; it was a combination of sulphur, dampness and decay.

"Through here," said Feldon. He pressed the tip of the torch to the ground, squelching it out in the wet muck, leaving them in almost total darkness; only a little light filtered through the hanging moss. Taking a deep breath, Feldon separated the mossy weeds with his hands and stepped through. A stronger wave of the foul smell enveloped them and the twins almost retched. They held their breath and followed the little Giant through the opening.

They emerged on the side of a mossy hill and as soon as they stepped down from the opening, they were knee-deep in sludgy, slimy water, startling a water snake that slithered quickly across the surface then disappeared under a thick clot of rust coloured reeds. They had to breathe through their mouths to make the air bearable and even then, it was almost nauseating. The ghastly stink would linger in their nostrils for days to come.

In front of them lay a large swampy mess of murky water, muddy mounds of filthy earth and a few stunted and grotesque looking trees, all of which hung heavy with more of the disgusting mossy seaweed. The air itself seemed thick, no doubt a result of the heavy greenish layer of smoky fog that lingered a few feet from the water's surface. Here and there hovered little pockets of tiny insects and then, to their amazement, they spotted a few not-so-small insects which appeared to be mutated versions of their own mosquitoes. They were almost a metre long with thick, veiny wings and long, dangling legs. Their heads were the size of basketballs and the protruding proboscises were as long as hockey sticks. Their high-pitched buzzing noise echoed through the marsh, causing a constant, eerie humming sound that sent goosebumps crawling across their flesh.

The water appeared to be at a low boil though it was only warm to their skin, and occasionally a bubble or two would rise to the surface and pop audibly, releasing a puff of fine brown mist that smelled like the outhouses at summer camp. All in all, Tenebrous Marsh was a pretty awful place.

As the last of the remaining Giants stepped out into the marsh, Halford pointed to a large mound of rocks and brownish-green, stubby grass that vaguely resembled a small shanty. Jutting out from the top was a crooked pipe and from the pipe spilled a lazy stream of grey smoke. "There," he said.

"Do the Boffles know about those tunnels?" asked Alistair. He couldn't help but wonder if the passageways may have made the earlier part of their journey just a little easier.

"Some of them," replied Halford. "I don't know if they are aware of this one in particular."

"Can you get back to Loxbury from here using them?" asked Allison. It was the first thing she had said since leaving the bakery aside from periodically expressing her disgust with the tunnels by muttering a few random "ewww"'s and "yuck"'s.

"You can, yes," he said, then clapped a hand over Allison's mouth as she began to question why they hadn't simply used the tunnels in the first place. Just as Alistair was about to ask what Halford was doing, he spotted something near the large mound. The Giants all pulled heavy rocks from their pouches and slipped them into the pockets of their slingshots, ready to open fire if necessary.

"Burcheeze," whispered Halford.

In the distance stood a true giant of a man, huge even by human standards, dressed in grimy old trousers that were torn and threadbare. He wore what appeared to be an old plaid shirt that had seen brighter days and on his feet were large black boots, his big toe poking perversely out from one of them. His hair was long and frizzled and he wore a beard that seemed to engulf most of his face, only a bulbous red nose and squinting eyes peering through his massive head of fiery red- and silver-streaked hair. His hands looked like he wore baseball mitts with fingers the size of Allison's wrist. They could see something hanging from Burcheeze's neck, about the size of a large frying pan.

"And he has the key."

SIXTEEN

Burcheeze lumbered around in front of his mud and stone hut for quite some time, grumbling to himself as he almost absentmindedly stacked large pieces of firewood, mended a small section of a dilapidated wooden fence and for reasons only Burcheeze could know, dug a large hole, piling the dirt quite high and obscuring their view. All the while, he was singing little snippets of a song, deep and out of key, between his random mutterings.

"What's he doing?" mumbled Allison through Halford's beefy hand. Halford shrugged wordlessly, then told her to 'shhhh'. Alistair stood motionless, his attention so fixed on their adversary that he didn't notice that a large bug had landed on the fleshy part of his exposed leg until it took a gluttonous bite. Alistair's reaction was immediate and instinctive. And poorly timed. Burcheeze had only just stopped singing, pausing to wipe sweat from his brow and lean on his shovel, when Alistair let out a sharp "Ouch!" and squashed the bug with an audible wet *slap*.

Burcheeze's head jerked toward them as he let out an inquisitive grunt.

"Whoozat?" he growled, taking a slow forward step. He held the shovel like a club, ready to strike. "Whoozat?" he repeated.

Alistair, Allison and Halford hunkered down, the water now soaking their bottoms. Feldon and the other Giants also crunched low, pulling their slingshots taut. The bite on Alistair's leg began to itch almost immediately and it was all he could do not to scratch it with wild and abandoned frenzy.

Burcheeze took another half step, and then lowered the shovel.

"Bahhhh," he grumbled, "guess I'm hearin' things." He turned back toward his hole but at that point Alistair couldn't take it any longer. He madly began to scratch at his leg, which had begun to swell terribly, having turned an angry shade of red around the little chunk of missing flesh. Suddenly, he was itchy all over and seemed to have lost his mind as he jumped up and down uncontrollably, scratching all over his body as though he were pitching some sort of fit.

"Alistair, no!" hissed Halford, but it was too late. The boy had jumped back to his feet, foul water splashing in every direction. He clawed at his torn and waterlogged jeans, unfastening them and kicking them off with a wet *ploop*. He all but ripped his shirt off and tossed it aside as well. It was absolute agony as the red blotchiness began to creep up Alistair's legs, across his flabby belly and chest, down his arms and up his neck. In a matter of seconds, he was a disturbing shade of deep crimson from head to toe as he stood scratching like a crazy person, dressed only in a pair of underpants with little sailboats on them.

Burcheeze came bellowing toward them, shovel held high over his head, and the Giants opened fire, sending a volley of rocks sailing toward the huge and angry man. The rocks had no effect on him, however, most simply thumping and thudded into him, bouncing away as though they were paper spit-balls.

The shovel swung wildly as Burcheeze attacked, bashing some of the rocks away like a big league batter. Everyone scattered to try to take cover except Alistair, who simply splashed around, scratching himself raw. He only stopped when Burcheeze's shovel glanced off the back of his skull, eliciting a loud *clank*.

The Giants doubled their attack efforts and the rocks finally started to take their toll on their enormous assailant. Burcheeze stumbled then fell to one knee, picking himself up slowly as he was repeatedly pummelled with stones and rocks. Staggering slightly and with a cut over his left eye that sent blood gushing down his face, Burcheeze turned and fled, his shovel having sunk to the bottom of the boggy marsh when he fell. He wailed madly as he retreated, hands clenched into tight fists which he waved high in the air, and disappeared behind the mound of dirt. They heard a heavy thud as he shut himself up in his hovel.

Alistair lay face up in the bog, floating motionlessly except for the waves of the settling sludge. His entire body was bloated to almost twice its normal size, covered in a violent red rash and his breathing was wet and laboured. Halford scooped him up effortlessly and set him gently on the soggy bank. Allison watched, silent tears streaming down her face, her hands cupped over her mouth, which hung agape. The Giants huddled around the boy as Halford knelt down beside him.

"He's been bitten by a Thunderbug," he said to Allison as he removed a small water skin from his pouch. "Very poisonous. He's actually lucky he's so portly. Had it been you . . ." he paused. "Well, the venom works quickly. We must hurry."

He pulled a stopper from the skin and poured its contents over the gaping wound on Alistair's leg. It hissed and bubbled, foaming up in mucousy yellow froth and Alistair's entire body tensed as he wailed in pain. Feldon held him down, bracing his arms and another of the Giants held his legs. A strange cobweb of yellow seemed to course through his veins and in a matter of seconds, he was covered in fine yellowish threads that seemed to have spider-webbed just below his skin, reaching from his toes to the his forehead. After a few minutes, he began to relax and the twisted look of agony that had crossed his face dissipated. The redness in his skin began to fade as the fine yellow tendrils started to enlarge. Within ten minutes, he had returned to his normal size and was no longer red. Instead, he was a sickly colour of yellow that reminded Allison of mushed baby food. Against his newly yellowed skin, his natural freckles and stark red hair seemed to blaze on his body.

"He'll rest now," said Halford, glancing cautiously over his shoulder, in the direction of Burcheeze's shack. "I think we've set Burcheeze straight for a little while anyway. He's in there planning another strategy, I'm sure."

"He's ok though?" she asked nervously, meaning Alistair.

Halford offered her a reassuring smile. "Yes," he said, "he'll be fine. As I said, Deadlylion nectar mixed with Tangleroot has remarkable healing powers." He handed Allison the skin. "Take a sip," he said. "It will make you immune should you happen to become bitten by a Thunderbug. Or anything else for that matter."

Allison took a sip, her face twisting in revulsion.

"Ugh!" she sputtered. "It's awful!"

"Yes, but it works," he said. "Just a little more."

"Do I have to?" Her face was still scrunched up as the vile taste lingered on her tongue. Halford nodded toward Alistair. "OK," she said and took another sip, this time plugging her nose as she did so. It didn't help the taste in the least, but with great effort she managed to drain the skin dry.

Alistair began to stir, groaning softly at first. He propped himself up on his elbows and looked quizzically at his sister and Halford, who hunkered in front of him.

"What happened?" he muttered, rubbing his head. Then he noticed he was completely yellow. And almost entirely naked. "Allison!" he gasped, "get out of here!" He grabbed a handful of weeds and leaves, covering his midsection, eliciting a good natured chuckle from Halford and his men.

Halford explained what had happened and Alistair had never been happier to be the fat kid. If he had been skinny, like his sister, he would have been a goner.

Alistair had made Allison turn around as he dressed, to which she rolled her eyes and said "Boys" as she faced the opposite direction.

"Did we get the key?" he finally asked. He was trying to slip into his soaked jeans, which clung to his skin, making the process incredibly difficult. "Not yet," said Feldon. "But we will."

Alistair looked at the Dibble watch and his heart lurched into his throat. It was broken. The crystal had been smashed and the minute hand was bent to a ninety degree angle, pointing straight upwards. The hour hand was missing completely and the second hand had simply stopped. He had no way of knowing whether time had ceased or not.

***

They cautiously approached Burcheeze's hovel from behind. There was a single window laid into the wall, but it was dirty and caked with grime, which was rather fortunate for them as there was no way they could be seen from inside. Feldon and two of the Giants went ahead of the group, their slingshots at the ready, with Alistair, Allison, Oscar and Halford in the middle. Three more Giants took up the rear.

They could hear Burcheeze inside, growling and muttering to himself, though the words themselves were indistinguishable through the stone and mud walls. Something heavy scraped across the floor inside and bashed against the wall where they stood, sending a shower of dirt and debris down on the group.

"What do you think that was?" whispered Alistair worriedly, though no one answered. Whatever it was, Burcheeze moved another one, bashing the wall and sending more debris sifting down on them. This was repeated several times, and then there was silence.

They waited a few minutes, listening to Burcheeze's heavy footsteps clomping around in the tiny hut. Then they heard the door open and slam shut, the entire hovel shuddering with the impact. Burcheeze was laughing loudly at the front of the shack as he trod away, splashing off into the marsh.

"Where's he going?" Allison whispered.

Carefully, Alistair stood up and tried to peek through the window. It was so grimy and soiled that even when he rubbed the thick layer of sludge away, the glass remained murky, as though there were a film of grease on the inside.

A crooked chair that had been crudely fashioned from tree branches stood in front of a stone fireplace, which still had glowing embers smouldering within. The door was directly adjacent to the window and on it hung what looked to be a half eaten animal of some description. It had been skewered and apparently cooked over the open fire. A small pile of bones lay near the door and among them skittered a few black Stinkrats like they had seen in the Obsidian Woods. They were busily scavenging the bones for any meaty remnants, though it looked as if Burcheeze had done a fair job of cleaning the bones himself. In the centre of the room stood a rickety old table, leaning with a decided tilt as one leg was noticeably shorter than the rest. However, it was the thing that lay on the table itself that caught Alistair's eye.

"Oh man!" he exclaimed, spinning to look at the rest of the group. "It's right there."

"The key?" asked Allison, her eyes wide. "He just left it there?"

"Yeah," he said. "It's just lying on the table."

"It's a trap," said Halford. "He has something in mind. He's probably hiding just on the other side of the marsh, ready to attack the minute we enter the shack. We'll be sitting geese."

"Ducks," corrected Allison.

"I beg your pardon?"

"We'll be sitting ducks. Not geese."

"She does that all the time," said Alistair. "You get used to it. Do you think we can get through this window?"

Without a word, Feldon stood up, grabbed the crude window frame and tore it from the side of the hovel as though it were the simplest of tasks.

"I guess so," said Alistair.

"Alright," said Halford, "I'll go in and get the key. If Burcheeze comes, you will run. Do you understand me? Run back to the tunnels and do not stop." He pointed a thick, stubby finger at all of them, holding a little longer on Alistair. Everyone agreed.

He lifted himself up and tried to squeeze through the opening but it proved to be too small for his broad chest and shoulders. It quickly became obvious that only one of them could fit through.

"Allison," Halford said softly, "you'll have to go."

She shook her head vigorously. "Uh-uh," she said.

"You're the only one who can fit," said Alistair. "You gotta go."

"I'm too scared."

"It's OK," said Halford. "We'll be right here. If you go quickly and quietly, we can get the key and get away from this awful place."

Allison stared at him, knowing that he was right. She was the only one who could do it. If she didn't go, everything they had done so far was worth nothing. She closed her eyes and took a deep breath.

"OK," she huffed.

Using Halford's back as a stoop, she climbed up and slipped through the tiny gap into Burcheeze's home. It was quite dim and gloomy and difficult to see, the only light coming from the smouldering embers and a small candle which burned just to the left of the window sill. As she climbed through, she slipped slightly on a pile of loosely stacked wood, which gave way under her weight. She scraped her knees when she fell but was otherwise alright. Pausing to take a cautious look around, she expected to be charged at any second. When no attack came, Allison slowly approached the table. The key was tarnished brass, with a long barrel and an ornate handle, which depicted an hourglass within a circular clock face. She looked at it for a few moments, amazed that something so simple was quite literally the key to the future of an entire race of people. With her eyes shut as tightly as possible, she quickly snatched it from the table, well aware that the key could be booby-trapped. It wasn't.

"I've got it," she whispered loudly, turning back toward the window. "I've got the k-"

Her words were cut short as she stopped dead in her tracks, staring at the wall which she had just come through.

It was as though she had stepped out of her life and into some sort of cartoon where the traps were unnecessarily complicated and convoluted. The pile of wood she had slipped on was not a pile of wood at all. Before her sat two large barrels, each of which had a long waxy wick jutting from the top and piled about them were hundreds of sticks of old fashioned explosives. This was what had been pushed up against the wall. Though far from being an expert on the subject, she knew dynamite when she saw it, having done a school project on the building of the Trans-Canada highway the previous year.

The candle she had seen was burning away at a thin piece of cord which ran to a hook in the ceiling. Looking up, she saw that a small tin plate was carefully slung in a loop at the other end, dangling from the hook. On the tin plate sat a large a few burning embers from the fire, glowing an angry blackish-red. Any minute now, the cord would burn through and the embers would fall. Within seconds, the entire hovel - and perhaps most of Tenebrous Marsh - would be blown sky high. Whether the display was convoluted or not did little to lessen the anxiety Allison felt, knowing full well just how deadly dangerous the situation had suddenly become.

"Allison," Halford called softly though the window, watching her stare blankly at the wall. "What's the matter?"

She slowly looked up at Halford.

"We're in big trouble," she said. With a grunt, Halford pulled himself up and poked his head through the hole, first spying the candle and then the explosives.

"Allison, get out of there!" he screamed, but Allison remained still, frozen in terror as the candle flame finally burned through the chord. The tin plate dropped and clattered to the floor as the embers clattered between the sticks and fell out of sight. A few seconds later, she could hear a soft hiss.

Halford dropped from the window and pushed everyone back. "Go! Go!" he screamed, but Alistair ducked under his arm and dashed around to the front of the hut. Feldon grabbed for him, but his fingers just brushed the nape of his shirt collar. Alistair figured that even if Burcheeze was lying in wait, they had nothing to lose at this point and it was obvious that Allison wasn't going to try to save herself.

Charging through the heavy wooden door and grabbing his sister by the wrist, Alistair managed to yank her back to her senses. The room was beginning to fill with smoke and it was only due to the moist conditions that the explosives didn't go up immediately.

They bolted from the hut, running as fast as they could through the mushy-bottomed bog. In an uncharacteristically swift move, Alistair managed to narrowly avoid the pit that Burcheeze had been digging by deftly leaping over it. They then charged toward the tunnel entrance and what would hopefully be their route of escape. At first, Alistair couldn't even make out where the entrance was as everything suddenly looked the same in every direction. The Giants, running just ahead of them, crashed through the tunnel opening with determined ease. Allison, Alistair and Oscar were close behind, and then came Halford followed by Feldon. A few seconds later, thick, black smoke began to billow out of the broken window of the hovel.

The very second that Feldon's toes slipped through the wet, dangling moss, having dived headfirst through the entrance, a thunderous roar tore through the marsh as Burcheeze's hovel exploded into a million tiny fragments. The explosion echoed through the tunnels as the group charged blindly through the underground passage. Behind them, flames ripped into the cavern before collapsing the roof of the tunnel entrance, cutting off the route from which they had first come. Chunks of dirt, rock and debris came showering down on them yet again as the roof threatened to cave in right over their heads.

SEVENTEEN

Everyone was on the ground, arms curled over their heads, waiting to be buried alive. It didn't happen.

"Is everyone alright?" Halford asked, his voice echoing through the darkness.

"Yeah," groaned Alistair. "I'm OK."

"Me too," said Allison as Oscar let out a nervous *growlf*.

"How about the rest of you?" Halford asked. Five of the six Giants grunted a response.

"Feldon?" Halford said loudly. "Are you alright?" There was no answer. "Feldon, are you hurt?"

Alistair pressed the light on his Timex and a soft green glow illuminated his face. He carefully crawled around the narrow tunnel, dimly illuminating everyone. Finally, he found Feldon and Allison let out a shrill scream.

He was lying deathly still, half buried by the fallen rocks and dirt. His face was turned away from the rest of the group and Halford quickly scuttled to his fallen comrade, bloodying his knuckles as he began to desperately heft rocks from the pile of rubble and toss them aside. Feldon slowly turned his head to look at Halford. Feldon's savage, scarred face was covered in dirt and grime and Halford finally stopped trying to dig him out, knowing it was a futile quest.

"Go," Feldon whispered, followed by a heavy, wet cough. He spat something thick and dark onto the ground and Allison turned away with a slight whimper. "Go," he repeated.

Halford cradled Feldon's head in his hands, bending low to his ear.

"Hold on," Halford sobbed as he fumbled with the elixir skin. "Hold on, Feldon."

Feldon grunted weakly in Giantese and then in English said, "It's too late for that. Save them." A wet, gurgling sound spilled from his throat. "Get . . . Get them home." His eyes slowly slipped closed and his head was suddenly very heavy in Halford's hands.

Feldon was gone.

Halford turned toward the rest of the group, his face eerily green and shadowed from the soft light coming from Alistair's watch. The deep lines in his face now seemed like bottomless chasms, and his eyes shimmered with tears as he said a silent goodbye to his friend.

"He *will* pay for this," Halford hissed as Allison slipped the key around her neck. "We must go." With that, he pressed past Alistair and marched down the pitch black tunnel.

"Come on," he called from the darkness, his voice echoing loudly. "This is the main passage. It will take you where you want to go."

They followed blindly down the cavernous passageway, unseeing, listening for Halford's footsteps. Alistair and Allison each held a hand against the hard dirt walls to guide them, occasionally passing another opening or a smaller passageway. No one said a word for quite some time until Halford informed them it was time to rest. Alistair was truly grateful that he had done so, because he was extremely tired and very, very hungry. After a brief stop, they continued on for another few hours with nothing spoken between any of them. Finally, a soft glow appeared ahead of them and they had suddenly realised that they had walked through the tunnels all night.

As the opening became more pronounced they could see that large roots jutted downward like stalactites. Some were as thick as tree trunks while others were as thin as a string of thread. All of them seemed to be moving, though ever so slowly, the way a cat's tail might casually sway back and forth when it is sleeping peacefully. However, when Halford reached up and grabbed one of the mid-sized roots, they began to quiver wildly. With little effort, he gave the root a twist and snapped it off, tossing it to Alistair. He grabbed a smaller one and broke it off as well, handing it to Allison.

"Eat," Halford had grunted after he handed them the roots. While the little Giant had previously been quite pleasant and amicable, there was now a dark shroud that seemed to envelope him, and in the gloomy darkness of the semi-illuminated tunnel opening, he looked disturbingly dangerous.

"What is it?" Allison asked, inspecting her piece of root suspiciously. It was a greyish brown with several thin strands protruding from it. A sticky syrup seemed to ooze from the broken end, dribbling down her hand.

"Tangleroot," he growled. "Eat it, you must be hungry." As soon as he said this, a sound emerged from Alistair's stomach that resembled a piano being rolled across a hardwood floor.

"Sorry," he blushed.

"We're below the Eating Garden," he said and the twins both paused, each having just cautiously brought the Tangleroot to their mouths. Halford noticed the fear that sparked in their eyes.

"Don't worry," he reassured them. "The fruit has the sleeping effects, not the root itself. Although you might be grateful time has begun to move so slowly. If not, these roots would have ensnared us the second we were close enough."

Allison looked down at the sludgy floor of the tunnel and her stomach threatened to erupt at the thought of what they might be standing in.

Halford again grunted in Giantese and one of his men slipped through the opening.

"I thought only Boffles were effected by time," Alistair said.

"Not just Boffles," Halford replied. "Anything that is alive and native to Dibble is affected, including these plants."

A few minutes later the Giant reappeared and grunted to Halford. Halford then grunted something in return and then all of the Giants began to grunt indecipherably to each other.

As the Giants held their private conference, Allison reluctantly took a small bite from the root. Alistair took one tiny nibble, then gluttonously bit off a large chunk and chewed noisily. Tangleroot, it turned out, was deliciously sweet, even more so than its bulbous fruit. Halford nodded his head and turned back to the twins.

"The Eating Garden is safe for now," he said. "Your clock shouldn't be too far that way." He pointed toward a small opening in the south wall. "It's inedible and should be in one piece. It shouldn't be too hard for you to get it now."

"Wait," said Alistair though a mouthful of Tangleroot. "You're not coming with us? How will we get back to Loxbury?"

"The same way you got here," said Halford matter-of-factly.

"But the Obsidian Woods . . ." Allison began, clutching the key to her chest as though using it as a protective shield, but Halford abruptly cut her off.

"You won't be going through the Obsidian Woods," he said impatiently. "Our tunnel has collapsed and cut off our return route. All you have to do is follow the coastline until you reach the Shallows. It will take you to the bridge and from there you can find your way back to Loxbury. Now if you're finished asking foolish questions, I'll tell you how to get your clock, get back to Loxbury and go home."

Allison stared at Halford, her piece of Tangleroot forgotten, as her eyes began to well with tears. "Why are you being so mean to us?" she asked weakly.

"Yeah," said Alistair. "Why are you suddenly such a jerk?"

Halford reeled toward the boy, his face compressed with anger and impatience.

"We have no time for the petty problems of children," he growled. It was obvious he was working very hard to maintain his temper. "We got you to your key and we got you to your clock and in doing so, a very good friend of mine has died. Our job is done. We have new business."

"Geeze, Halford," said Alistair loudly, "we didn't want anyone to get hurt. It's not our fault your friend -"

"I know," he snapped, his already ruddy face becoming flush. He then paused for a moment to regain his composure before continuing. "I know it's not your fault," he said with forced calmness. "But I have every intention of making the man who is responsible pay for what he has done."

"Burcheeze?" asked Allison quietly. Halford turned to her, his temper simmering.

"Yes," he growled.

"But once we get the Boffles back in time -" she began, her voice trailing off slowly.

"What are you gonna do to him?" Alistair asked, but Halford didn't answer.

"This opening will lead you into the Eating Garden," he said instead. "You'll find your clock."

"Are you sure it's safe?" Allison asked. Halford nodded.

"Take these," he said, snapping off a few more Tangleroots and placing them in his pouch. He then handed the pouch to Alistair, who let out a grunt at the weight of it, still loaded with several rocks. With great effort, he slung it over his shoulder. Halford then handed him his slingshot.

"All you have to do -" Halford began, but Alistair raised a hand, a shrewd look on his dirty face.

"I'm familiar with a slingshot," he said smugly.

"Well then," Halford said, tucking the weapon into the pouch, "you should be fine."

"Why do we need a weapon if you said it was safe?" asked Allison.

"I'm sure it is," Halford said reassuringly. "But it never hurts to be prepared. It's better to have it and not need it than the other way around."

Alistair nodded in agreement, as if this were the most obvious statement he had ever heard. Allison, on the other hand, wondered if their luck was on the brink of change, and not for the better.

They climbed through the passage, pushing through the tangled grasses that obscured the opening. It took a moment to adjust to the sudden brightness, despite the fact that dusk was already upon them.

"Mom's probably got the cops looking for us by now," Alistair said. By his watch, it was almost half past six on Monday morning. He wondered what punishment they might get for disappearing without letting anyone know where they had gone. Whatever it was, he was willing to bet it was going to be a walk in the park compared to the way this punishment had turned out.

A feeling of cold steel ran down the twin's spines as they looked around the Eating Garden. The Deadlylions loomed malevolently as some of their spikes were in mid-flight at unseen prey; two of the yellow spears hung suspended in the air, as though hanging from invisible wire. Alistair ran a hand over and under one of them, wondering if maybe it was some sort of simple trick, but nothing seemed to be holding the spears in place. Looking closely, he could see that they were, in fact, moving, though at an incredibly slow speed. The rest of the flowers loomed ominously as well, several of them appearing to be frozen mid-strike. Several of the sparkling rose-like flowers with rows of razor-sharp teeth were poised just above their heads, petals spread wide, lunging downward. The twins laughed heartily as Oscar lifted his leg and relieved himself on one of its spiky leaves. Only inches in front of the rose hung a Stinkrat in mid leap, only seconds away from becoming an unfortunate victim of the Eating Garden.

"This is pretty freaky," said Alistair, his back to one of the Deadlylion spikes, which was aimed directly at his backside.

"Remarkable," Halford replied, running a hand down the smooth stem of one of the tulips. It was cool to the touch and very smooth. "No one who has touched this stem has lived to tell about it. Incredible." After lingering with his palm pressed to the stem, he turned to Alistair.

"One more thing," Halford said, tearing a strip of fur from his tunic. "You may find this to be useful." Halford then plucked the Deadlylion spike from mid-air and wrapped it in the strip of fur. "Remember what I said about the healing agent?" Alistair understood and tucked the spike into the pouch, burying it under the heavy stones so he didn't accidentally jab himself.

Halford grunted something in Giantese to the others and they swiftly trudged away, quickly becoming lost among the stems, petals and leaves. Their footsteps became more and more distant until there was no sign of them at all. Allison and Alistair were alone on their journey once again.

With nothing left to do but continue on, Alistair began to walk in the direction Halford had told them. After only a few steps, however, he realized that Allison was not following him.

"Waddya doin'?" he asked, turning back to face her. She stood absolutely still, the key resting across her chest, obviously quite heavy in her thin arms. Looking at her, Alistair couldn't help but feel a touch of pity. Her clothes were filthy and torn and her hair was no longer neatly braided. Instead, it frizzed out in every direction, one blue rubber band dangling down in a wiry tangle. Her glasses lay crooked on her face, resting on the tip of her nose (she had given up pointlessly adjusting them) and her knees were scraped and her left elbow had at some point been bloodied, though now it was a dry and crusty scab.

"What's the matter?"

"You saved me," she said quietly. Alistair rolled his eyes, blushing slightly below the grime that covered his chubby cheeks.

"Oh, come on," he said, pretending to be annoyed by her apparent silliness. "I didn't save you, I just . . ." He didn't know what to say.

"Why did you do that?" she asked, slowly approaching him. Oscar trotted along behind her, tail wagging slowly.

"I dunno," he shrugged. "You're my sister, I guess. I didn't want you to get hurt. That's all. It's no big deal."

"Yes it is," she said. "I was being pretty stupid and wasn't being very nice to you (even though you deserved it), but you still saved me. You could have been killed."

"Yeah, well," he said awkwardly. "Forget it. Now we're even. It cancels all the stupid stuff I did to ya. OK?"

Allison's face lit up as a smile drifted across her face. "OK," she said. "Let's go."

***

The Tangleroot was far less ominous than it had been previously. There was little resistance as they manoeuvred through its spindling vines. One thin vine tried to slip around Alistair's ankle but he easily pulled himself free.

The twins followed the tangles until they happened upon a large heap of them, tightly woven together, as though creating a sort of protective covering. Between the interwoven tendrils were many shiny glints of metal. Slowly they began to pry the long vines apart, revealing a horde of valuable (and not-so-valuable) objects; among them were watches, rings, a necklace and something that looked like a little steel box that Allison said might have been a pace-maker. All of these objects were metallic and therefore indigestible and the meaning of them even being there was unmistakable. These objects were the only remaining evidence of the people who had ever had the misfortune of coming too close to the Eating Garden.

The vines themselves were heavy and awkward and it was exhausting work to move them aside. They were tightly entwined and more than a few times both Allison and Alistair wondered if they were ever going to find the clock at all.

After struggling with the ivy for well over a half hour, Alistair and his sister slumped in exhaustion, sweat pouring down their faces leaving semi-clean streaks through the grit and grunge.

"We're never going to find it," Allison huffed. "It's impossible."

"We have to keep trying," said Alistair as he lowered himself onto his back to rest. As the sun arched higher into the pristine, cloudless sky, the sky again became a melting pot of deep crimsons, golden yellows and brilliant oranges. Alistair stared skyward, quickly slipping into a dreamy slumber, but was awakened sharply by a sudden burst of noise from Oscar.

He was barking wildly, the hair on his shoulders raising menacingly, his teeth bared as a low growl rumbled from somewhere deep inside. The twins looked at each other fearfully, wondering what else could possibly happen to them, when they heard something approaching briskly, breathing heavily.

Alistair pulled the slingshot from the pouch and slipped a stone into the pocket, pulling the leathery strap as tightly as he could manage. When the thing was finally in view, a dark silhouette against the brilliant sky, he let the stone fly, striking his target squarely on the head.

"OW!" it grunted, stumbling backward. Alistair reloaded the slingshot and readied himself to fire another rock.

"Lower your weapon," a low voice rumbled as a few more intruders climbed into view. "It's us."

Halford approached them cautiously, hands stretched before him, prepared to ward off any rocks that may come hurtling his way. The remaining four Giants came behind him then began to pull away the entangled vines with minimal effort.

"I thought you were leaving," Alistair said with an air of confusion.

"We decided you might need some help," Halford said, taking the pouch and slinging it over his own shoulder. "Apparently not with a slingshot, however."

"I told ya," Alistair said proudly.

The Giants began to grunt loudly, shouting to Halford. "Aguk! Aguk! Tug ni aguk!"

"Ug nik tug agog, tuk gakak!" Halford grunted in return, but to the twins it sounded like little more than strange, guttural rumblings.

"They've found it," he said with a smile. "Come on."

Three of the Giants held the heavy tangles of vines out of the way as the fourth heaved the clock face from its crevice. It was larger than they had expected it to be, easily a metre in diameter, its plain white face surrounded by a gold coloured frame. It had once been protected by heavy glass, but all that remained were a few jagged shards that jutted dangerously from the frame. The hour and minute hands were also gold coloured, stopped at 3:17. The second hand wasn't moving. On the back of the clock was a hole the same size and shape as the barrel of the key.

They had done it. They had found the Grandfather Clock. Excitedly, Alistair grabbed the key from Allison and jammed it into the hole, twisting it around and around.

"Yeah!" he whooped as he turned the key with all his might.

"Alistair, NO!" shouted Allison. Halford grabbed the boy's wrist harder than he meant to, leaving a deep bruise that would take several weeks to heal.

"OW!" moaned Alistair, finally letting go of the key handle. The clock began to tick rhythmically. "What was that for?"

Before anyone could answer, the vines below them began to rumble and writhe beneath their feet. There was a loud series of creaks and groans as the Eating Garden slowly returned to life. The distinct sound of the Stinkrat's fearful squeal slowly began to drift through the air, followed by a sickening crunch, cutting the sounds off almost as soon as it had begun.

Alistair looked at his feet for a moment, not sure what was happening, and by the time he realised what he had done, it was far, far too late.

"Oh yeah," he said as Tangleroot vines quickly wrapped around his ankles. They were all immediately trapped in the vines, struggling desperately to pull free before it had reached its full strength once again, but it only made things worse. One of the Giants grabbed hold of the clock as they were dragged into the constricting depths of the Tangleroot's crevice, leaving the Eating Garden eerily silent as the flowers and Tangleroot waited for their next unsuspecting victim.

EIGHTEEN

Alistair, Allison, Oscar and Halford lay together in a disoriented heap, arms and legs twined together rather uncomfortably. There was a smell of old, mildewed paper and cardboard, rotten vegetables and the bawdy scent of damp earth that lingered about them and a soft yellowish light glowed beyond their closed eyelids. Slowly, they began to stir as Oscar let out a mournful groan and licked Alistair's face several times in long, soggy laps. Alistair's head thrummed madly, having thudded against something blunt and solid and Allison's left arm was wrenched back painfully, pinned under Halford's unconscious body.

"Are we . . . ," Allison moaned, trying to free her arm. "Are we . . . dead?"

"I don't think so," replied Alistair. "I think Heaven would smell better."

Allison let out a painful grunt as she finally pulled her arm free.

"What makes you think you'd wind up in Heaven?" she asked wryly.

"Well, you're here too, aren't you?"

She had no reply for that.

"Well, we seem to be in some sort of dungeon or something. Do you think we've been kidnapped?"

They were in a dank, dingy room, littered with what appeared to be cast-off clothing and belongings from former prisoners. Old musty clothes lay in heaps and mouldy cardboard boxes were stacked one atop the other while others had fallen, spilling their contents on the hard-packed dirt floor. One single light bulb, glowing faintly, cast a yellow hue around them, creating the illusion that everything was sheathed in a muddy film.

"Wait a minute," Allison said in a bewildered tone. She was staring into the blank, one-eyed face of a spooky little moth-eaten doll's head. "Alistair, do you know where we are?"

"Yeah," he said slowly, pulling himself to his feet. "But how?"

Halford finally began to stir, slowly crawling onto all fours, then standing upright, though he wobbled dangerously, grabbing the arm of a mouldy old sofa to steady himself. He shook his head a few times, as if shaking cobwebs from his brow.

"Where are we?" he moaned, rubbing his eyes with two dirty fists.

"Home," said Alistair.

Halford shot him a shocked look, his eyes suddenly very wide. "Home?! What do you mean?"

"He means we're home," replied Allison. "*Our* home. Well, Auntie Bernice's home, anyway. We've come back through the clock."

"But... But... This is impossible," he marvelled, looking around quickly. "Auntie Bernice? Home? Where are my men?"

"They must not have come through," said Alistair softly. "They must not have escaped the Tangleroot."

"No," Halford whispered forlornly. "What have I done? I lead those men to their deaths. What have I done?"

He crumpled to a heap on the floor, dropping his head into his hands. He shook violently as silent sobs wracked his entire body. Allison slowly knelt beside him, placing her arm around his shoulder. He pressed his face deep into her shoulder and wept.

"Halford, I'm really sorry," Alistair said after a few minutes. "But maybe they aren't dead. We don't know what happened to them, do we?"

"You're right," he said, looking up at Alistair. His eyes were red and swollen, shimmering with tears. "Yes, you're right, of course. They were brave, resourceful warriors. It's quite possible that they escaped. We must get back to Dibble at once."

"That might not be all that easy," Allison said carefully.

"What's the big deal?" asked Alistair. "We can just hop through the clock and go back to Dibble."

"No, we can't," sneered Allison. "The clock might be at the bottom of the Tangleroot by now. We could be killed the second we popped out the other side."

"Oh yeah," he said slowly. "Good point."

"There must be another way," said Halford. "We can't just give up. We just have to think."

"Well, there's always the other clock," a voice said from the darkness. The three wheeled around, startled, as Oscar let out a sharp and frightened yelp. Instinctively, Halford pulled his slingshot and loaded its pouch, poised to strike as a large figure loomed from the darkened corner of the cellar.

"Hello, Halford."

Halford lowered his weapon and squinted into the darkness as Alistair and Allison stood in silent awe. Auntie Bernice stood before them, clad in her multi-coloured muumuu, her jet-black hair tidily stacked high atop her head. She also wore a smile that was warm and inviting as she held her hands forward in a welcoming gesture.

"By the Maker," whispered Halford as recognition washed over him. "Can it be? Bernice? Is it really you? You look so . . . so . . . *different.*"

"Wait a minute," said Alistair. He was terribly confused and the scene before him made absolutely no sense what-so-ever.

"How do you two -" Allison began, but Auntie Bernice cut her short.

"It's been a long time," she said as Halford slowly stepped toward her, his full height measuring just above her ample waist. They embraced and Halford's thick, bulky form was almost lost in Auntie Bernice's massive arms and bosom.

"What the heck is going on?" Alistair finally said. Auntie Bernice and Halford relinquished their grip on each other and looked at the twins with amused expressions on their faces.

"Let's go upstairs," their Aunt said jovially. Any hint of the overzealous, haltingly saccharine Auntie Bernice had all but disappeared and suddenly the thick make-up and garish muumuu no longer seemed to suit her at all. To Allison and Alistair, it seemed as though the Auntie Bernice they had known all their lives no longer existed. Instead, there now stood a woman in a sort of costume, as if poorly disguised in an effort to hide her true identity.

***

They sat in the living room, the television turned off, as the rain still pelted the dusty window panes. Auntie Bernice sat in her chair as Halford rested comfortably on the chesterfield. Allison and Alistair sat cross-legged on the floor with Oscar snoozing between them. The warm aroma of freshly brewed tea lingered in the air and each of them held a steaming mug from which they sipped casually as they talked.

"Halford and I have known each other a very long time," explained Auntie Bernice. She smiled at the little Giant, who blushed deeply.

"We haven't seen each other in years," Halford continued. Not since . . . " He and Bernice exchanged a cautious, concerned look, as if considering whether or not to continue with this particular line of exposition.

"We'd better tell them," Auntie Bernice finally said. Halford nodded in agreement, took a sip of warm tea, and began to explain how it came to be that he, a Giant from the Land of Dibble and she, a simple woman from Schmendricktonville, Saskatchewan, had known each other for a great many years.

"As a little girl, my Grandmother would tell stories about a magical land where people lived in peace and harmony. These people, whom she called Tick-Tock People, were always happy. There were no wars, no starving families, and no depressions in their land. The Land of Dibble. Oh, it was such a wonderful place and I would always beg her to tell me more and more and she never ran out of stories, although my brother always scoffed and said her stories were pure hogwash."

"Wait a second," Alistair interrupted. "Your brother? What brother?"

"I'll explain," she said, "now don't interrupt. It's rude."

"Sorry."

"She would tell me how her sitting room clock, which never kept proper time by the way, was a magical doorway to this great and wonderful land and I would stare at it for hours, just waiting to see even a glimpse of one of these wonderful Tick-Tock

People of which she so often spoke. Of course, I never saw one and as I grew older, I began to realise that Gran was just telling stories, as my brother had always said. I eventually concluded that she was just a lovely old lady telling wonderful stories to entertain her naïve little granddaughter. When she passed away, I was very sad, and the only thing I asked for was that wonderful, magical clock. My brother laughed at me for ever thinking it was magical but it held so many delightful memories, I simply had to have it. It stood right in that corner (she pointed to an empty corner of the room, just to the left of the fireplace) for many, many years, before I moved it to the cellar."

"Why did you move it to the cellar?" Allison asked.

"I'll get to that," she said kindly, "but as I said to your brother, it's not polite to interrupt."

"Sorry."

"Well, it wasn't long before the world was in a terrible state," said Auntie Bernice. "War, poverty, depression . . . It wasn't bad here in Schmendricktonville, but it was bound to come sooner or later and people were terribly frightened. I was a nurse in the Army, you know. I saw things overseas that would make your blood turn cold. Inhuman things inflicted on men by other men. Burty died there. I still have nightmares about it, all these years later. After we returned home, a group of us decided that perhaps we could go somewhere, live in peace and harmony, away from the threats and fears of the world. I remembered the Land of Dibble, wishing such a place existed, and suddenly something Gran had said to me during her stories came to mind during her stories. Twice a day, she said, the gate was open and you had only one minute to step through. At 3:17, to be precise. Well, the clock hadn't run properly for as long as I could remember and I had stopped winding it years before. Then, one fateful day, as I looked at the clock, I wondered . . . So I got up, opened the crystal, set the time to 3:17 and waited for something to happen. At first, nothing did and I was beginning to feel somewhat silly for even thinking that it would. But then I remembered that the clock hadn't been wound. Once I wound it and it started to keep time once again, I immediately began to feel dizzy, as if I had stood in the middle of the room and spun around and around and around. The next thing I knew, I was standing in the courtyard of the most delightful little village. I was greeted and welcomed with open arms and I knew then that Gran hadn't been making up stories at all. I was in the Land of Dibble.

"I explained myself to a little man who called himself Sender and he remembered old Gran, who had visited Dibble many times in her youth. He encouraged me to bring my friends and live with them in their village, away from the war and poverty of our own world. Oh, that place was so delightful that I returned home and gathered up my little group. It took some convincing, but eventually I managed to get them to come with me. We met Halford and the Giants, of course, and taught them English. They taught us a little Giantese as well, though I've forgotten most of it now." She grunted something indecipherable to Halford, who grunted something equally indecipherable in return. They laughed together at their private little joke before she continued.

"At first it was wonderful. Everyday was a celebration with feasts and marching bands and life seemed absolutely perfect; it was a virtual utopia, unspoiled by the touch and influence of human hands. They had told us of a vile creature called Burcheeze, but I never saw a wink of him. I just assumed he was a myth, really, and every day was a joyful celebration. But soon, some of the others began to have ideas. Terrible ideas. You see, they began to think that as humans, we should become the Boffles' leaders. We were much larger than Tick-Tock People and I suppose they thought of we humans as more intelligent, even superior, and they were convinced that we could overtake them; '*Civilize them*', they said. Well, most of us wanted none of that. It was a terrible mess and eventually they separated from us because we wouldn't follow them. They seemed to just disappear, but returned several months later with guns and explosives, ready to take up arms at any time. It became evident that they were a genuine threat to the Tick-Tock People, so we banded against them. There was a terrible battle and many people were hurt, even died, including several Boffles. The dissenters were defeated and went off to live in exile. As for the few of us who remained, well, we felt so terrible for bringing such horror to their little community that we chose to leave before we caused them even more trouble. We had created a society that mirrored our own, the one from which we had so desperately tried to escape."

She paused here, her eyes vacant, as though she were reliving a vivid memory deep in her own mind. Finally, she said, "When I came home, I told everyone that I was upset at the death of my brother and had gone on a mission for the Peace Corpse. I also said that I never wanted to speak of it again. Then I had the clock put in the cellar, where it has remained for many years. To be honest, I had almost forgotten about it, but when I heard the crash from downstairs, I somehow knew that it was the clock. I rushed down there immediately and was horrified to discover that you were nowhere to be seen, though I knew exactly where you had gone. Oscar showed up at my doorstep shortly after that and it occurred to me that you might just need his help, so I sent him through as well. I knew he would find you. He's a very resourceful fellow, Oscar is. All I could do, then, was wait and hope that Sender would get you back."

"You mean you've been waiting in the basement for three days?" Alistair asked.

"Oh no," she chuckled humourlessly. "Our time and Dibble time are not one and the same. As far as this world is concerned, you've only been gone for about three *hours*."

"But my watch -" Alistair started, but Auntie Bernice chuckled again with the wave of a meaty, bejewelled hand.

"You can't rely on your own watch in Dibble," she said. "I don't expect you to understand. It can be very confusing. Even I get confused from time to time."

"You said you had a brother," said Allison, glancing at the wall of photos. "Is that him in the pictures?"

"Yes," she said sadly. "That's him, poor thing. He was very handsome, wasn't he? I was quite a looker once myself, I don't mind saying."

"Yeah," said Allison as she slowly approached the wall, carefully looking at the photographs. "Mom told us not to talk about him. She says it will upset you."

"Well, it's very sad," said Auntie Bernice. "I do miss him, though he wasn't a very nice man in the end. I was very sorry when he died in the war. He always taunted me for being so idealistic. I truly thought that he would see things differently, given enough time."

"I don't think you would have gotten your wish," said Allison as she was inspecting one of the pictures so closely that her nose was almost pressed to the glass. Alistair stepped along side her as she wiped away a layer of dust with her thumb, revealing the image of Auntie Bernice's brother. To Alistair Allison said, "Doesn't he look familiar to you?"

The man in the black and white photos stood easily six and a half feet tall. Auntie Bernice, even now, was over six foot and the man in the photos was at least a head taller. His features were somewhat blurry in most of the pictures but the resemblance was unmistakable. He had a full head of hair and wore a neatly trimmed moustache. He was wearing an Army uniform and stood handsomely beside Auntie Bernice, who was wearing a plain white dress and nurse's cap. She and Burty were standing arm in arm, grinning from ear to ear.

Alistair looked carefully at the image, a stunned look on his face. "Wait a sec," he said, "isn't that . . ."

"I think it is," said Allison.

"Auntie Bernice," Alistair said, slowly looking at his Aunt, "what was your brother's name again?"

"Burt," she said with a quiver of curiosity. "Everyone called him Burty. Why?"

"Well, I don't know how to tell you this," said Alistair, "but I don't think Burty is dead."

"What?" she exclaimed, bolting from her chair and spilling her tea on the floor. "How can you know that?"

"They call him Burcheeze," said Alistair. "And he's going to slaughter the Boffles."

"That's impossible," Auntie Bernice whispered, almost to herself. She slumped into her chair, which groaned mournfully as her hefty form wedged deep into the soft cushion. "Halford, did you know?"

"I had no idea," he said, staring at the photo in wide-eyed astonishment. "This can't be possible. The tale of the Vermilion King . . . the Marsh Hag . . . It's just not possible. Halford looked carefully at the photograph. There was no doubt about it. The man who stood beside Bernice all those years ago was the same man who was about to destroy the Boffles. "How did he even get to Dibble?" he queried.

"I just can't believe this," Auntie Bernice finally said as she dropped down in her chair once again.

They explained about the Dibble clock having been stolen, Burcheeze's plan to tromp the Boffles into oblivion and all the adventures the twins had encountered since they were first drawn into the old clock. Auntie Bernice seemed to only half listen. When they told her of their encounter with Burcheeze in Tenebrous Marsh, however, she suddenly snapped to attention.

"So him then? You're sure?" she asked when they had finished recounting their adventures. There was a tentative hopefulness in her voice that the twins found endearing and somehow also dangerous.

"Yes," said Halford. "He's alive. But he's a killer, Bernice. He's not the same man you once knew. He killed my best friend and who knows how many others. Time has started again in Dibble, so the Boffles stand at least a chance to fight back. But unless we return to help them, they won't defeat him. They have no weapons - nothing to defend themselves with."

"Plus Burcheeze still has guns," said Alistair. "And he's obviously not above blowing people to smithereens." Auntie Bernice gave him a sour, cheerless look. "Sorry," he said softly. "But it's true. The Boffles are in *big* trouble."

"Bernice," said Halford. "You mentioned another clock."

"Yes," she said, "there is another clock like mine. It's smaller and I don't know where its counter-clock is. To try and use it would be terribly dangerous. Who knows where you would end up?"

"We must try," said Halford. "The fate of the Boffles depends on it. Bernice, I am sorry to say this, but Burcheeze must be stopped. By any means possible."

She stared at her old friend for several moments, a look of deep seated sadness etched into her suddenly tired features. Over the past couple of hours, her usually colourful make-up had somehow become dull and smudged and for the first time, Auntie Bernice looked less like a strange circus character and more like a sad, lonely old lady trying desperately to keep a grip on something - anything - that could make her happy. Whatever she had found to do so in the past, it no longer seemed to be working.

"I know," she finally said. Her voice was shaky and sounded congested, as though something thick was lodged deep in her throat. "I know."

"The clock," whispered Allison. "Auntie Bernice . . . Where is it?"

"Don't you know?" she said, glancing at her dishevelled niece.

"I think I do," said Alistair. Auntie Bernice smiled at him and he thought he saw just a glimmer of hope in her eyes.

NINETEEN

Under different circumstances, the sight may have been funny. Allison and Alistair, filthy from the tips of their noses to the tips of their toes, their clothes ripped, torn, soiled and ragged, walked briskly down the street, huddled together beneath a colourful umbrella festooned with garish pink, orange and green polka dots. Oscar, with half his fur shaved off, strode between them, trying rather unsuccessfully to remain dry. Ahead of them, Auntie Bernice lumbered along in large, heavy rubber boots and a yellow rain slicker the size of a three-man pup tent, the hem of her multi-coloured muumuu peering out from below the slicker itself. She held another umbrella, which was identical to the one the twins were holding, and hunkered down so that Halford, who stood three feet shorter than she, wouldn't be drenched in the silvery splatters of heavy, fat raindrops. Of the motley group, however, it was Halford who seemed the oddest. He wore an old pair of Burty's cut-off blue jeans and Alistair gave him his green sweatshirt with a picture of a cartoon moose and the caption *'Where in the World is Schmendricktonville, Saskatchewan?'*. The sleeves of the sweater were rolled up as well, and it looked like he wore two thick bands around his wrists. A yellow rain hat sat crookedly on his head, pulled down well below his large ears and over the sweatshirt was slung his leather pouch. Auntie Bernice had offered him a pair of shoes, but his feet actually proved to be too large for them so he remained barefoot as he went splooshing through large, wet puddles down the street.

They stopped at a bus stop, eliciting a great many stares from the few people forced to crowd into the tiny bus shelter. When the bus finally came, Auntie Bernice motioned for them to climb aboard, but the driver refused them.

"Sorry," he said, staring at them with a look that was both curious and indignant, "no dogs allowed." With no choice but to continue on foot, the doors hissed closed before them and the passengers stared at the outlandish little group as the bus rolled away.

By the time they reached their destination, they were soaked to the skin, despite the umbrellas. Oscar looked particularly unhappy, offering random whines and groans of dissatisfaction throughout their journey.

"The other clock is here?" Allison asked incredulously. "It's been here all the time?"

"Yes," said Auntie Bernice. "I made sure it was in good hands, somewhere that I knew it would never be put to use."

The five of them stood in the rain, peering into the McAllister's living room window. The pictures had been re-hung, the smashed glass swept up and Mr. McAllister's chair had been righted once again. The newspaper was folded neatly and lay on the coffee table, a steaming cup of coffee resting on top of it.

"Where's Mom and Dad?" Allison whispered in a hushed voice. As though waiting for their cue, Mr. And Mrs. McAllister entered the living room. Mr. McAllister wore a pair of track pants and a t-shirt and Mrs. McAllister wore a pair of jeans and a sweater, the sleeves rolled up to the elbows. The twins knew that these were their regular 'clean-up uniforms'. A dish towel was slung over Mrs. McAllister's shoulder, smeared in red blotches that were quite obviously spaghetti sauce. They were talking to each other, smiling and laughing, as Mr. McAllister made hand gestures that seemed to indicate that he was re-enacting the 'Great Spaghetti Incident', as it would later be called whenever the story was retold. He laughed heartily as he picked up his coffee cup, shaking his head and the pair left the living room.

"There," said Auntie Bernice. "On the mantle."

Mr. McAllister practised photography as a hobby and the mantle was literally cluttered with framed photos of everything from family and friends - including their wedding photo which showcased Auntie Bernice and her hideous wedding attire - to trees and trains, another of Mr. McAllister's fascinations. Also on the mantle sat Mrs. McAllister's surviving ceramic unicorns. Almost completely obscured by the multitude of pictures and nick-knacks sat the clock.

"But how do we get in without Mom and Dad seeing us?" asked Allison. Already, Alistair was devising a series of potential and in his opinion, deviously clever, diversions. Before he had an opportunity to offer any of them, Auntie Bernice spoke up, quashing a plan that involved the slingshot, Mr. McAllister's car and a small incendiary device that he was pretty sure he could whip together using a few simple ingredients from the garage.

"Simple," she said. "We wait."

After twenty minutes of standing in the rain, they heard the garage door rumble upward and the McAllister's station wagon backed out of the garage and drove off, the garage door rumbling closed once again.

"How did you know they were going out?" Alistair asked.

"Dinner was ruined, wasn't it?" she said. "You kids were out of the house; they had to clean up a terrible mess, from what I understand. Logically, then, they would be going out for dinner."

"But how do you know they weren't going to just order Chinese food or something?"

"Well," she simply said with a shrug, "lucky for us they didn't, isn't it?"

They were careful to wipe their feet as they entered the house. The smell of spaghetti sauce still lingered in the air but it was now combined with lemon scented cleaner and air freshener. Alistair quickly grabbed the clock from the mantle, careful not to knock over any pictures.

"Got it," he said. "Let's go." With that, he raised the clock directly over his head and grinned mischievously at the group. "Me first."

"Alistair, wait -" started Auntie Bernice, but it was too late. Alistair let go of the clock, which dropped heavily onto his head, knocking him cold.

When he came around a few minutes later, his head throbbing painfully where the solid wood clock had connected with his skull, everyone was huddled around him. Oscar offered a look that seemed somewhat pathetic, but gave him a bevy of slobbery kisses just the same.

"Ohhhh, my achin' head," the boy moaned as he pushed Oscar away and sat up slowly. "What happened?"

"You knocked yourself out with the clock, you big nerd," sneered Allison. Alistair shook his head vigorously, and then looked up at Auntie Bernice. She wore a bemused grin on her face and held out her hand to help him to his feet.

"Why didn't it work?" he asked groggily.

"You forgot the most important thing," she said. Auntie Bernice picked up the clock and manually moved its hands, pausing just before it reached the 3:17 mark.

"Are you ready?"

"Aren't you coming?" asked Allison.

"No, no, I'm not coming," said Auntie Bernice. "I'm in no shape to join a fight against Burty or anyone else. You'll have to do it yourselves. With Halford's help, of course. Besides, I have to wind this clock so it will begin to keep time and then reset it once you've gone through. If your mother or father should happen to come near it while it was open, well, wouldn't they be surprised to suddenly find themselves in the Land of Dibble?"

Halford looked at Bernice for a long time, watching her as she spoke to her niece and nephew. She had changed a great deal since he had last seen her, but he could see that her heart was still as pure and kind as it had ever been. Her days of visiting the Land of Dibble were behind her, he surmised, and it was entirely possible that this was the last he would ever see of her. A great sadness overwhelmed him and tears began to shimmer in the corners of his eyes.

"You take good care of these two," Bernice said to Halford as they embraced and Halford was all but lost in her massive grip. "And please . . . Try not to hurt him."

"We'll try," said Halford, understanding that she meant her brother. "But we have to stop him one way or another."

"I know," she sniffed. "It's just . . . I've already lost him once."

"We'll do our best," said Halford. By now he was blubbering like a baby, still entombed in Auntie Bernice's huge arms and bosom. "You take good care of yourself. I'll see that these two get home in one piece."

Auntie Bernice finally relinquished her embrace and placed her hand on the clock as Halford joined Oscar and the twins.

"Remember," she sniffled, "I don't know where this comes out. If there is any danger - any at all - you must turn around and come straight back through. The gate will remain open for one minute. Are you ready?" They were. "Alright. Here you go." She wound the clock one revolution and it slowly began to tick. After a few seconds, the room seemed to spin wildly as Allison, Alistair, Oscar and Halford began their return journey to Dibble.

Prepared for it this time, the sensation was just as Auntie Bernice had described. It was as if they had twirled around and around and around in circles, the world spinning dizzyingly into a strange black and white nothingness. In just a few short seconds, only Auntie Bernice stood in the McAllister's living room.

TWENTY

When they finally opened their eyes, they didn't know what to think. It was cold and dark and they were all cramped together in a tiny room. There was an acrid, ashen smell that seemed to envelope them and something hard was jabbing Alistair between his shoulder blades. It appeared that they had emerged in some sort of small storage space full of crates and cartons. Slivers of glowing, orange light sliced though several wooden slats which covered two small windows, offering only the tiniest amount of illumination. From somewhere in the distance, people were laughing and singing. A hopeful air seemed to fill the tiny enclosure.

"Is that the Boffles?" asked Allison, listening to the off-key song that rang through the air. "They sound worse than ever." Indeed, the music that filtered toward them was terribly out of tune and the lyrics themselves were somewhat crude and discoloured.

"I don't think so," said Halford cautiously.

"Of course it's the Boffles," Alistair chided. "Who else would it be?"

"Um, you guys?" Allison whispered nervously, "you might want to look at this."

She stood before a large open crate that sat against the back of the small room. It was one of a half dozen that were stacked together amongst piles of neatly folded blankets, old shoes and boots and a gleaming pile of old, cast-off jewellery and nick-knacks, among which lay an old mantle clock that had the same ornate design on its face as that of the McAllister's living-room clock. Peering inside the open crate, Halford 's breath caught in his throat and then came out in a deep, breathtaking sigh.

"Holy cow!" blurted Alistair as he snapped up a small silver handled pistol. It was heavy in his hand and Allison quickly knocked it from his grip, sending it clattering to the wooden floor.

"Are you crazy?" she hissed. "You should never pick up a gun. How do you know it isn't loaded?"

"Don't be stupid," he hissed back. Their voices were raspy as they whispered and none of them had realised that the music had suddenly ceased. "The Boffles wouldn't keep a loaded gun lying around. They . . . Wait a minute," he said, turning to Halford. "I thought you said the Boffles didn't have any weapons."

"They don't," he replied cautiously. He had opened another crate and inside were more guns and ammunition. "I think we're -" He stopped speaking mid-sentence and quickly held up his hand, indicating immediate silence. He was watching Oscar, who was sniffing the air. The distant music had stopped and the abrupt silence was hauntingly eerie. The little hairs on the back of Oscar's neck were raised and for the first time since both Alistair and Allison had known him, he bared his teeth and began to emit a low, menacing growl. The music suddenly burst back to life, louder and cruder than before, and Halford let out a deep sigh of relief.

"I don't think that's the Boffles," he whispered. "I've never known them to sing such vulgarities and I doubt very much they would have a large store of human weapons. No, this is something else entirely."

Quietly sneaking back toward the window, Halford peeked through the slats, beyond the dusty glass. Outside it was dark, the only light coming from a few flickering torches which were posted a few feet away. Further, visible only due to the brilliant glow of a large bonfire, was a small group of strange looking people, little more than inky silhouettes against the roaring fire, and it was obvious that these were the foul musicians whose lyrics and tuneless instruments now assaulted their ears. Most were huddled around the fire while a few danced grotesquely, whooping, howling and clapping every time a dirty or suggestive word was sung.

"Just as I feared," whispered Halford.

"What?" asked Alistair, joining Halford at the window. "Who are they?"

"Pirates," he replied flatly. "Vile men and women who would kill and maim for the sheer joy of it."

"Pirates?!" Allison exclaimed. "That's crazy. There's no such thing as pirates. Not any more." She paused. "Right?"

"Oh, pirates are real, alright," said Halford. "And by the looks of things, we're sitting right in the middle of their camp."

Oscar shuffled alongside Alistair quietly, a low whimper trickling from somewhere deep inside him.

"Are we still in Dibble?" Alistair asked.

"Yes," Halford replied. "But I think we're on Perilrock Peak, a volcanic island that has been threatening to erupt for several weeks. Judging by the smell in the air, it's really beginning to heat up. We had better get out of here while they're still distracted."

"But didn't you just say this was an island?" asked Allison. "How do we get out off?"

"We use a boat, stupid," Alistair snarled.

"Oh, I see," she replied mockingly. "We're just going to go over and ask the pirates if they have a boat we could borrow to escape the exploding island. Sounds like a great plan."

"Actually, we're not going to ask," said Halford. "But they do have boats and they won't be far from here. I think we can sneak away undetected, but we have to act now. Let's go."

Together they crept toward the door. It was a simple latch and fortunately for them, it was unlocked. Carefully and quietly, after telling Alistair and Allison to stay close to him and low to the ground, Halford slowly opened the door. They hadn't realized how stuffy and dry the little room had been until they were greeted by a gust of cool sea air as they stepped into what appeared to be a small compound of tiny huts and shacks. A few windows glowed from within some of the huts but as far as they could tell, no one was lurking about besides themselves.

Oscar crept before them, leading the way as they inched toward a patch of scraggly trees, which would hopefully offer them some cover. As it stood, they were completely exposed with nowhere to hide should one of the pirates chance to look in their general direction. They were only a few feet from the edge of the darkened woods when Oscar suddenly stopped. He stood motionlessly, staring into the darkness, his body coiled low to the ground, as though ready to pounce.

Just as Alistair was about to give him an encouraging tap on the rump to move him along, something black and ugly burst from the darkness, with wild yellow eyes and massive, jagged teeth. In an instant, Oscar was airborne, colliding solidly with the beast in mid-leap. They crashed to the ground, thrashing wildly, sending arcs of sand into the air as Allison, Alistair and Halford watched in horror. Allison began to shriek like a wild animal when something grabbed her from behind.

For a moment she was sure she was about to be ripped to shreds, that her attacker was another of the ugly black beasts. When the sharp claws didn't tear into her flesh, she realised that she had been grabbed by powerful, calloused hands, one of which was clamped around her mouth as an arm wrapped around her upper body, pinning her arms to her sides. As Alistair lunged toward Oscar screaming "NOOOOOOO!" as he went, but he too was snatched into someone's grasp. He proved to be somewhat less easy to subdue as he struggled violently to help his faithful companion. He was finally overtaken, though it took two more sets of hands to finally manage to pin his arms and legs to the ground.

"Let me go!" he screamed as he helplessly fought against their tremendous grip, thrashing helplessly as he watched Oscar and the beast battle it out. "No, he'll be killed. *Oscar! OSCAR!*"

Halford dashed toward Alistair, his eyes wild, slingshot drawn and loaded, when he was hit from behind with something large and heavy. He crashed to the ground with a dull *thud*, where he lay unconscious, a trickle of blood dribbling from a gash in his scalp.

The noises that came from the two animals were deep and guttural; a primeval sound that would send shivers up the spine of the bravest of men. Oscar let out several blood-curdling yelps as the black beast repeatedly bit him about the face and neck, never quite managing to chomp down on his jugular. Oscar himself tore a large chunk of flesh from the creature's ear, sending it into a brief retreat. For a moment, as the black fiend backed up, Alistair thought it might just bolt off into the darkness, but instead, it seemed to redouble its efforts, lunging once again at Oscar. Oscar must have thought the same as Alistair, for he appeared to have been taken by surprise, twisting helplessly under the creature's violent attack. He kicked madly with his hind legs, his sharp claws digging deep into his attacker's fleshy underbelly. A spine-chilling yelp tore through the night air as the brute bit Oscar, its teeth sinking into the back of his neck. The defeated dog's body immediately went into powerful, spastic convulsions, and then finally fell to the soft sand, where he lay perfectly still. The beast looked up at the twins and Halford, licked its chops and then slowly lowered its gnarled snout to Oscar's neck. It reeled back and was poised to make the final kill when a loud *CRACK* sliced through the air. The creature violently reeled away from Oscar and went tumbling across the sandy ground. The black beast, which looked like some sort of cross between a pig and a wild dog, quickly regained its footing as a man with long, silvery hair rushed from the darkness. He was wielding a shotgun, its twin barrels smoking softly, and he loaded two more shells as the beast pounced. Another deafening *CRACK* ripped through the night air, but the shot was wild and thrashed through the scrubby brush as the creature began its assault. Upon impact, the stranger's shotgun was sent flying from his hands and landed uselessly in the loose sand several metres away.

As the pair wrestled wildly, the silver-haired man managed to keep the creature from ripping its teeth into his neck by jamming his thumbs deep into its eyes. It let out a wild cry that made everyone's blood turn cold. He then clamoured onto the beast's back, one arm wrapped tightly around its neck, and began punching rigorously about its face and snout. The beast bucked and jilted, trying to throw him off, but he somehow managed to hold on. The creature had suffered a shotgun blast and a wet, gaping hole in its side pumped what seemed to be buckets of blackened fluid with every racing heartbeat. The man, who now seemed to be attempting to strangle the creature, was covered in deep scarlet blotches. His clothes were thrashed and torn and they could see that he had a large gash sliced across his ribs along with multiple wounds on his arms, legs and face.

The monstrous beast reeled onto its hind legs and allowed itself to fall directly backwards, crushing the man with a wet *crunch* as it landed with its full weight on top of him. With a single swipe of its massive paw, the right side of the man's face was slashed open. The creature then regained its footing and began to circle the man slowly, who now lay on his back, wounded and stunned. He slowly tried to roll onto his hands and knees but only fell back to the ground on his stomach, his arms pinned beneath him. His were the groans of a dying man, a man whose life was about to come to a violent and painful end, defeated by a ruthless enemy. The monstrous fiend let out a muted growl and lunged a final time, intending to strike at the base of the man's skull. With a single deft movement, however, the man swiftly rolled onto his back with one long-bladed knife gripped in each bloody hand. As the beast lunged for his throat, he sunk the knives deep into either side of the creature's neck, the blades cutting through layers of muscle and tendon, sinking up to their hilts. The creature thrashed violently as a shrill cry of pain and anger erupted from its gnarled snout. Severely wounded and bleeding, the animal reeled and thundered into the dry brush, the sounds of its retreat gradually diminishing as it returned to whatever vile lair it came from.

With great effort the man weakly got to his feet. He was the very picture of morbid carnage. His clothes were ravaged and soaked with gore - both his and the creature's - and his silver hair was now streaked a mottled, macabre crimson. A hideous gash pulsed at his ribs and his right cheek was literally shredded and swollen. Although the swelling made it difficult to tell for sure, it looked as though he had actually lost his right eye in the bloody battle.

Oscar lay motionless in the sand as tiny crimson bubbles rippled weakly around his nostrils.

"You killed him! You killed him and you got what you deserved, you big ugly freak!" Alistair was screaming in the direction of the retreating creature, his voice cracking due to his hysterical wailing and

his cheeks were soaked as tears spilled like open faucets. He weakly fought against his captor's iron grip, finally collapsing in anguish and exhaustion. Allison remained stunned, horrified by what she had just seen as she hung almost lifelessly in the grip of her own vanquisher.

Another man emerged from the darkness. He was tall, thin, with long stringy brown hair and a scruffy beard. Behind him came more men of similar description as well as a few women. All wore dirty, well worn jeans or khakis; some were shirtless while others wore tatters that had once been t-shirts or sweatshirts. They were all armed either with guns or dangerous looking spears.

"Looks like we have visitors," wheezed the bloodied man as he pointlessly tried to wipe some of the gore from the left side of his face. He smiled wide and menacingly. "Welcome to The Peak." His knees then buckled and he crumpled to the ground.

Somewhere in the distance there came a deep and thunderous rumble. The sky overhead, however, was clear, the stars perfect silver pinpoints on a sea of imposing blackness. Beneath their feet, the ground shook violently and Halford began to stir. Two spear-wielding pirates struggled to keep their balance as they stood over him, their weapons aimed sharply at his stocky form. Two of the others tended to their fallen companion, gathering him in their arms and carrying him off toward a hut near the fire pit.

"What happened?" Halford grunted. The sharp point of a spear was then sharply pressed against the underside of his chin, an obvious warning that any attempt to overtake the armed guards would be a pointless gesture. He held his meaty hands in the air, indicating he had no interest in testing them.

"That thing," wailed Alistair, clutching Oscar and rocking slowly back and forth. He was gasping for breath, almost as if he were fighting to get the words out. "That pig thing . . . it was . . . it . . . it was gonna kill Oscar. I think maybe it did. But then . . . that guy . . . he jumped out of nowhere and scared it off. I think Oscar's dead!" He began to wail uncontrollably and Oscar let out another feeble whimper.

Halford reached for his pouch but the sharp edge of the spear pressed deeper into his neck.

"My weapon," he said, indicating the slingshot that jutted from the leather pouch. "Take it." Cautiously, a woman dressed in a tattered brown dress reached down and slipped the slingshot away from him, never taking her eyes from his. As an afterthought, she also grabbed the strap of the pouch, intending to remove it from his shoulder. He quickly grabbed her by the wrist, eliciting a sharp welp of pain from her.

"Let her go," one of the others said and there was the distinct click of a gun being cocked. Looking up, Halford saw that the brown-haired pirate had drawn a pistol and was aiming it directly at his head. "Let her go *now*."

Halford released his grip and she pulled the pouch from his shoulder and handed it to the gun-toting pirate, who quickly examined its content.

"Rocks and stones," he mocked. "How primitive." Another loud rumble rippled through the air and the ground shook again.

"Please," Halford said softly. "You can have my weapons. But I need something else from that pouch. I can heal this dog. And I can heal your friend."

The pirate eyed him suspiciously. "How?" he asked leeringly.

"In that bag you will find a spike of Deadlylion," he began, but the pirate cut him off.

"What do I look like, some kind of idiot?" he shouted. "I *know* what Deadlylion is."

"You don't understand," said Halford, somewhat impatiently. "I also have some Tangleroot. When combined they create a sort of salve with healing qualities. I can save this boy's dog and I can save your friend. He's badly hurt. He won't live. I can save him." The pirate stared at him for several moments. "I can save him," Halford repeated imploringly. The look of sincerity that showed on his face seemed almost out of place in contrast to his usually rocky, hardened demeanour.

The pirate considered this for a moment, first glancing at Oscar, whose eyes were now closed and was taking shallow, gurgling breaths, then toward the camp where his companion had been taken. "Him first," he finally said, lilting his head toward Oscar. "And it better work."

The spear-wielding pirate stepped back, leaving a thin red line where the blade had dug into Halford's neck. If not for his thick skin, the spear would undoubtedly have pierced his flesh and perhaps been fatal. The gunman kept his weapon aimed steadily at Halford without a hint of fear or nervousness. This was a man prepared to survive by any means necessary. He ordered the woman who held the pouch to remove the Tangleroot and Deadlylion spike. She did so apprehensively, knowing full well what would happen in the pointed spike were to puncture her skin. As she unwrapped the spike from the soft fur wrapping, she looked as though she were holding something repulsive.

"I'll need a dish," said Halford, "or a small bowl and I'll need one of my rocks from the pouch."

"No rocks," said the gunman.

"I have to mix this somehow, mash the ingredients together. If they are mixed improperly, even by the slightest margin, the outcome could be severe."

As one of the pirates returned with a small porcelain bowl the pirate finally agreed. "But don't forget," he said, handing over a medium sized stone, "one wrong move and I pull this trigger."

"And you call *me* primitive," Halford grumbled almost inaudibly.

He broke off a piece of Tangleroot about the size of his thumb and crushed it into a slick muddy pulp in the bottom of the bowl. He then carefully held the spike over the bowl, tapered end toward himself, and gently squeezed it about its centre. He slowly worked his thick, powerful hands down the spike as amber nectar dripped from the raw end into the dish. Once satisfied that he had removed enough of the Deadlylion nectar, he again took the rock and proceeded to mix it thoroughly with the remains of the Tangleroot. After a few minutes of constant mashing, the entire concoction began to sizzle and bubble, turning into a thick brownish-yellow paste. A strange and grossly pungent green haze began to mist up from the bowl's contents as the paste fizzed and sizzled. The fizzling quickly subsided as Halford continued to mash the concoction together, pausing every few seconds to gently blow into the bowl. Once the sizzling finally stopped, Halford was ready.

He crossed to Oscar and prompted Alistair and Allison to carefully lay him onto the ground. They did as they were told, still weeping, and watched helplessly as Halford slowly and deliberately poured dribbles of the strange elixir into Oscar's wounds. Upon contact, the gashes and cuts began to bubble and hiss and that pungent aroma rose once again, though this time it was much fouler than it had been before.

Halford carefully rolled Oscar onto his other side, the dog whimpering softly as he did so, and continued to pour the contents into his wounds.

"Now watch," said Halford as he drew away from the dog.

Nothing happened for several seconds and the gunman was beginning to show distinct signs of impatience as he began to shift from foot to foot. Just as he was about to declare Halford a fraud, the wounds in the dog's shaved flesh suddenly began to miraculously knit together. After a few minutes, all that remained of the open gashes were a series of deep purple scars that looked like nothing more than minor surface scratches. Halford then knelt in front of Oscar and held the remaining mixture before his nose, enticing him to drink it.

"It's OK, boy," Alistair sniffed through tears of relief, "go on. Drink it up."

"Come on, Oscar," Allison encouraged him, "you can do it, boy. Come on now."

Finally, Oscar's tail thumped a few times onto the soft ground and he slowly lapped his elongated tongue into the dish, scooping out its contents little by little until the bowl was empty. Slowly, his breathing began to become less shallow and the wet gurgling sounds began to subside until he was breathing normally. His tail flopped once more in the soft sand, then again and before long, he was wagging his tail wildly, as he was prone to do, and he scrambled to his feet, showering both Allison and Alistair, who were bubbling with relief, in slobbering wet kisses.

"Incredible," said the female pirate. "I've never seen anything like it."

At first the gunman seemed speechless as he watched the dog miraculously come back from the brink of death. The rest of the pirates were

equally stupefied and all seemed to have momentarily forgotten that they were holding three hostages. Finally the gunman came back to his senses and shifted his attention back to Halford.

"Now my friend," he said stiffly.

Slowly Halford stood up, his three foot form significantly shy of the gunman's more than six foot frame. He lifted his head and met the man's gaze. A stony expression crossed his face as his eyes narrowed and his hands clenched into imposing fists.

"No." he said defiantly.

"Halford, are you nuts?" Alistair almost shrieked. "He could kill us."

"We don't know that he won't anyway," Halford replied, not taking his steely eyes from the gunman's. "If you want this mixture, then you will let these three go first."

"Halford, no!" Allison exclaimed, but she fell silent when Halford raised his hand sharply in her direction. The gunman levelled the pistol at Halford's head, directly between his dark, impenetrable eyes.

"What makes you think I won't just shoot you? I watched you mix that stuff, we don't need you any more."

"If you shoot me," said Halford coldly, "your friend will die. There's a technique to mixing that potion that can be deadly if not handled in just the right manner. But if you want to try, then go right ahead. But just know that if you do it wrong, your friend will not only die, he will die painfully and violently."

"Hurry," the woman shouted. "We don't have much time!"

The gunman considered Halford's warning for several moments, his eyes drifting from one of his accomplices to the next, each of whom were fidgeting nervously. Finally he returned his attention to Halford.

"Alright," he said. "They go, you stay. You will teach us how to mix the batch and give it to him. If he lives, you live. But understand me clearly, Giant - if he dies," he leaned into Halford until their noses were only a few centimetres apart, "*you die.*"

"Understood," Halford said.

Alistair and Allison burst into tears once again, this time in fear of their friend's life. "Halford, no," they said. "They could kill you."

"They might," he said, boldly turning his back to the gunman. "But you'll live. You have to get back to Loxbury. You still have a job to do and you still have to get home."

Another large explosion erupted around them, the night sky suddenly alight in an angry orange glow as the earth trembled violently under their feet. Overhead they could see the precipice of the volcano, previously invisible in the extreme darkness, glowing hotly as molten rocks spewed viciously into the air. Thick, black smoke belched from the peak as another terrible quake rumbled violently beneath them.

The world seemed to vibrate around them, making it all but impossible to remain standing for very long.

"GO!" Halford screamed at the twins. Showers of sparks and red-hot rock, some as small as bowling balls and others as large as automobiles, began to hammer the ground around them. The dry brush quickly caught fire and in moments, the entire island seemed poised to become a blazing inferno.

"Not without you!" screamed Allison, her face twisted in horror and fear.

"Come on or we'll all get killed!" screamed Alistair.

"NO!" Halford bellowed as a large blazing rock narrowly missed bashing him in the head. "I made a promise to this man that I would save his friend. You two get out of here now. I'll catch up with you."

The group of pirates were scrambling madly, running helter-skelter in every direction, desperate for an escape route. The heat was becoming unbearable and the thick smoke was suffocating, each breath becoming increasingly difficult and painful. All around them, thick ash and showering rocks sparked fires wherever they touched down. In a matter of minutes, the island had become all but engulfed in a raging firestorm.

"Listen to me," said Halford as he gathered the twins into his arms and held them close, "you have to stop Burcheeze. You are the Boffles' only hope now. You have to go. I'll catch up to you. I promise."

Allison and Alistair bawled as they hugged Halford tightly, positive they would never see him again. He had saved their lives more than once on their adventure and the last thing they wanted to do was leave him behind, where he was sure to meet a terrible end.

"Ezekiel!" the woman screamed again as she rushed toward the gunman. "We have to get out of here before the ammunition store blows us all sky high."

"I know," he screamed back as he grabbed Halford by the back of his shirt and tugged sharply.

"Let's go!" he shouted. "Tell them to go to the water. They'll be safe there. Go!"

"Alistair," Halford bellowed, "you heard him. Go to the water. Get your sister out of here before it's too late for all of us. You're a good warrior, son. You can be proud of what you have accomplished. Both of you can. Now get out of here while you still can. I'll meet you in Loxbury. I promise."

"OK," Alistair finally said. He wiped the tears from his eyes and stood up straight, shoulders blocked and head held high. Despite his rotund physique, he looked every bit the hero as he wiped dark, gritty ash and soot from his tear-streaked face. "Come on," he said to Allison. "We have to go now. We have to save the Boffles." Allison nodded and gave Halford a quick peck on the cheek.

"We'll meet you in Loxbury?" she asked. Halford nodded as the gunman named Ezekiel tugged again on the back of his shirt. "OK. See you then."

Alistair lead the way through blazing scrub brush and smouldering boulders, manoeuvring carefully between the rocks and debris that still pelted down around them, touching off fires with each blazing impact. One rock, about the size of a large watermelon, crunched to the ground in a small shower of cascading sparks. He narrowly dodged out of its way but the map had slipped from his pocket and began to waft about in the turbulent air.

"Alistair!" screamed Allison as she tried to snatch the map from the air. He looked back and realised what had happened.

"There's no time!" he screamed as he grabbed her by the wrist. "Come on!"

"But the map!" she screamed. "We need it!"

Just as she said this, another shower of small glowing embers practically assaulted them, immediately burning hundreds of tiny holes into the dry parchment until it finally caught fire. They ran for the edge of the water, looking behind them as they went, and watched the map drift to the ground as it curled and blackened, eventually consumed by fire and reduced to ash. The map was gone.

When they reached the water they saw that there were indeed several small rowboats, however most had already been cast out to sea by escaping pirates. A few of the boats were filled to capacity and even beyond while others carried only two or three passengers. Others were splashing about as they tried to swim toward or climb into the almost empty vessels. Behind them, the peak was ablaze as molten lava, heavy, red and angry, began to spill down the mountainside.

"There!" Allison screamed as she pointed to the only boat remaining on the beach. It was creaky and dilapidated but there was no time to question whether it was sea worthy. It was their only hope of escaping the island before it was reduced to nothing but ash and tinder. Oscar let out a loud *growlf* as they darted toward safety.

TWENTY-ONE

Directed by Ezekiel, Halford darted toward a small wooden hut. Its thatched roof was ablaze and the woman who had summoned them screamed hysterically at them to hurry.

Inside the hut lay the silver-haired man who had beaten the black beast. He looked to be on the very edge of death and his wounds had begun to dry and cake due to the extreme heat of the blazing roof. Fortunately there was a layer of wooden planks between the dry fronds that made up the thatch covering and the ceiling of the room below, slowing the spread of the flames.

Mixing the precise ingredients proved incredibly difficult for Halford. The walls about them shook and shimmied with each violent earth quake. Fine grit and bits of wood fragments sifted down onto them and it was almost impossible for Halford to keep any harmful elements from tainting the precarious potion. Ezekiel stood behind him, steadying himself against one shaking wall, the gun poised directly at the back of Halford's head.

"Don't forget, Giant," Ezekiel growled, "if he dies . . ."

"He just might if you keep breaking my concentration," Halford growled back. Ezekiel fell silent and allowed Halford to mix his concoction.

"Alright," Halford finally said after the mixture had ceased fizzing, "I think it's ready." Ezekiel motioned wordlessly with the barrel of the pistol and Halford slowly approached the mortally wounded man. The hard-packed ground beneath their feet shuddered violently once again and a fissure quickly cracked through the room, leaving a three centimetre gap in the ground and splitting the timbers of the walls.

"Hurry on!" snarled Ezekiel. Halford paid him no mind and carefully dressed the other man's wounds, beginning with the worst of them. Gashes had all but obliterated the left half of his face and the eye was gone altogether. He then proceeded to dress the gaping wounds on his ribs.

"Hold his head up," he directed the woman. She carefully lifted the man's head with both hands and then Halford trickled the remaining mixture into his slackened mouth. All that was left was to stand back and wait for the mixture to take effect.

The woman knelt beside the wounded man, stroking his hair gently and Halford couldn't help but notice that there was a strong kinship between the two.

"It's not working," she said with a sob. Her body quaked with grief as she continued to stroke his blood-streaked hair.

From the corner of his eye, Halford could see that Ezekiel was becoming agitated as they waited for signs of recovery from the silver-haired man. The ground continued to shake as thunderous tremors ripped through the air and the fissure in the ground cracked open another few centimetres.

"Why isn't it working?" Ezekiel screamed and thrust the gun into Halford's face. The look in the pirate's eyes was a combination of indescribable fury and terror as he eased the hammer back, poised to fire.

"Wait!" shouted the woman. "Look!"

The man's wounds began to stitch themselves together ever so slowly. The woman stared in disbelief as she slowly moved next to Halford, clutching him about the shoulders as she sobbed uncontrollably.

Over the next few minutes, the silver-haired man's wounds had closed into an ugly but completely healed series of scars. His eye socket meshed together, leaving a bruise-coloured and sunken cavity where his eyeball had once been. The wounds on his ribs had knit together nicely as well, leaving only deep red scratches much like Oscar's but otherwise there was no hint that there had ever been any gashes at all. Another few seconds passed and the man began to stir, groaning softly.

"You live," Ezekiel said plainly to Halford, then lifted the silver-haired man to his feet and shuffled him toward the door with great difficulty. Halford slipped under one of the wounded man's arms and eased the weight for Ezekiel, who looked at him puzzlingly for a moment before the two of them awkwardly eased him toward safety, the woman not far behind them.

The short distance was a challenging one as the small hut had filled with thick, suffocating smoke. Flaming bits of ceiling pelted them from the engulfed roof and twice they had to stagger out of the way as a large section of ceiling collapsed almost directly on top of them. Outside, all that could be heard was the roar of the blaze as the entire camp was quickly engulfed by flame. It was only by some divine miracle that the ammunition hut hadn't gone up, which would surely level most of the small encampment. There was an audible creak above them just as the small group reached the door and suddenly the roof collapsed in a fiery avalanche of blazing fronds and wooden planks. They shoved the semi-conscious man through the doorway and into the outer encampment as the section of roof crashed down on them, knocking Ezekiel unconscious and leaving Halford and the woman both badly stunned.

Most of the ceiling and roof had come down and they were surrounded by a searing black and orange inferno, the sky blotted out by a thick layer of suffocating smoke. A large crossbeam had come crashing down across the doorway, blocking their path. Despite his greatest efforts, Halford's weakened and stunned condition made it impossible for him to pry the heap of flaming wood away from their only means of escape, forcing him to admit his own defeat and bravely face his demise. His eyes stung from heat and smoke, watering terribly and making him all but blind as he waited to be enveloped by the flames. Then, in his state of resigned defeat, Halford wasn't sure that he was seeing what he thought he was seeing. It looked as though something large was surging toward them from behind the scorching veil of blistering flame.

There was a loud crash as the heavy planks that criss-crossed before them came crashing down and Oscar charged through the wall of fire like a flaming angel of mercy. He let out a loud and surprisingly heroic *WOOF!* as he charged to the rescue. Not far behind him came Alistair and Allison, arms covering their faces in an effort to ward off the sweltering heat. With Halford's help, they were able to push the charred planks to the side with their bare hands. Once uncovered, Halford sprang to his feet and dragged Ezekiel out of the hut, followed by Oscar. Allison and Alistair managed to heft up the woman and carry her out of harms way just as the walls of the flaming hut collapsed on themselves, leaving the tiny shack little more than a scorching pile of deadly rubble.

Ezekiel was beginning to stir and managed to weakly stand on his own two feet, though he needed some assistance to remain stable. He held onto Oscar's collar as Halford scooped up the silver-haired man and hefted him over his blocky shoulder. "Let's go!"

The twins lead the way, struggling to carry the still dazed woman, as Ezekiel hobbled behind them, clutching Oscar for much needed support. Behind them followed Halford, carrying the silver-haired man as though he were little more than a sack of potatoes.

As they staggered away from the camp and toward the beach, they looked behind them to see the entire area was a raging bonfire the likes of which none of them had seen before or since.

It was impossible to determine whether all of the pirates had escaped, though many had managed to cast off and were now rowing away from Perilrock Peak across Dibble Sea. The boat that the twins had planned to use was still beached and Halford carefully placed the semi-conscious man within, and then helped Ezekiel into the boat. Once the twins were aboard and Oscar had hopped in, Halford pushed off, the keel scraping sharply against the rocky coastline, then climbed in himself and began to row as hard and fast as he possibly could. Behind them, the ammunition hut finally erupted with a deafening explosion and they could feel the searing force of the blast despite being several hundred metres from shore. As they rowed into the blindingly darkened night, the brilliant orange glow began to fade and fade and fade until it was little more than a glimmering orange speck on the horizon, finally winking out of existence.

TWENTY-TWO

As the sun peered over the horizon, the coal black sky began to bleed magenta as though the edge of the world were an opening wound. They drifted lazily, Halford having collapsed from exhaustion several hours before. Oscar lay in the bottom of the boat, snoring loudly as the twins huddled against each other, lost in their own depths of exhausted slumber. Ezekiel and the woman were leaning against opposite sides of the boat as the silver-haired man half lay across them, his head resting in the woman's lap.

Allison was the first to open her eyes and all she could see in every direction was the clear empty nothingness that was Dibble Sea. Somewhere behind them, far beyond the horizon, she could still see the wafting black smoke from the volcano.

Finding no solace in the fact that the nearest landmass was a blazing inferno, she shifted her attention to the strange birds which drifted casually high above them, swooping and gliding as though they hadn't a single concern. She watched them for several minutes, finding their peaceful resolve somehow relaxing after such recent and ultimately horrific events. Finally she prodded Alistair, who mumbled something that sounded like "Peanuh-budder-samidges", but she couldn't be sure. A second sharp jab to his ribs with the end of the oar finally awakened him and he rubbed his bleary eyes with his pudgy, soot-covered hands.

"Where are we?" he asked wearily as Oscar's head jerked up at the sound of his voice.

"I don't know," Allison replied. "In the middle of the sea, I guess."

Ezekiel suddenly jerked awake and fumbled for his pistol, but it had been lost somewhere between the hut and the beach. He sat almost almost motionlessly, only swaying gently back and forth with the movement of the boat as it gently crested the tiny waves. He stared at the twins suspiciously and then darted his eyes toward Halford before taking a quick look at the silver-haired man and the woman.

"Where are the others?" he asked slowly, scanning the seemingly endless cobalt seascape.

"Dunno," shrugged Alistair. Allison simply shook her head in dismay.

The wounded, silver-haired man began to stir and Ezekiel immediately cast his attention to him. Leaning down, he placed a hand on his shoulder and with the other he brushed away a small shard of charred wood from his hair.

"Ezekiel," the man choked, but the words caught in his throat and sent him into a frenzied coughing fit which awoke both Halford and the woman.

"Easy now," Ezekiel said softly. "You need to rest for a while."

"What?" he coughed. "Where?" It was all he was able to manage. The woman began to stroke his brow once again, sweeping long, sticky strands of magenta and silver hair from his face.

"The island's gone," Ezekiel said sadly. "Erupted."

"How many?" the man gagged.

"No way to know for sure."

"The . . . the . . . Boarhound?" He was asking how he had survived the attack from the vicious black beast.

Ezekiel smiled softly and there was a kindness about him that had not been present before. "You almost didn't make it. If not for him . . ." His voice trailed off as though the thought of what may have been was far too difficult to speak of. He gestured toward Halford. "He saved us all." The man turned his head slightly and looked at Halford, who was scooping water from the sea and held it in his cupped hands for the man to drink.

"Thank you," the man choked through a weak smile and slowly sipped the water. Halford shrugged casually, as though it were the simplest task in the world, never to be mentioned again.

"Now you rest, Pop. You'll need your strength."

The man's eyes drooped and he fell into a deep sleep almost immediately.

"Pop?" Halford said in a surprised tone. He had never heard this expression before.

"Yeah," replied Ezekiel as he extended his hand. Halford took it, Ezekiel's hand lost in the massive mitt of the tiny Giant. "This is my father. Ambrose Rubottom. My name is Ezekiel and this is my sister, Ella."

"We owe you a great debt," Ella said in a weak but kind voice. "And an apology."

"No apologies necessary," Halford replied. "You were trying to save your father."

"Where are we?" Alistair asked.

"Well," said Ezekiel, looking around. The telltale plume of smoke was now only a dark thread against the bright blue sky. "If the Peak is directly behind us, we're heading east."

"East?!" exclaimed Allison. "Then that means we're headed toward Tenebrous Marsh."

"Eventually, yeah," he replied, "but it'll be some time before we get there. It's a two day journey under the best conditions."

"Yes," she continued, "but that means we can change course and go almost directly to Loxbury through Mayomay Bay. All we have to do is head North East. It'll take us right there."

"Or we could wind up being lost in the middle of Dibble Sea. Without a nautical chart, we could be way off course."

"No, we aren't," she said. "I remember the map. Perilrock Peak is South West of Mayomay Bay *and* Loxbury. We're heading east. If we just change course, we can be there in a day, as long as we all pitch in."

"How do you remember all this?" Ella marvelled.

"She reads a lot, lady," Alistair replied. "Trust her. She's right."

"Then we do it your way," said Halford as he took up the oars and sliced them though the water. "To Loxbury."

***

They had decided to take turns at the oars, with Alistair taking over for Halford. As they skimmed across the water, Ezekiel and Ella told them of how they and the other '*pirates*' had once been Burcheeze's compatriots but exiled him for taking things too far. They had wanted to start their own community, a sovereign nation that didn't have to abide by society's laws and limitations. In the beginning it had been a grand plan. They would live peacefully without war and hunger, without prejudices and without any single authoritative leader. Theirs would have been a community of equals where everyone had a say in every item of business, whatever that business may be.

He told them of Burcheeze's charismatic and clever personality, how he had a way of speaking that made the things he said - the crazy, horribly devious things - make sense. Soon they were raiding villages like Loxbury and taking whatever they wanted. Others in their group had tried to stop them, just as Auntie Bernice had said, but their efforts to dissuade the marauders were futile. Once Bernice and her people had left, Dibble was theirs to plunder.

Burcheeze had by then become power-hungry and highly dangerous and it was decided that they no longer pursued the same goals. There was a terrible battle and many people were injured, even killed. Outnumbered and defeated, Burcheeze finally ran off to live alone in Tenebrous Marsh. The *'pirates'*, labelled as such by the people of Dibble, chose to live apart from the rest of them as well, ashamed of their misdeeds and not daring to show their faces again.

"Why didn't you just go home?" Allison asked Ezekiel.

"We couldn't," he said. "Most of us didn't have homes. None to speak of, anyway. We were escaping a world that seemed terrifying and unfair. Most of us, the ones who stayed back with Burcheeze, had nothing to go home *to*. At least here we had each other. A family."

"But you had your father," Halford interjected. Ezekiel said nothing. Instead, he simply bowed his head as though he were ashamed.

"I wasn't much of a father," said Ambrose. Everyone started at the sound of his croaking voice as none of them knew he had awakened.

"Dad!"

"I'm alright," he groaned as he sat up in the boat. His face was deeply scarred and was turning pink from the blazing sun but otherwise he appeared to be in relatively fine form. "Just a few aches and pains." He ran a hand across his ribs, and then slowly pressed his fingertips to his marked face. "I thought maybe it was a dream," he said softly.

"I did what I could," Halford said. "I'm sorry."

"Sorry?" he chuckled mirthlessly. "Sorry you saved my pitiful skin? Don't be ridiculous. It's more than I would have done for you."

"I don't understand," said Allison, "Halford saved you. You would have been killed for sure. You would have burned alive if you didn't bleed to death first."

"You're right, you *don't* understand," he said to her. "What I meant was I couldn't have done what he did. I don't even *know* what he did, but I know I would have thought about my own hide first and foremost. You saved me and I hardly deserve it. In fact, I deserve much less. I'm grateful."

"Dad, are you OK?" Ezekiel asked. He had never seen his father show anything like gratitude to anyone. Ever. He was a tough nut, difficult to crack, as Ezekiel well knew and for him to open up to anyone, especially a stranger, was a surprising, to say the least.

"Sure I'm OK," he grinned tiredly. "Why do you ask?"

"I just . . . I've never seen you so . . . so . . . nice."

"Bah!" he grumbled, suddenly taking on an air of grizzled peevishness that somehow didn't come off as genuine. "I'm just an old pirate that's been whacked on the head a few too many times. Forgive me if I periodically slip into a momentary lapse of reason."

"There's something I don't understand," Allison said to Halford. "How did Burcheeze - I mean Burty - get to Dibble? And why does he hate the Boffles so much?"

"I don't know," Halford replied. "Probably from living in Tenebrous Marsh for so long. You see, through no fault of your own, it seems humans are terribly flawed, weak and easily corruptible, prone to violence. Look at you two," he said, meaning Allison and Alistair. "When we left our village you were concerned about the use of guns. During your argument, Alistair, you threatened to shoot your sister in the bottom. Did you mean it? Doubtful. But that's how it starts. Minor threats, often unfounded, until it escalates into a war. It's a human condition that seems engrained. And you hadn't even stepped foot in Tenebrous Marsh. Imagine if that had happened after taking on Marsh Fever. Human weakness. Whatever sorcery lies in the Marsh, it feeds on human weakness. It's not in all humans, I don't think, but enough."

There was a profound silence for a very long time as Halford finished speaking, the only sound was that of the gently lapping waves and the oars as they splashed through the water and clunked against the creaky sides of the boat.

"I'm glad you're all having such a pleasant little chat," Alistair finally grunted as he heaved the heavy oars through the water. Sweat was pouring down his face as the morning sun crested high in the clear blue sky, beating down upon them. "I'm touched. I really am. But my arms are killin' me. Whose turn is it?"

They rowed on for what seemed to be days. Halford divided what little Tangleroot remained in his pouch and everyone nibbled their rations, well aware that there may not be any more food for an undeterminable amount of time. They recounted their adventure to Ezekiel and his father. Ambrose burst into a painful laughing fit as Allison described the scene of Alistair riding Oscar down the stairs and as they told of their dizzying adventures, it hardly seemed possible that they had ever happened. Their tattered clothes, Allison's scratched glasses and now obliterated braids, their cuts and their bruises were all testimony to their extraordinary journey.

Clouds began to drift toward them from the North West around mid- afternoon. Within a half hour, the sky turned from a striking pale denim colour to a slate grey as storm clouds churned and rumbled overhead, flickering brilliantly from within as lightning threatened to lash down at them at any moment.

"Well, this is just great!" Alistair bemoaned. "You gotta be kiddin' me. Can anything else *possibly* go wrong?"

As if waiting for a cue, the clouds opened up and dumped torrents of rain down upon them. It was as though someone had opened a large faucet somewhere above the clouds and was deliberately trying to sink their small craft. If that were indeed the case, they would have been doing a fine job as the bottom of the boat quickly began to fill with rain water.

Thunder boomed all around them, reverberating as though a hundred cannons were being fired simultaneously. Lighting flashed and flickered like electric blue forks and it was only a matter of time before they were struck.

"Start baling!" Halford screamed over the driving rain. He emptied the contents of his pouch into the raging sea and began to use it to scoop water out of the boat. Oscar had curled up behind Alistair, cringing and whimpering with every crack of lightning as they fruitlessly tried to scoop water out of the boat by hand. There was just too much of it, however, and it was coming too fast and too furiously. They were sinking.

"We'll have to swim!" Ezekiel screamed, though he was barely audible over the sounds of the furious storm. A half-second later, the boat crested a large wave and tipped sideways, toppling Alistair into the frigid water.

"Alistair!" screamed Halford, reaching over the gunnels toward him. "Grab hold!"

"I can't!" he glubbed through a mouthful of water. His head disappeared beneath the large waves several times and with each disappearance, their hearts raced, silently wondering if it would be the last time they saw him. Allison was screaming for someone to help him as his head finally bobbed back to the surface. Alistair flailed helplessly, his arms splashing about in the churning sea like out of control propellers. He was choking on sea water and obviously drowning. Just as Halford stood up, steadying himself in preparation to dive into the water, Allison tossed him her glasses, then jumped head first into the icy swell and began swimming toward her brother.

She slipped one of her arms under his armpits and around his torso, then struggled against the water as she swam back toward their craft. It was as though she were fuelled by some supernatural strength that she could never explain. Even so, it was a difficult and exhausting rescue as she fought against the raging current and if the boat had been even a single metre further away, she was not sure she would have made it. Halford reached out and grabbed Alistair by the front of the shirt and hefted him into the boat. Allison climbed aboard and collapsed against Halford, breathing heavily as Ezekiel held Alistair, who was coughing out mouthfuls of sea water.

"Swimming lessons," she gasped, looking up at an incredulous Halford. "Level five."

"LOOK!" Ella bellowed. She pointed toward a massive wave that was bearing down on them. The wave was at least twenty metres high and the foamy white cap was crashing over them before anyone could even respond. Halford scooped Alistair into his arms and dove to the port side, Ezekiel, Ella and their father to starboard and Allison and Oscar jumped from the stern. The crushing wave reduced the boat to splintered tinder as its former occupants were now helplessly engulfed by the stormy waters of Dibble Sea.

Halford heaved the semi-conscious Alistair onto a large section of splintered keel as Allison and Oscar swam toward them. Ezekiel and Ambrose managed to hang onto a smaller section of the obliterated boat. All were at the mercy of the storm, helpless to do anything but wait for it to pass and hope that they survived.

***

The storm raged on and all hope seemed lost as wave after crushing wave pummelled and buffeted them. Allison somehow managed to hold onto Oscar as she, Halford and Alistair clung for dear life to the broken section of the boat. Ezekiel and Ambrose had been washed further out to sea, leaving Ella alone, clinging for life to a splintered section of the boat. In Alistair's weakened condition it was very difficult for him to cling to the make-shift raft and Halford had to hold onto him with one arm while trying to keep them afloat by holding the broken planks with the other. Twice Halford's grip slipped and he and Alistair dunked under the surface, but managed to come up again. Halford then heaved the boy onto the flat of the board until only his arms and legs dangled in the water. His grip then slipped a third time and he disappeared under the rocking waves, only this time, he didn't re-emerge.

"Halford!" Allison screamed as she splashed her way toward the spot he had gone down. "Halford, where are you?" To Alistair she screamed, "Where did he go?"

"Gone," Alistair gulped and wheezed. "Dunno."

As Allison splashed around blindly under the surface, hoping to grab hold of Halford's shirt collar or pant leg, Oscar suddenly began to bark wildly at something above their heads. She tried to look up and see what he was barking at, but the sweeping sheets of heavy rain offered her only a silvery veil to look through. Then, before she could even register what she was seeing, a small, cigar-shaped insect buzzed madly over her head. It was one of the same strange insects they had seen in the Eating Garden and again in Sender's cottage. It zipped first to the left, then to the right before it finally zoomed down toward them and paused briefly, hovering before her eyes, then buzzed toward Oscar and then Alistair before plunking into the water and disappearing. A few minutes later it reappeared and soared off into the violent sky. All that Allison could hear was the deafening rattle of thick, torrential rain hammering the surface of the raging water until a few minutes later, when a weak buzzing sound, somehow familiar, reached her ears.

Several dark forms quickly began to blur into view through the driving rain. They were flying high in the sky at an alarming speed, careening toward the stranded group. Allison's heart leapt as she realized what they were and she knew that they were saved.

One of the dark forms bore down upon her and deftly clipped her out of the water and within seconds she was soaring high into the sky, dangling precariously by one pincered claw. A hand reached down from somewhere above her and hefted her upwards.

"You looked like you needed some help," Sender shouted as she settled in behind him on Thurgood's back.

All about them swarmed a dozen Whipperloopers, each fitted with their own leather harness and guided by a Boffle. Alistair and Oscar were plucked out of the water and soared high up into the sky as well. As Allison shielded her eyes from the pelting rain she watched one of the Whipperloopers zoom straight up into the air, then make an abrupt turn and dive straight down, its long, narrow wings tucking tightly to its side, resembling a torpedo. Its rider leaned low until he was lying almost flat atop the Whipperlooper's back, holding tightly to reigns that were part of the harness assembly, and together they sliced into the water and disappeared below the surface. When they emerged a few seconds later, an unconscious Halford was heaped in front of the rider, who held him tightly so he wouldn't fall off. As they soared away from the fragmented remains of the obliterated boat, Allison could see that three more Whipperloopers carried Ezekiel, Ella and Ambrose.

"How did you know where to find us?" Allison shouted. The wind that roared past her ears, coupled with the rain, made it difficult to hear.

"I sent out a Fleeting Glimpse," he shouted back over his shoulder.

"You mean that little bug thing?"

"Yes," he replied jovially. "It's called a Fleeting Glimpse. I send them to look for people when I think they're in trouble. They seek them out and when they find them, they return and tell me where they are. Quite remarkable creatures, really. We've had Glimpses looking for you for two days. Ever since time began to run normally again."

"What about -" she began, but Sender cut her short.

"I'll explain more when we get back to Loxbury," he yelled. "Now hang on. This is going to be a very bumpy ride."

Sender was right; it was a bumpy ride indeed. With the severity of the storm, it was far too dangerous to risk rising to an altitude where they could fly above it. Instead, they flew only a few hundred metres above the rocking sea, hammered by relentless winds and rain that felt like a solid punch with every savage drop. Twice Allison thought she might fall from her harness but she managed to remain seated and finally, far, far below them, she could see a solid dark mass approaching that was obviously land.

They finally touched down in the middle of Town Square in Loxbury. There was no fan-fare this time, aside from the lone tuba player, who stood drenched to the skin, bleating and boomping his instrument. Verona came running to Halford's side, weeping with worry and relief. She held him tightly, kissing him about the face for several minutes before moving on to Allison and Alistair. She even hugged Oscar, whom she had never met, and then Ezekiel, Ella and Ambrose.

Once through the heavy double doors of the Town Hall, the storm sounded almost hollow as the pummelling rain thrummed madly on the roof, though thunder crashed every few seconds and lightning illuminated the dim and grey afternoon.

"The key," said Halford forlornly as they entered the Mayor's empty office. "We had it. It's gone."

"Yes, yes," said Sender. "We'll deal with that in good time."

The doors burst open as Mayor Maynott waddled hurriedly into the room. He was a frazzled bundle of nerves, his hands flailing wildly in the air and his face contorted in fear, confusion and relief.

"Oh, they've come back!" he exclaimed as he rushed around and around in circles. Once again, his little rant was slung together as though he were speaking one long, single word. "We were so worried. So worried, indeed, yes. You did it! You managed to wind the clock. We were ever so worried. Oh, it was terrible, just terrible. Thank goodness you're alright. You are alright, aren't you? Oh dear, perhaps you're not. Perhaps we need Doc Foober. I'll get him right away. Oh, but what if he's not in? But of course he's in. Where else would he be? This is terrible, just terrible. Yes, I think I'll get Doc Foober. Doctor! Doctor Foober! Come quick. Oh, I do hope he's in."

The small, waterlogged group watched wordlessly as the Mayor left the office once again, still muttering and worrying that the doctor may not be available.

"I failed," Halford said softly. Everyone looked at him, wondering just what he meant.

"But time is running once again," said Sender. "I would say you succeeded quite nicely, actually."

"I lost Feldon," Halford replied. He seemed particularly interested in the condition of his own fingernails, not willing to meet Sender's gaze. "He died. Killed. By Burcheeze. As for the rest of my men . . . I don't know what happened to them."

"That's a terrible loss," Sender said softly as he rested a hand on the Giant's shoulder. "But Feldon knew the risks when he joined you. Let me ask you this. Would Feldon feel like he failed you if you had died while carrying out what I can only describe as a successful mission?"

"I just . . . I . . . no, I don't think he would." Allison took Halford's hand and squeezed it tightly. He finally looked up and glanced around the room. Allison and Alistair looked as though they had been through a threshing machine. They were filthy and bedraggled, their clothes a horrendously tattered and mangled mass of fabric. Alistair's exposed leg was scraped and scabbed, the cuts on his elbows were ugly brownish red blotches and he had scrapes, cuts and bruises about his neck and face. Allison was in no better shape. Though somewhat less ragged, her clothes were destroyed beyond repair as well and she, too, was covered in cuts and bruises. Her blazing red hair had lost its lustre and her tidy braids were a distant memory. Suddenly remembering he still had her glasses, Halford reached into his pocket and retrieved them, handing them to her. Once she slipped them on her nose, Allison looked a little more like the girl he had met not so long ago. A little. Even Oscar, who had started out with only half his fur intact, looked battered and worn. What was important, however, was that they were still here. He had almost abandoned them and if he had, perhaps they would never have made it back to Loxbury. But here they were. Alive.

"You also saved us," said Ezekiel, who had been standing quietly in the corner with his father.

"Yes," Sender said suspiciously, his eyes narrowing slightly. "I seem to recall having met you gentlemen before."

"That was a long time ago," Ambrose said softly. He stepped forward and offered his hand. "We made some terrible mistakes and for that we are truly regretful. But now, if you will, you can call us your friends."

Sender glanced toward Halford, who nodded his head ever so slightly. Finally, Sender took his hand and they shook, forming a new alliance.

"But the key," said Allison. "And the clock. We left them in the Tangleroot."

"Ah," said Sender. "So you did." Just then the doors opened and a group of Giants entered, followed by Nessa Littlejohn, who cradled their swaddled child in her arms. Halford jumped to his feet and began to grunt in Giantese, the guttural noises sounding like a mixture of both glee and confusion. He and the other Giants hugged and shook hands for several minutes as Mrs. Littlejohn and Sender beamed with genuine delight. Oscar chuffed in confusion and Allison was perplexed.

"I don't understand," she began.

"We arrived yesterday," Mrs. Littlejohn explained as she embraced her husband. "When you went back through, the others were able to wrestle themselves free and return to the village with the clock and key. Sender immediately had Thurgood bring me here. You did it. The Boffles are saved."

"I knew we could do it," mumbled Alistair, who sat slumped in one of the Mayor's barber chairs. "It was a cinch."

TWENTY-THREE

Mayor Maynott returned with Doc Foober a short time later, who proceeded to examine the group. He declared all to be in relative good health and ordered them to rest and get something hot to eat. Eager to take his advice, they all sat down to a delicious meal of hot soup, fresh baked bread and steaming mugs of Dibble Tea.

The storm continued as the afternoon receded and night made its stealthy approach. Sender told them of how the Giants had returned, clock and key in tow, and the grand celebration that followed. Allison, Alistair and their group then told of their adventures since leaving Loxbury.

"I should have warned you about the Serpensilicus," Sender had said. "I apologize."

"Yeah," said Alistair, "it might have been nice to know. I'm not big on getting swallowed whole by giant snake thingies."

"Alistair!" Allison hissed, jabbing him in the ribs.

"Well I'm not!" he jabbed back.

The Tick-Tock People

"We still have an important issue to consider," said Halford. "Burcheeze is still out there and I'll wager he still has visions of destroying Loxbury and everyone in it."

"Yes," said Sender, "I was thinking the same thing. I'm sure that when time started again he was absolutely furious. I have no doubt that he's going to attack at any moment."

"Then we must be ready."

"Ready?!" the Mayor said worriedly. "Ready how? We've no weapons to speak of, no way to effectively defend ourselves. We'll be crushed."

"Look," said Alistair reassuringly, "if I've learned anything over the last few days, it's that anything is possible as long as you think things through."

A crescendo of thunder ripped through the air as they sat at the table staring at the boy whose actions were well known to be frequently reckless and questionable.

"What?!" he finally blurted.

"You're right," Sender agreed. "We can't just sit back and do nothing. We must fight back. We may not survive - not all of us - but if we simply do nothing, Burcheeze will surely emerge victorious."

"Don't forget," said Halford, "you have a dozen Giants at your side, not to mention five capable humans and the bravest dog I've ever seen."

***

Mayor Maynott bustled around his office for almost twenty minutes, his hands fluttering in every direction as he blithered about how dangerous it would be to fight Burcheeze, how they could hide - though where they could hide was a question he couldn't answer - or try to talk to him very nicely.

"Too bad we don't have any guns," said Ezekiel.

"No," said Sender. "We don't want guns here."

"We don't need them," said Halford. "Burcheeze is as stupid as he is big. We can outsmart him if we set the appropriate trap."

"Trap?" asked Alistair. "What kind of trap?"

"I have an idea," Halford said in a hushed tone as he looked around the room.

***

An hour later, the plan was set. If successful, it posed minimal threat to the Boffles, though some damage to Loxbury was undoubtedly unavoidable. The thunder and lightning had begun to subside as the storm finally began to dissipate. A slick steady rain still fell but it wasn't the driving stream it had been when they had arrived. In the Town Square, Thurgood and another Whipperlooper named Archibald stood silently with their giant, translucent wings flittering in the breeze as the twins settled into the saddle harnesses."Are you sure you want to do this?" Sender asked. "It's very dangerous."

"Are you kiddin'?" Alistair chuckled. "I wouldn't miss this for the world."

"Neither would I," grinned Allison. She held a small round object tightly in her hand, its warmth and energy pulsing within. Alistair held a similar object in his own grip as a muffled buzz becoming more and more pronounced. Finally, they opened their hands to reveal what looked like two tiny, armour plated brown spheres. They slowly began to unfurl and became elongated as two pair of wings sprouted from between two of the plates. Another second or two passed as their wings began to vibrate and hum and then the Fleeting Glimpses quickly zipped into the air and hovered for a moment before darting off into the late afternoon sky. The Whipperloopers' wings began to thrum and they slowly lifted off the ground, Alistair and Allison waving at their friends.

"Remember the plan," Halford shouted at them though cupped hands.

"We will," Alistair shouted back. "Don't worry."

But Halford did worry. The twins were setting off to find Burcheeze, unguarded and weaponless, and attempt to lure him directly into Loxbury's Town Square.

TWENTY-FOUR

It was difficult for either of the twins to follow the Glimpses movements but the Whipperloopers eyesight was far superior and could easily monitor their course. Before long, the tiny insects were gone from sight, though the Whipperloopers appeared to maintain a steady flight pattern. They soared high above the open fields and pastures of Dibble, over the Eating Garden and Tangleroot and began to follow the coastline of Mayomay Bay toward Tenebrous Marsh. The Obsidian Woods loomed below them, nothing but a thick, imposing mass to tightly clustered trees. Even though the evil and hideous secrets that hid within the woods were invisible from such a height, it still sent chills through the twins' spines.

The rain had finally stopped and the water-slicked landscape below looked crisp and fresh. Far off in the distance they could see the hollow peeks of the Bumblehive Mountains and in the other direction they could see the smouldering remains of Perilrock Peak. Two unpiloted

Whipperloopers had joined them; one flanking either side, as the Glimpses suddenly zipped back toward them. They buzzed around their heads, swooping in erratic circles and humming loudly. They had found Burcheeze. The Whipperloopers then went into a steep dive, following the Fleeting Glimpses as they made their descent. They had doubled back and were heading toward the outer edge of the Obsidian Woods. As they drew closer and closer to the ground, the twins could see a large object charging along the emerald sea of grass and brush.

"There he is!" Allison shouted.

Indeed, Burcheeze was stomping along at breakneck speed, carrying a large wooden mallet in one hand and resting on his opposite shoulder he held a long wooden club with a spiked ball and chain dangling heavily from the other end. Looking a little worse for wear, Burcheese's clothes were tattered rags and the open toe of his boot had torn so much that the entire front half of his foot jutted out, his gnarled ugly toes digging sharply into the moist earth. The Whipperloopers tucked their wings to their sides and they glided along silently. Below them, Burcheeze stopped dead in his tracks and jerked his head slightly, as though listening for something in the distance. He quickly began swinging his arms around his head and as they drew closer, the twins could see that he was trying to bat away the Glimpses, which were buzzing around his head like a couple of blood-starved mosquitoes.

Burcheeze dropped his weapons and began clapping his hands together sharply, the wet skin-on-skin sound echoing through the now eerily silent afternoon. He spun around twice in a comical ballet-type swirl, almost losing his balance, before he steadied himself and brought his hands together once more. This time he let out a resounding "HA!" and wiped something mucky on his soiled trousers - he had squashed one of the Glimpses.

Alistair and Thurgood dove directly at Burcheeze and knocked him in the back of his knees before swooping out of harm's way. His knees buckled from the surprise move and he toppled backward, landing in the soft grass with a muffled *crunch*. He grabbed the mace and began to swing it wildly, not really knowing what he was swinging at, and then spied Allison and Archibald, who were mounting an attack of their own.

They flew directly toward Burcheeze's stomach as though intending to knock the wind out of him. He swung the mace again and only missed hitting them by a matter of centimetres. Archibald quickly ducked to the left and flicked his heavy tail, knocking Burcheeze's feet out from under him. Again, he crashed to the ground with another audible wet *crunch*.

Burcheeze let out a bellow of rage that shook their eardrums as he once again clamoured to his feet, snatching the mallet as he went, and swung it around like a mindless beast.

Alistair whooped as he and Thurgood made another pass. Burcheeze swung the mallet and it glanced off of Thurgood's tail and opened a deep wound whick knocked him slightly off course before he regained his balance. "Alistair, come on," Allison shouted as she swooped toward her brother and Thurgood.

"Yeeee-haaaaaaaaaa!" he screamed as he waved his arm in the air. He felt like he was a rodeo rider on a bucking bronco. With that, he grabbed the reigns tighter and nudged Thurgood with his heels. "Let's go!"

They flew at an altitude of about ten metres, just high enough and slow enough to keep Burcheeze interested by being irritatingly out of reach. He stormed after them shouting obscenities and flailing his weapons every which way. He showed an impressive amount of stamina as they approached Pointing Rock but was beginning to show signs of exhaustion. He was slowing down considerably and his arm movements were becoming sluggish. It was then that the next part of their plan went into effect.

Once having decided that their foe was adequately run down, the two accompanying Whipperloopers swooshed toward him and snatched his pant cuffs with their pincered feet. It took both of them and all of their might to lift the massive man off the ground and it was all they could do to remain airborne. Burcheeze, dangling precariously upside down, dropped his mace, which thumped to the ground and was left behind. He managed to maintain a grip on his mallet, although he was too exhausted to heft it upward. With his free hand, however, he tried in vain to pry one of the Whipperlooper's pincers loose. Finally, either through absolute exhaustion or simply knowing a losing battle when he experienced one, he ceased trying to escape and simply allowed himself to be carried over the landscape.

The shallows of Mayomay River were fast approaching and Alistair couldn't help but wonder what might happen if they were to simply drop Burcheeze and allow the Serpensilicus have its way with him. He grinned mischievously at the thought but it wasn't part of the plan. As the bridge and Mayomay River passed beneath them, Alistair set his sights directly ahead. Within a few minutes they would be approaching Loxbury, where Burcheeze would finally get his due.

The large tower in the centre of town finally came into view, the Grandfather Clock now reaffixed in its proper place. The smaller clocks which jutted from every angle all read the correct time - 6:28. All but one.

Toward the bottom of the tower was attached a small, non-descript clock that didn't tick. It hadn't kept time for years, according to Sender, and its counter clock was believed to have been lost many years before. It was this clock that would be Burcheeze's final resting place. Its hands were set to read 3:17.

As they approached, not a single person or Boffle stood in front of the tower for fear of being drawn into the clock and whisked off into the unknown realm of between-time. Instead the townspeople all stood in front of Town Hall, cheering madly as they swiftly made their approach. The marching band was at the ready, their eager eyes, lips and fingers ready to strike up a victory song the moment Burcheeze finally disappeared. Halford and Mrs. Littlejohn stood side by side as the other Giants huddled around them. They clapped and cheered, as did Ezekiel, Ella and their father. Oscar ran around in tiny circles, his tail wagging madly to and fro as he barked in the shrill tone that indicated pure delight.

The sight of the cheering crowd seemed to spark a new wave of anger in Burcheeze as he realised what was about to happen. He began to struggle violently and one of the Whipperloopers accidentally allowed him to slip free. With only one of the large winged insects bearing his massive weight, they immediately went crashing to the ground, skidding through the wet muck and mire of the rain-sodden earth, well before the intended target zone.

Burcheeze skiffed along the ground for a few metres, finally crumpling in a dazed and addle-minded heap. The Whipperlooper tried to right itself but only managed to tumble head over tail toward the large group of onlookers. Everyone screamed and scattered, careful not to run in front of the tower. It finally crashed head first into the large double doors of the Town Hall, where it lay unconscious.

"Oh no!" Allison screamed. She and Alistair zoomed down to ground level, jumping from their saddles before Thurgood or Archibald had even placed all six of their feet on land.

Burcheeze screamed in absolute fury as he pulled himself to his feet. He picked up his mallet and began to swing at anything in sight, bashing holes in roofs, walls and sidewalks. He brought his weapon down on a building, shattering Doc Foober's sign and store front.

Boffles raced indoors, tried to hide under push carts full of produce or simply scrambled around in mindless zig-zags as they looked for safe cover.

Within minutes, most of the Town Square had been demolished. All that remained standing and untouched was the clock tower; Burcheeze knew enough not to get too close.

In the heat of the moment, Burcheeze hadn't noticed that Alistair and Allison had scrambled away with Halford and the others. Prepared for the possibility that he might somehow manage to escape, they quickly re-emerged from the blacksmith's shop wielding make-shift slingshots, which Halford had crafted while the twins were summoning Burcheeze. They each held a wooden 'Y' shaped weapon which had been strung with an elastic-like vine called Memory Vine. It was a resilient and stretchy plant that had many of the same characteristics as rubber and proved to be the perfect substance to create the launching sling for their slingshots. They had also wrapped their hands in thick strips of fabric so they could handle their ammunition; red hot pellets which had been heating up in the fire for several hours. They loaded the pellets into the slings and waited for the signal.

"NOW!" shouted Halford. Alistair and Allison shot the first volley, sending the tiny glowing orbs arcing through the air. There was a distinct *hiss* as they connected with the exposed flesh of Burcheeze's face. He let out a blood-curdling roar of anger as he swatted the pellets away from his skin, spinning to face his attackers.

"NOW!" Halford screamed again and this time Ezekiel and Ambrose opened fire. Ezekiel's volley proved useless, sailing harmlessly over Burcheeze's head, but Ambrose's handful of red hot ammunition hit their target. Burcheeze dropped his mallet and clawed at his face as the pellets seared his flesh and lodged in his eyes.

"NOW!" Halford screamed once more and he and his men sent a final volley; hundreds of pellets, these considerably larger than the ones fired by the others, went arching into the air. They pelted Burcheeze about the hands and face, sizzling into his flesh, while a few more found their way down the open collar and loose sleeves of his shirt. He dropped to his knees, and then crashed to the ground, clutching and gasping at himself as he tried to find the searing pellets that were now scorching his skin beneath his clothes. His roars were ear-splitting and his thrashing legs smashed into the already severely damaged buildings, causing even more destruction.

The pellets that hadn't found their mark hissed on the ground as they cooled rapidly due to the enormous amounts of moisture that had soaked the entire village, eliminating the possibility of sparking any fires.

Burcheeze again managed to find his way back to his feet, though he now teetered and tottered dangerously, as though he could fall again at any given moment. He was dazed, confused, burned and battered as he lowered his hands from his face. The flesh on his cheeks, forehead and across his nose were blazing red, scorched and cauterized with every fiery impact. His hands were pocked with deeply embedded steel pellets and large holes had been singed into his shirt and trousers. As he stood staggering and almost completely defeated, Halford slowly approached the massive man. He had picked up the mallet, which was almost as long as he was tall, and hefted it onto his shoulder. There was a steely look in his eye that was almost murderous and his chest heaved up and down in great, angry breaths.

"YOU!" he screamed as Burcheeze wearily looked down at him. If not for the deadly serious implications of Halford's final confrontation, seeing the two of them standing side by side would almost be amusing. "You killed Feldon."

Burcheeze looked puzzled by this, as though he had no idea who, or what, was a Feldon. Halford brought the mallet down on the exposed section of

Burcheeze's foot, and the huge monster of a man crumpled to the ground with a resounding roar of rage and agony.

"You killed Feldon and you tried to kill these Boffles," he growled as he hefted the mallet high over his head, ready to strike. "And now I will kill you, you vile piece of -"

"WAIT!"

Those who had not gone into hiding were crowded around the fallen adversary and were paying no attention to anything but the scene that was unfolding before their eyes. Everyone turned to the shrill yet familiar voice that had come from behind them.

"Let me talk to him."

"I . . . I . . . I don't believe it!" Sender said in an astounded tone. "Can it be?"

"He's my brother," said Auntie Bernice as she slowly approached. "I'll take care of him."

Auntie Bernice stood beside the Dibble clock, her massive form looking just the way it had when the twins had seen her last, dressed in her multi-coloured muumuu, her jet-back hair piled high atop her huge, round and frighteningly colourful head. As she studied the grizzly form of her brother, she leaned against her cane, which again bowed under her impressive weight.

"What are *you* doing here?" Burcheeze grumbled weakly as he tried to pull himself to his feet. He managed to do so only through the help of his sister.

"You've been a bad boy, Burty," she said coolly.

"Yeah? What do you know about it?" He spat a thick wad of blood and saliva which splattered to the ground between their feet, and then wiped a singed hand across his bearded chin, his eyes scouring the scene with an air of loathing.

"I know that these people have done nothing to you," she said. "I know that I *should* let them kill you."

Burcheeze emitted a humourless chuckle as a sneering grin crossed his angry, frazzled face. "Let them try," he sneered.

"No," she said simply. "I won't do that."

"He deserves it," Halford growled through gritted teeth. His formidable hands tightened on the mallet handle, turning his knuckles white.

"I know he does," she said. "But I won't let you sink to his level. There is a code in place that says people like him should be tried and convicted for their crimes. We cannot become judge, jury and executioner."

"Why not?" Halford shouted. His face was becoming engorged with blood as his temper flared. "A man like this-"

"A man like this is what *you* will become if you strike that fatal blow," she shouted back. "Look around you. Look at this town. This is what happens when you try to take justice into your own hands. Your intentions are valiant, I know, but when justice comes at the cost of people's lives - innocent people - and their homes, their way of living . . . We don't have that right. We cannot simply take the law into our own hands and punish the criminals! When we do that, we cross the line. We *become* the criminals!"

All was silent as Auntie Bernice stood before them, Burcheeze swaying weakly beside her.

"I'll take him home," she finally said, "and tell everyone that he just appeared on my doorstep. Then I'll figure out what to do with him. Alistair and Allison, you two will follow us but not until morning. Understand?" The twins slowly nodded their heads in agreement.

As Auntie Bernice turned toward the tower, they noticed that the small clock had been changed, its gate no longer open. Instead, the Grandfather Clock was set to 3:16. One more minute would open the gate and she and her brother would slip through, the Boffles' terror of Burcheeze finally over.

As they stood before the clock, Burcheeze looked over his shoulder at the small group, grinning, and gave them a wink. Then, before anyone knew what he had done, he pushed Bernice with all his might, sending her crashing heavily to the ground. He then spun around and roared as though he were some sort of savage beast and began stomping around the Town Square. He reduced the shattered store fronts to absolute rubble as he tore through the walls and window frames. He brought his fists down and flattened an overturned produce cart. The people of Dibble, who had begun to emerge from their hiding places, certain that the danger had passed, were now scattering once again, screaming in terror. Bernice lay on the ground, her ankle badly sprained, as she shrieked at Burcheeze to stop his rampage, but her beseeching words fell onto deaf ears.

Halford swung the huge mallet in every direction but couldn't connect with the attacker. With a casual swoosh of his arm, Burcheeze sent him toppling into Sender, rendering both men dazed and unresponsive. Before anyone realised what was happening, the air was alive with sound and motion. A loud buzzing hum reverberated through the ruins of the town and the very next moment, hundreds of Bumbles were swarming the Square. The Grandfather Clock ticked away under its own volition as 3:17 came and went. No one slipped through to Bernice's basement.

Ezekiel and Ambrose pulled Bernice out of harm's way as Burcheeze continued his rampant tirade. Burcheeze screamed and bellowed as Bumble after Bumble sunk their barbed singers into his skin. He dropped to his knees as black spikes jutted from his flesh in bloodied random patterns, the Bumble's tearing away from their stingers with each crippling jab. Even Oscar joined the fray, nipping and biting at Burcheeze's ankles.

Unnoticed due to the commotion, Alistair bolted to the tower and grabbed the hour hand of the small clock face and pulled it to the number three. He then pushed the minute hand to the seventeen after mark, careful to stand behind the clock itself. The clock shuddered briefly beneath his weight and he could feel a strange pressure in his fingertips, as though a powerful magnet had tried to drag him toward it.

"Halford!" he shouted through the din of the attack. Halford heard and realized what Alistair had done. So, too had Allison, Ambrose and Ezekiel. Together with the help of Ella and the other Giant's, they grabbed hold of Burcheeze and dragged him toward the tower. With one mighty heave, they shoved him in front of the clock.

For a brief second nothing happened and their hearts hitched into their throats as Burcheeze erupted in a fit of humourless laughter. Then, before their very eyes, Burcheeze seemed to almost melt as his midsection began to swirl like a strange vortex. His eyes widened and his jaw dropped as his laughter was replaced by an eerie, high pitched wail and he was literally swallowed into the swirling clock face. Halford then heaved the mallet toward the clock, smashing it into a mangled heap of twisted metal, springs and gears. The mallet disappeared with a strange pop.

Burcheeze was finally gone.

***

The aftermath of the brief battle was brutally devastating. Most of Loxbury had been demolished. Only a few buildings within the Town Square remained intact and even they were badly damaged and on the verge of collapse.

Thurgood had regained his wits and was resting near the Town Hall, his tail oozing a slick green fluid where Burcheeze had struck him with the mallet. Several Bumbles lay in the street, having given their lives in the face of battle. A few of the townspeople had been injured, but miraculously no one had died. Doc Foober administered the Tangleroot elixir to those who needed it while others began to pick up the debris.

"That's it then," Sender finally said as he surveyed the damaged town. "We won."

"Yes," said Halford. "We won. But at what price?"

Oscar came bounding toward Alistair and Allison, smearing them with his long, wet tongue, his tail swishing gleefully through the air.

The rubble that lay heaped in front of Town Hall began to rumble and clatter as someone pushed their way through the demolished doors. Slowly and carefully, Mayor Maynott emerged, his face slackened and his eyes as wide as saucers. His suit was crusted and filthy with fine dust and grime and his moustache was frazzled like thousands of tangled white wires. He looked around with quiet disbelief, his hands on top of his bald little head.

"Oh dear," he muttered. "Oh dear, oh dear, oh dear." He then turned around and went back into the Town Hall, pulling the battered doors closed behind him. One of them fell from its hinges and crashed to the ground. Without looking back, he simply slipped back into the darkened building muttering "Oh dear, oh dear, oh dear" as he went.

The tuba player began to oompha-bloompa on his tuba as people were solemnly picking up debris. Other members of the marching band gradually joined in and before long, they were playing one of their upbeat - if not exactly in key - melodies. This seemed to lift the spirits of the beleaguered Boffles, who stopped what they were doing and looked at the situation for what it truly was.

A victory.

"I can't believe it," said Allison as Oscar darted in circles around her, leaping with joy. "I never would have believed we could do it."

"But you did do it," said Halford. "You and Alistair, Oscar and all the rest. We came together and defeated Burcheeze."

"I hope you discovered something about yourself," said Sender as he wrapped an arm around both Allison and Alistair. They looked at him with equally puzzled expressions.

"What?" Alistair asked.

"You," said Sender proudly as he held the twins tightly to his sides, "are pure potential. When you put your minds to it, there is absolutely nothing you cannot accomplish."

The twins blushed and Alistair sheepishly dragged the toe of his shoe through the dirt in loose circles. Oscar growlfed once more and pranced around the three of them, offering a congratulatory swipe of the tongue with each pass.

That night there was a grand feast. Auntie Bernice's ankle had been healed thanks to Doc Foober's concoction. Halford, the twins and Ella, Ezekiel and Ambrose were the guests of honour. They were presented with awards for bravery and even Oscar got a special treat - a wonderful mixture of Rattweed and Bumbleberries that helped grow back his hair.

It had been decided that they would spend one more night in Dibble and in the morning, Auntie Bernice, Oscar and the twins would return home. Ambrose, Ella and Ezekiel were invited to stay on with the Boffles but they had decided that they were going to set off in a few days to try to find any survivors from Perilrock Peak.

Halford and Mrs. Littlejohn, along with the rest of the Giants, accepted the invitation to remain in Loxbury, for which they and the Boffles were eternally grateful.

As Thurgood, Archibald and the rest of the Whipperloopers rested quietly, the band played on well into the night, louder than they ever had before. Their wrenching notes drifted clear across Mayomay Bay and not a single person had any complaints.

Except one.

EPILOGUE

As the first week of school rapidly approached, Allison had decided that after experiencing the real thing first hand, her volcano was nowhere near authentic enough to hand in, even though it was strictly for bonus marks. Instead, she and Alistair spent the remaining few days of summer almost glued to each other.

Mr. and Mrs. McAllister were pleased with themselves when they had retrieved the kids from Auntie Bernice's that Sunday evening. Not only had they survived a weekend with Auntie Bernice (a feat neither Mr. nor Mrs. McAllister thought they could manage), they actually seemed to like one another. They had been astounded at the twins' appearance, however, but Allison claimed that Alistair and she had been wrestling in the basement when the clock fell on top of them.

"Don't worry, Mother," Allison had said. "We're fine. It's just a few scratches."

Auntie Bernice acknowledged their story (it wasn't exactly a lie, really) and said she had examined them carefully. There were no broken bones, just a few scrapes and bruises, certainly nothing to worry about.

The Friday before school started, Alistair was in the garage, carefully prying the lid off of a large bucket of ball-bearing grease as Allison approached with reserved apprehension.

"What are you doing?" she asked. Beside her brother lay a pair of their father's skis, a bike helmet and elbow pads and a pair of old crutches.

"Nothin'," he said flatly. Oscar, who lay on the concrete beside him, chuffed softly, his midsection almost completely grown in once again.

"You're not thinking of trying to ski down the driveway with that stuff, are you?"

He looked at her as though she had asked the most ridiculous question in the entire world.

"Of course I am," he said. He was looking around the garage for something with which to smear the grease onto the floor. He finally decided on a ping pong paddle.

Allison tisked, clicking her tongue on the roof of her mouth.

"What?" he asked, poised to scoop a paddle full of grease from the plastic container.

"You'll never get it even like that," she said, snatching the paddle from her brother. She grabbed a window squeegee and skimmed a layer of grease from the bucket. "That's better." In a few minutes, they had a perfectly level layer of grease running the entire length of the garage and driveway, a dozen or so pop cans stacked in a pyramid at the end.

"Me first," Allison said as she plopped the helmet onto her head and slipped her feet into the skis. Just as she grabbed the crutches and readied herself for the ride, Mrs. McAllister came into the garage to toss out a bag of trash.

"What on earth?" she said, startled not by their stunt but by the fact that it wasn't Alistair strapped to the skis. "What do you think you're doing?" Her voice suddenly became cold and threatening. "Do you want to spend your last weekend of summer back at your Auntie Bernice's?"

Allison and Alistair exchanged a knowing smile, and then Allison pushed off, rocketing toward the pile of pop cans.

Oscar looked at Mrs. McAllister with big, sad, brown eyes, as if to say that no matter how bad things look, it wasn't his fault.

Made in the USA
Monee, IL
17 October 2020